Paxton's Worlds

Paxton's Worlds

Mary Jane Frost

Published by Time Bottle Books

Edited by Elizabeth Sims

Cover design by Robim Ludwig Design Inc.

Print Formatting: By Your Side Self-Publishing

Library of Congress Control Number: 2016951237

Time Bottle Books: Buffalo, New York

This book is dedicated to
Beatrice Portinari
and all women like her.

Introduction

Paxton Frost died. I cannot overemphasize that point. Paxton Frost died. If you don't believe that, his story won't make sense. Is he still dead? I don't know.

My name is Mary Jane. For a while, I was Paxton's best... I was his only friend. You could say we were part of each other. 'I am in the Father, and the Father is in me.' John 14:11. Yeah, we were that close.

This is his story. Part comes from firsthand experience. Part is from what I learned from others. Part is what I could infer.

One more thing. When I was with Paxton, it was funny why the chicken crossed the Mobius strip. It's not funny now. That means I'm dying.

Mary Jane Frost

PART ONE

Midway upon the journey of life
I found myself within a forest dark,
For the straightforward path has been lost.

The Divine Comedy
The Inferno
Canto I

Dante Alighieri

Chapter 1

Paxton Frost carried Mary Jane through the European High Energy Collider complex located at the University of Yorkshire. Everyone they passed glanced at her.

Well, she is the prettiest girl on the block and she is my best hope for... What? For keeping the madness at bay. Does she know how much I depend on her? Paxton furrowed his brow. "This collider isn't as big as the Conseil Européen pour la Recherche Nucléaire's, or the International Linear Collider in Japan," he said. "It was built for one purpose."

"Ventriloquists have a reputation for being a little mad," Mary Jane responded.

"Huh?"

Mary Jane's soothing voice continued. "The EHEC was built to test M theory. Bosonic string theory postulates there are twenty-six dimensions of space-time. Right?"

"Right. CERN and the ILC are bigger subatomic particle colliders. They can do everything. We focus our effort, equipment, money, and most of all, time on one outcome, M theory. We're stopping at the cafeteria. I'm buying a bottle of water. Would you like something?"

"No thank you, Paxton. I'm too nervous."

"Mary Jane—I need to bring something up. You can be a bit raunchy at times."

"Don't worry about me, Paxton. I know how to stay in control. Do you?"

Paxton always ate alone. Today would be different. Mary Jane hammered into him the need to join the members of his team. His team members had heard of the visitor he was bringing in. When they saw Paxton, they made room for him, chairs screeching.

"Mary Jane, I'd like to introduce you to Cecilia and Marie."

Marie smiled and said, "Hi."

Cecilia grunted.

Paxton said, "Here are Isaac, and Max."

He pulled out a chair. Mary Jane snuggled on his lap and gazed doe-eyed at the group. Paxton asked, "Where are Charles and Niels?"

"They're still working in their pods," Max said between mouthfuls of a triple decker Cricket Club sandwich. "Another problem with the interfacing came up."

Mary Jane looked at Paxton. "Is there going to be a test on this?"

"If there is I'm sure you'll do fine."

Mary Jane sighed. "Sometimes my head feels like it's made of wood."

"That's because you're a ventriloquist's dummy."

Mary Jane leaned forward to see Cecilia at the far end of the table. "Cecilia, I heard you went to Brighton for a holiday."

Cecilia glared at the big dummy. Then she turned her attention to Mary Jane. "I had a miserable time."

"Miserable is, as miserable does." Mary Jane sing sang.

Marie gripped the table. "Alright you two... three... two, don't make me put you in time out chairs, again. Cecilia, be the adult and learn to work with Paxton."

Marie took off her glasses and pushed the heels of her hands against her eyes. She pushed her hands back to her temples. "Mary Jane," she said softly now, "tell us about you and Paxton."

"We've known each other for about a month. We met in Paris." Mary Jane gazed up at Paxton. "Can I tell a story Paxton?"

"Does it have a wow finish?" Paxton love whispered.

"I don't know the finish yet," said Mary Jane. She turned her attention to Paxton's teammates. "You should have seen the dismal flat on the Left Bank he rented. We later went to the Champs-Élysées where he bought this beautiful blue—"

"I don't remember buying anything blue."

"Paxton," she said, "that blue teddy you bought."

Paxton blushed. "You promised to tone it down, Mary Jane."

Looking out over the table, Mary Jane confided, "He was stoned on Pernod and Purple Afghani the whole time."

Mary Jane swiveled her head to look at Paxton, and then turned to the group. "It's like we have a psychic connection. Like I can read his thoughts."

Isaac's eyes watered as he blew his tea out of his nose.

How did I lose control of her? How did I lose control of myself?

"What's she made of?" Isaac coughed.

Mary Jane replied, "Some glass, a lot of silk, machined, not stamped bearings, but mostly wood. Some people say my father was a son of a beech. Others say he was a son of a birch. But everyone agrees my mother was the best piece of ash in the woods."

"Is she microchipped?" Max asked.

"I've given her a mem chip. It records my social interactions. I copy them to my laptop every day to review." *I need to get the conversation on a new topic.* "Let me show you a trick." He held up the bottle of water he'd bought.

"Not the old 'you're going to drink water while I talk' trick," said Mary Jane.

"No, this is going to be different. You're going to drink the water while I talk."

"Wait a minute! Where's the trick in that? Don't forget, I'm not waterproof. Did you think of buying me adult diapers? Make me drink water and I'll piddle all over your lap! You'd enjoy that, wouldn't you?"

How can I get her on a new topic?

"So this is the visitor you promised us," said a voice from behind.

Mary Jane swiveled her head to look behind her.

"Mary Jane, this is the project manager, Albert."

"Of course, I'd know you anywhere. You're the debonair and handsome one."

Albert was a taller, thinner, and darker-haired version of the famous Albert, Einstein. He took the pipe from his mouth. "Don't hornswoggle me, Mary Jane. You're not going to distract my best team member from his work, are you?"

Paxton understood. *Play all you want, but get your work done.*

"Any news on the repairs to the interface phasing?" asked Cecilia.

"When you get back to work everything will be ready for another test."

"That's good news," said Max. He took two more wolf-sized bites from another triple decker Cricket Club sandwich. "There still is enough anti-Helium 3 to power another test."

Wide eyed, Mary Jane turned to Paxton. "What's with the antimatter?"

"The matter antimatter reaction powers the subatomic particle collisions. Quantum gravity waves generated from the collisions form the wall of the wormhole. The tachyons provide definition and stability to the wormhole." Paxton's armpits were soaked from all the social interaction. "I should get to my pod. Come on, Mary Jane. I'll show you the Bottle Room where I work."

Paxton ran to the corridor with the lifts. He shouldered open the door to the stairs, and forced it shut with his back. He leaned against it, panting. The stark concrete and steel of the stairwell felt safer than the warm, bright cafeteria.

"Paxton, you went out of your way to be snippy with Cecilia."

"I thought it was clever."

"Did saying that make you feel good?" asked Mary Jane.

"No."

"No? The first chance you get; we're apologizing to her. Understand?"

Paxton lowered his head. "Understood."

"So where are we going?"

"The lowest level. Sub-level nine."

"You can't keep building walls to keep out people."

"I tried to interact before."

"No, you didn't. That's why Roseann's dead." Mary Jane paused. "Paxton, you're crying."

"Maybe stealing you from the psychologist's office wasn't a good idea. Maybe I told you too much, too soon."

"You're carrying me down nine floors. You want to avoid people that much?"

"It could be worse. It could be nine floors up. Have you been putting on weight?"

"Half of that kilo you bought."

Paxton's laughter echoed in the concrete well. "And people call me a pothead."

"So tell me about sub-level nine."

"The matter antimatter reactor is in the centre module," Paxton explained as they jogged down the stairs. "Our workstations or pods make a circle around the reactor. There are pods with equipment, utility pods, a break pod, medical pod, and a conference pod."

Paxton shouldered open a door and stepped into the sub-level nine hallway. A lift opened and Max stepped out. Max's pod was close to Paxton's, so they wound up walking together. Students in the art school had decorated the circular hallway. The murals blended into one another. There were scenes of goals, and conflicts, then disappointments, and renewed efforts. Clockwise, the ceiling depicted dawn, to day, to dusk, then night, and back to dawn. Traveling counterclockwise reversed the process.

"Not to feign interest, but where is everyone else?"

"Albert went to a meeting. Isaac is picking up betting slips. Cecilia and Marie went to the loo. You know women. They can't go alone. Some herd instinct. Cecilia's still mad at you. You're twenty-five, the newest of the team, and you got the position in God's Room."

"Cecilia should learn to control herself," said Paxton.

"She should learn to use her head," Mary Jane giggled.

Paxton slapped Mary Jane's face so hard it spun three hundred sixty degrees.

Max chuckled. "You're having fun with the dummy, aren't you?"

"Paxton's okay. Tell me Max, what's he like?"

Max paused. "This is weird. You know him better than I do."

"No. He keeps a lot hidden. Even from me. So what's he like?"

"He's a great co-worker."

Mary Jane leaned in to press her question. "No. What is Paxton like?"

"Umm. Err." Max wiped his sweaty hands on his pants. "He's okay. You have to watch out for him. He can be normal one minute, the next minute, surprise!"

"Tell me Max, how tall are you?" Mary Jane looked up with teddy bear eyes.

"About one point eight metres."

"How tall am I?"

Max looked down. "With Paxton carrying you, about one point six metres."

"You're looking down the front of my blouse, aren't you? You want to know what I look like down there. Hey Max! My eyes are up here!"

At the Bottle Room, Paxton used the facial scanner to unlock the door. Mary Jane continued to face Max. "Tell me Max, have you ever had a real good piece of wood? I'll bet you're afraid of getting Dutch elm dis—"

"After you left the cafeteria," Max shot back, "we sat around trying to decide which one of the two of you is more stiff and wooden."

Hearing other team members exiting a lift, Paxton closed the door. He liked working in the Bottle Room. That part of the project gave him the most time alone. The beige-coloured room featured grey industrial grade furniture, cold fluorescent lights, and silence like a winter night. It all fit Paxton well. At least it did until he brought Mary Jane into it. Now the bland utility of the room embarrassed him.

Mary Jane shivered. "Is there a reason it's freezing in here?"

"The A/C is stuck on full blast. They can't seem to get it fixed. It's been freezing for as long as I've been here."

Mary Jane looked at Paxton. "That conversation went well for a start. Next time why don't you have me ask, what are you like? Remember to get the other person to talk about himself." Mary Jane rotated her head. "While I love what you've done with this place, it could use a woman's touch. A few matching throw pillows." Mary Jane looked at the Hang in There Kitty! poster on a wall, one corner unstuck. "That is so boring! This place could use some needlepoint on the walls. Tell me about this room."

"Some people call this God's Room. Others call it the Rabbit Hole or the Wonderland Room. I prefer the generic Bottle Room. This is where we hope to bump multiverses into one another. Well, just a tiny fraction of some of the folded dimensions of subatomic particles of different phased multiverses together."

"What'll that be like?"

"If we do it right, we'll produce enough energy to develop a wormhole."

"From where to where?"

"We don't know yet from where to where, or from when to when."

"Where's the bottle?"

Paxton pointed to a disc embedded in the floor, three metres in diameter. It looked like frosted crystal, a silver and electric blue-mirrored metal wrapped around the outside. Three metres above, was an identical disk. The lower and the upper disks had gold plated instruments, the size of euros imbedded in them.

"Where's the flux capacitor? Is this dangerous?"

"This is the safe part. The wormhole can only exist in a quantum gravity field that we call the bottle. The tachyons modulate the bottle. That prevents background radiation from leaking into the wormhole. We can't have anything falling in at one end and popping out at the other."

Mary Jane looked at Paxton. "What?"

Paxton pulled up a chair for Mary Jane. "It's complicated. Over here we're going to be using instruments located inside and outside the field or bottle, to measure for potential leakage."

The phone rang. Answering it, Paxton heard Cecilia's shrill voice. "Paxton, it's Cecilia. What are you doing?"

"Showing Mary Jane around. Then I'll tweak some instruments."

"There's been another delay. Just thought I'd let you know."

"Thank you Cecilia. Hang on. Someone wants to talk with you."

Mary Jane's sweet voice came on the line. "Cecilia, I hope you don't think too ill of me because of what I said in the cafeteria."

8

"No, you're funny."

"Cecilia, don't you feel odd talking to a dummy, like she's a real person?"

Cecilia fell silent for a moment. "No, you have more personality than some of the human dummies I have to work with." The line went dead.

Mary Jane turned her head to look at Paxton. "She was talking about you."

Paxton's shoulders slumped. "I know."

"You've always found working with things easier than working with people."

"What makes you say that?"

Mary Jane leaned in close to whisper. "We'll always have Paris."

A long guilty pause came from Paxton. "I needed some place to practice."

Mary Jane's eyes bored into Paxton. "What? Ventriloquism?"

"What else?"

"Look, Paxton, I was there the whole time. You don't have to sell me if you say it was about ventriloquism. Remember, I was with the psychologist when we hooked up."

"You have a degree in psychology?"

"No, but sitting back and watching her and her clients, even a dummy can learn a few things."

"Like what?"

"I'll bet it started early. You always strove for perfection, and come adolescence you always wanted the prettiest girls."

"You don't have to be a perfectionist, just a horny teen boy to want that. Besides, where I grew up, all the pretty girls had diseases."

"Your mother worked for the World Health Organization. You grew up traveling in undeveloped countries where she documented rare disease outbreaks. What about later?" She whispered, "When you attended Columbia?"

"Drop it." Paxton snapped.

"It was the means you employed, or perhaps the means you didn't employ, that led to your chronic failures. You always wanted to make sure things were just right so there could be only one outcome. By the time you finished lining up all your ducks, the moment and the girl were gone. Just like your work here. Think about what you said. 'We're focusing our effort, equipment, money, and time on one outcome only.' Paxton, before you can get laid, you have to learn how to be friends with the girl. Even that won't mean you'll get a piece of ass, but you'll have her for a friend." Paxton's face remained immobile. "Paxton, if I can get you in the sack with a woman, can I watch?"

"You're almost as sad as I am."

Mary Jane leaned toward him. "I am you."

"You shouldn't play with other people's heads, Mary Jane."

"You play with mine all the time."

The creepy crawlers feeling on his skin started again. "I'm going to tweak the instruments inside the disc. You stay here at the gauge panel."

Mary Jane looked at the panel to acquaint herself with the instruments and their meanings. "Okay, I'll monitor the gauges for any fluctuations from standard deviation."

"There won't be any fluctuations."

Paxton took his hand from Mary Jane's back. Her head and eyes turned towards him, one eyebrow rose, and stayed there. Paxton stepped on the disc to tweak instrument N40 with the screwdriver in his Swiss Army knife. He did this many times before, but never in Mary Jane's presence. Rubbing her silk and glass together built up a static charge. Her wood frame allowed the charge to grow. The cold, dry air contained the charge on his hand, until it could find a ground. Instrument N40 was supposed to be grounded.

A small spark from the static electricity on his hand jumped out. The pre-charged field on the disc intercepted the spark. It became a signal to the matter antimatter reactor. This initiated a discharge of types of energies not seen since the birth of the universe. That forced folded dimensions to open up and bump into their counterparts in an alternate phased multiverse. Without the tachyons generator to modulate their interaction, the quantum gravity reaction went wild.

Paxton found himself in what appeared to be a cloud-like tunnel. *Now what happened? The general electrical supply may have shut down. Wait for the backup power kicked in. No, that's wrong.* Now panic, pure, intense, unadulterated panic. *Wormhole! Have to get out. When the wormhole collapses, it will dissolve me into nothing but sub-atomic particles. Not even that much will be left. Nothing but pure diffused energy. Have to get out! How?* It was a tunnel, so he ran. There seemed to be gravity, seemed to be a floor for him to run on. He just plain ran without thought of any direction. The rational part of his brain dissolved, followed by his emotional core. Nothing remained but feral instinct. *Go! Run! Faster!* There appeared an end to the tunnel. *Back to the Bottle Room.*

Contempt swept Cecilia's face. All the instruments spiked, there was audible snap, a whiff of ozone, and everything shut down. She studied the readouts. *There's going to be an investigation into this.* She picked up the phone and switched to PA.

"Everyone, this is Cecilia. Lock your data consoles." She cradled the phone to ponder her data. The phone's ringing made her jump.

"Cecilia, it's Max."

She could hear him pounding his console.

"I got a discharge from the reactor. I thought you weren't ready for another test."

"I'm not." Cecilia's high-pitched voice rose another octave when she got excited. "The tachyons generator is down again. I had a spike in the instruments and then everything, I mean *everything* shut down."

"Same thing here. Well, at least we know the safety interlocks are working."

"Yob tvoyu mat. (*Fuck your mother.*) Did you call Paxton to find out how this affected the Bottle Room?"

"No, and I'm surprised he's not calling around having a hissy fit trying to find out. Let me see what my data suggests."

Cecilia hung up and as soon as she did, calls began coming in. Calls came from everyone, except Paxton. Soon everyone realized a major event had occurred.

Max called back. His voice shook. "I haven't heard from Paxton. I'm going to check on him."

Max stepped inside the Bottle Room and closed the door. It was so quiet it hurt his ears. It then hit Max why it was so quiet. *The A/C finally shut off.* "Paxton?" Mary Jane still monitored the instrument panel. There was no sign of Paxton. Max checked the readouts, then looked at the computer's LCD screen. Paxton's computer was devouring data; it was scouring other pods for data to feed it. The data was piling up like dirty laundry in a frat house. Max picked up the phone. When Cecilia answered, his voice dropped a half octave. "Since I'm talking to you, we know Paxton's phone is working."

"What's he doing?" Cecilia asked.

"I hope he went to the loo," said Max.

"I'm not getting any feedback from his computer."

"It doesn't look like he's analyzed any of the data from his instruments."

Cecilia said snidely, "One dummy may be trying to interface with the other dummy."

Max rubbed the fabric of Mary Jane's blue plaid skirt between a thumb and index finger. *Real wool. Nice.* He peeked up her skirt. *That answers that question.* "No, Mary Jane is by herself watching the gauges. Cecilia, it's been too long. Paxton should've done something by now." Max slammed down the phone and ran to the loo. He banged open a stall door. Wham! *Nobody.* More stall doors. Wham! Wham! *No body.* Wham! *Nobody's body.* "My God," Max screamed. "Oh, my God." He huffed and puffed back to the Bottle Room and stared at Mary Jane, trying to calm his conflicting thoughts and emotions.

PART TWO

In addition, of that second kingdom I will sing.
Where in the human spirit doth purge itself,
Moreover, to ascend to heaven to become worthy.

The Divine Comedy
Purgatory
Canto I

Dante Alighieri

Chapter 2

Paxton hit the ground hard. His breath came in spasms. *That was close.* Rolling onto his back, he wasn't shaking as much as convulsing. The trees around him seemed to spin. *What happened? What is going on? I have to get back to the gauge panel and see what happened.* He squinted hard.

Trees? I'm not in the Bottle Room. I'm outside, in a forest. Paxton's body convulsed more. Breathe, Paxton! His head spun, and then spun faster. He tried to get up, wobbled, and fell. Breathe deeply. Breathe slowly Okay, the air seems normal, rather warm. He tried to lift one convulsing arm, then a twitching leg. Gravity seems normal. I'm still on Earth, hopefully. He turned his head to look at the trees. Trees. Deciduous. Hardwood. Thick growth. Old growth?

Something rustled the branches in the tree above him. Paxton lay on his back. Now came a rustling in the leaves to his left. *Same thing? Its mate?* Paxton scrunched his eyes shut and covered his midsection. He tried to prepare for claws, claws that would rip into his rib cage. *O God, be merciful.*

Plop!

It hit him in the chest. Paxton screamed, then nothing. He waited. It was a small plop. Trembling, he raised his head to see his chest. *An acorn.* He turned his head and saw it, a red squirrel. He yelled, "I can't take any more of this shit!" The squirrel ran.

Thank God. Earth-like air. Earth-like gravity. Earth-like trees. Earth-like animals. To paraphrase that old saying about ducks, if it breathes like Earth's air, feels like Earth's gravity, has Earth-like trees, and Earth-like animals, it is probably Earth. Where? The Urals? North Korea? Anywhere, as long as it is Earth.

Paxton sat up cross-legged and pulled his cell phone out. *Call Albert. Hey Albert, a funny thing happened on the way to the next test.* He scrolled through his contact list and punched in Albert's number.

NO SIGNAL AVAILABLE

Maybe I am in North Korea. Get up Paxton. Check yourself out. His breathing returned almost to normal. Paxton checked himself. His pants pockets contained normal his stuff: keys and fob, cell phone, some joints in an Altoids tin, lighter, handkerchief, wallet, and some pound and pence coins. In his wallet: credit cards, driver's license, photos of him, Mary Jane, him and Mary Jane, National Health Insurance card, library card, shopper's club card, and paper money, worth fifty five pounds. In his shirt pocket: a laser pointer, and his ID badge for the project.

What now? Where now? Think, think, think. Paxton saw no signs of civilization. *Okay. There is a course of inaction. Sit here, stay here, and wait for help to arrive. Build three fires. Three of anything means hey, I'm lost and I'm over here. Two of anything is the reply. We see or hear you. First they have to know you're lost and in this area.*

There is a course of action. Find water. Follow the water. Water will always lead you to people. If you find a small stream, follow it to a bigger stream, then follow that body of water downstream. Keep following bigger and bigger streams until you get to people. Water will always lead you to people. He looked around. No water was evident. *Do a spiral search pattern. Try to find something of note about this place and walk around it in bigger and bigger circles. This is a forest. Trees have to get their water from somewhere. This is not one of the wastelands of your childhood. Go with option two.*

He checked his cell phone. *Try that for about an hour. What do I do if it doesn't work after an hour? Take one crisis at a time, Paxton. One crisis at a time. Maybe after that I should start crying.* He picked the Swiss Army knife off the ground, and started walking. *Fairly level topography. A walk in the park. If the park was all woods.* After less than an hour, he found a stream. *Hey, this is working.* The woods changed; the oak forest thinned to birch woodland. The stream led to a glade that became a bog. No people.

Okay, now what? Option three. Start crying. No, go back. Follow the stream upstream now. He continued upstream. Paxton resisted the urge to check his cell phone. There was no reason to believe there would be a signal now. He looked at the declining sun as if it were a countdown clock. A chunk of bile welled up in his throat, choking him. *Swallow, Paxton. Breathe. When I get out of this, I am going to kick someone's ass. I hope the data doesn't reveal it's my ass I must kick. What the hell did I do? I've adjusted that screw many times before.*

The faint sound of a bell slowly ringing caught Paxton's attention. He ran toward it, tripped, and ran until he broke out of the forest and into a field. It was a cultivated field, a grain field. *Yes! People.* He trotted across the field to some buildings. A farming village. As Paxton got closer, he could hear the sounds of animals, and the continuing tolling of the bell. When Paxton approached the village, he saw two young women in long plain-looking dresses herding cows into a pen.

The buildings appeared to be an historical re-creation of some sort. Childhood memories came to Paxton. He could be in Africa, or some place in Asia. It did not matter. It was like something you'd find in a developing country.

The cow herders, they're Caucasian. I'm some place in Latin America, perhaps. I can still sing Happy Birthday in Spanish. Three years of high school Spanish and all I can remember are a few phrases, how to count to ten, and how to sing Happy Birthday.

Paxton approached the first man he saw. The man's skin looked like worked earth. *Okay, Latin America it is.* The man sagged like a weary Atlas, carrying the weight of the world on his back. He was an Atlas with none of the needed muscle. The villager's eyes widened when he bumped into Paxton. When Paxton took a step forward, the man took a step back. The man wore homespun clothing, a brown, woolen, hooded tunic. His shoes looked homemade. Paxton noticed the shoes were a simple design, made to fit on either foot. He looked at the man's tunic and turned to look at the clothes of the others milling about. *No tee shirts. Nothing with a logo on it.*

"Excuse me, but does anyone here speak English? Hablas Ingles?" The man said nothing. "Hablas Espanol?" The man stared at Paxton. *Great. The first person I meet is the village idiot.*

Paxton looked around for someone else to talk to, maybe an aid worker. *If there is an aid worker, then they should have contact with the rest of the world.* As other people noticed him, they stepped forward a little bit and then retreated, either behind a building, into a building, or just away.

He looked around. *No cell phone towers. No power lines. Not even a paved road. This had to be as far out in the boondocks as you can get. How far into the boondocks can you get? Easy, halfway. After that, you start getting out again. It looks like I am halfway into the boondocks.*

The first man he met started gathering others around him. The hairs on the back of Paxton's neck rose. From the tone of their voices, he could discern their attitude. Yankee, go home. The first man approached him. With words and some gestures, he indicated that Paxton was to leave.

20

"Where? Where should I go?" Paxton then noticed the church. It was the most prominent building in the village. He went in that direction. If anyone was educated, it should be the parish priest, minister, or whatever. Going there, Paxton saw some people leaving the church. He stopped, stared. He couldn't believe what he was seeing.

When as a young boy he traveled the world with his mother, she explained such diseases were the result of sin, most of all, sexual sin.

"The purity of our faith keeps us well."

Supplemented, that is, by the vaccinations they were required to have. He'd seen pictures and videos of people with this disease. *Smallpox. This is impossible! Smallpox is wiped out. There are only a few samples of the virus left in some labs in the United States and in Russia. Maybe one or two other countries.*

What was going on here? An epidemic was impossible. That's it. I could be in Russia. Something happened. He had heard about it in the old Soviet Union. Some militarization of smallpox had gotten away from them and infected a town. *It looks like it happened again. If that's true, will the Russians let me out? Germ warfare will send international relations into a death-spiral. It will be a lot easier just to make me vanish.*

The mob of men followed him at a distance, urging him onward in their odd-sounding English. A crude path led out of the village. Paxton took it. Trotting down the dirt road, he again noticed the two young cow herders. One of them smiled at him. *Where am I going? What am I going to do?* The sun was close to the horizon. *That's good. Come night, I'll see the lights of a larger community somewhere in the distance and I'll go there.* He left the village and its church bell behind. Darkness came and there were no lights in the sky, other than the stars.

Paxton turned off the path and into the relative safety of the forest. His unspoken thoughts brought tears to his eyes. Panic rose in his chest again. Paxton massaged his throat. His taut windpipe threatened to cut off his breathing. He lay on the forest floor. The ground seemed designed for torture: cold, hard, and uneven. Worst of all it was full of real creepy crawlers. He flicked a spider from his arm and tried to pillow his head on a tree root. *Is it time for option three?* He pulled out his lighter and one of his precious joints. *What is the point of having it if you are not going to use it?* Paxton stopped just before the flame hit the joint. *What if I get the munchies? Whom am I kidding? I already have the munchies, and not a mini mart in sight. Who doesn't have mini marts?* Paxton lit up and waited for the magic to happen. *There's always that spider. I should smoke this outside more often.* He pointed a mellowed hand at the Big Dipper. *You aren't supposed to be over there.*

The twin girls entered their home. Nineteen years of age they were still fawn like. Their eyes adjusted to the half-light of the airless, windowless cottage. Elizabeth set about tending to little Thomas, their sick half-brother. Isabelle went to help Abigail, their mother, with the evening meal. Soon their stepfather arrived, his back bent in longstanding defeat. He sat on a bench at the table. Abigail set a plate of vegetables in front of her husband. Then she crossed her arms over her pregnant belly and waited for Jonah to speak.

"What do you want?"

"I want to know what you did."

"I went to the abbey."

"Jonah, what did you do?"

"What do you want of me?"

"You married me to double the size of your croft. You said we would be better off, with more food for us, and maybe a little something to sell in the village."

"And what of you, goodwife?" Jonah's voice pleaded. "The first boy you gave me to help work this land. That one was born with too large a head and strange slanted eyes."

"Yes." Abigail sighed. "Then we put his body in the earth."

Abigail looked down at her pregnant belly. "Ignatius arrived the spring he was conceived." Her head bolted up and her eyes accused Jonah. "That spring you stopped caring for me. After him, I came with child again. Thomas was born healthy."

Jonah spat back, "Now at four years he is sick. He can take down only a little water. His cough does not let him sleep. He doesn't have the pox, still near death." Jonah looked at Thomas's bed. Above the bed, a monk wrote a blessing. Lilith-A-Bi. It did no good. The pox swept the whole land. The twins had a mild form of it on their hands.

Abigail sat across from Jonah. "I heard our neighbors whispering, 'It was by the devil the twins were smitten lightly.' Can the monks, the church, God, help us or not?"

Jonah spoke slowly. "I went to the abbey—I begged God, the church, the abbot, for forgiveness—for whatever we've done. The abbot said we should give the twins to God. Put them in the convent school—under Ignatius."

Abigail sighed. "Ignatius is a religious man. Still a man. With a man's appetites. If he tries to pray with them, he'll have to watch their staffs."

Jonah grabbed his knife with a gnarled hand. He balanced his thoughts on either side of the knife's edge. Pushing his meal side to side, Jonah made up his mind. "Tomorrow I will meet with the monks. I'll put the twins in the convent school."

Staring at the sharp edge of the knife, he straightened up. *What of the stranger who entered the village?* "Maybe it was he who brought this pox to us. Maybe he has been nearby, unseen, for a long time."

"What did you say, father?" Elizabeth inquired, or was it Isabelle? Jonah did not realize he'd spoken aloud.

"A stranger tried to enter our village. Some of the other men and I drove him off."

The twins' eyes widened. The more freckled one said, "We saw this man as we brought in the cows. Perhaps he is from London." This place called London where the King lived seemed to have a mystical pull on the twins. Ever since they had heard of it, they asked everyone they could about London. Where was it? What kinds of people lived there? How did they dress? How many people lived there? People would make up fool stories just to get rid of the twins. This only seemed to whet their appetite even more.

"Did you see where he went?" Jonah asked in a low, slow voice.

The other twin replied, "Into the forest, towards the castle."

"I will hear no more of the stranger or London."

The twins knew they were the objects of scrutiny, and at times fear, by the other serfs. Through their own skill, they had developed their own nonverbal means of communicating. To others this made the twins seem even more distant and it increased the gossip.

Later, as they lay on their bed they made a pact. In the morning, they would take the cows out to the fields. They would then try to find the stranger in the forest. They talked to each other, again without speaking. "If he is from London, maybe he will take us there."

Chapter 3

The church bell calling Prime, the first day's call to prayer, woke up Paxton Frost. *This was the worst night of my life.* He wiped the sleep from his face, the film from his mouth, and shook the stiffness from the muscles in his body. *I can die a happy man if I never see a tree again. Paxton, what are you going to do when you get back to civilization? I will be grateful for small things. Hot showers. Beds. Vanilla ice cream. Being away from people, on my terms. People are complicated, and flawed.*

I'll bypass the village and make my way back to where I popped out of the wormhole. My teammates may have my coordinates and are looking for me. Paxton pulled out his cell phone to check for messages.

NO SIGNAL AVAILABLE

Check the time. Time? "Jesus Christ!" The truth he dared not admit now erupted. His agony cut off his breathing. Convulsions raked his body, shaking as when he had realized he was in the wormhole. His voice came out as a grating hoarse whisper. "My God, no, no, no. God help me!" Paxton fell to his knees and put his hands to his head. "Why did I leave the wormhole? Why didn't I stay there? When it collapsed, I would've been better off dissolved into diffused energy."

Paxton rocked back and forth, and side to side. *Maybe I'm not even that far from where the University will be. I'm centuries in the past.* Once again, ice-cold panic set in. *What can I do? I can't get back. I have to get back. I can't do anything. These people know nothing of my world. They know nothing of me. I have no skills for this time. I can't beg. I don't even know how to beg. I can barely speak with them. These people have run me out of their village.*

I'm alone. All alone. What is there left for me to do?

The analytic part of his mind left him. A black, bottomless well of despair entered into him. *One way out.* He climbed the nearest tree to a branch that overhung his head. He removed his belt, looped it around his neck, and slipped the end through the buckle. He wrapped the end around the tree limb and tucked it under itself. Paxton smiled, *I'm responsible for Roseann's death, so why not my own.* Hearing the bell tolling, he rolled off the branch.

SIX A.M. THE DAY AFTER THE EVENT

The Event, as it was already known, brought everything to a smashing halt. Two things were clear. There was a runaway event and Paxton Frost was missing. Albert's team worked through the night, drinking pots of coffee and crunching numbers. Finding Paxton should be the easy part. Everyone had to pass a biometric scan to enter the secure areas of the facility. The security computer logged the ID and time each gate was used. There were cameras in the open common rooms, such as the cafeteria and the halls and in the elevators. All evidence showed Paxton entering the Bottle Room. Searches by security and faculty members turned up no sign of Paxton in any part of the facility.

There were no cameras in the Bottle Room itself, only the computer recordings of instrument measurements and Mary Jane. She sat there, silent and somewhat creepy. Max texted everyone, "She wooden't talk."

By dawn, the team had reached two conclusions. An unregulated wormhole had formed in the Bottle Room, and Paxton Frost had disappeared into thin air, or somewhere else.

After Prime, the twins finished putting the cows to pasture. Now with caution they approached the edge of the forest. They froze in their tracks upon hearing unfamilar crying and wailing.

The sounds made Elizabeth think back to when she and her sister were younger, sinful girls. Their stepfather, Jonah, would taunt them. He told them he would take them deep into the woods and tie them to a tree. "Then the ghoulies and ghosties and long-legged beasties will come to eat you alive."

Elizabeth took half a step back, and then felt a sharp sting to her buttocks. With a yelp she spun around with her staff raised back high overhead. Her sister stood behind her with their mother's pout. "I'll have no retreating, Elizabeth." Isabelle pointed her sting-inducing staff at her twin. Holding their staffs at the ready, they looked at each other and summoned their audacity. They approached the edge of the forest. Every rustling, every scurrying shadow caught their attention.

They could hear cries of anguish that sounded like English, but not English, then silence. Venturing into the forest, they saw a man hanging from a tree, his legs dancing in midair, his arms flailing above him. With alarm for this sin that they saw, they ran to the tree. Elizabeth helped her sister to the branch from which the now-still man was dangling. When Isabelle got up on the branch, Elizabeth wrapped her arms around the man's waist to push him up. That loosened the belt enough for Isabelle to free it.

The lifeless man dropped to the ground. Elizabeth caught her sister as she dropped from the tree branch. They removed the belt from around the man's neck.

"He breathes not," whispered Elizabeth.

"He must," insisted Isabelle. "How else will we know where he is from?" Isabelle pressed her right foot hard on the man's abdomen. Air blew out of him, and life drew back in. He began coughed mightily and gasped for breath. As soon as some form of regular breathing returned, the man sat up shaking and moaning.

"Elizabeth, have you seen his hands? They're as soft as Thomas's is. And his skin is as white as a noble's."

"Be wary of such men, Isabelle. They achieve their desires by the fairness of their faces." Elizabeth took one step back and then struck him on the head with her staff.

"Ow. What the hell did you do that for?"

Isabelle looked at Elizabeth, (her older sister by one hour,) with a confused expression. Elizabeth returned with a look of disdain. Isabelle's body language conveyed her unspoken question, and her sister's expression gave her unspoken response. She decided Elizabeth was right. Paxton was looking at Elizabeth when Isabelle struck him on the head with her staff. Again, he cried out and turned towards his other attacker. "Why? Why are you torturing me?" Both women raised their staffs. Paxton waved his hands in front of his face. "All right, I get it. You're in charge." *Is this to be my fate? I can't even get a quick death. How am I going to die? Of what? These blows? Internal bleeding? Starvation? Dehydration.*

Paxton tried to wipe his dry lips with an even drier tongue. He formed his hands into a bowl and tilted them to his mouth.

Elizabeth drew a small loaf of bread from a pocket in her apron. Breaking off a piece, she tossed it near the man's hips. Paxton looked at the women and moved his hand to the bread, never taking his eyes off them. "Thank you."

His sharp, wary eyes gave the twins reason to think that this was no village fool. Elizabeth now took a chance. She broke off another piece of bread. She held it out to the man at arm's length. Cautiously, Paxton took the piece. The twins heard him whisper, "Thank you" again.

Isabelle crouched down close to the man, pointed to him, and asked, "London?"

Never taking his eyes off the staffs, Paxton replied, "Yes, I've been to London." The twins exchanged a smile.

Once again Isabelle spoke. "Dost thou live in London?" Paxton was slow to respond. Elizabeth wrinkled her brow. With this man's speech and clothes, perhaps he was a fool after all. She turned to her sister. "Perhaps his people did turn him out."

Isabelle pressed on. "Where art thy kith? Where art thy kin?"

Paxton chewed on the inside of his cheeks. *I've lived in England for years now. Right now, these girls are your only chance to survive.*

"My native land is far to the west of here. Far over the western sea. A place called Connecticut. I am a scientist. You would say teacher, or philosopher." *How do I explain falling out of the wormhole?* "I am lost. I came to England to work with my friends. I got separated from them in a storm." Now it was the girls turn to hesitate and to try to understand him.

Elizabeth pushed on. "Where art thou going? To London?"

Paxton's voice rose. "No! I will stay here. My teammates know I am lost. They will come for me. They will take me home." Paxton looked at the women, identical twins, in their late teens. Their thin faces were lightly freckled beneath blue eyes. Those eyes had the curiosity of kittens. They had the kind of golden hair that absorbed the sun's light and his attention. Long, straight, streams of gold flowing past their shoulders to their slim waists. Broad leather headbands held the tresses in place.

Paxton rubbed his throbbing head. It throbbed from interacting with the girls. As one of the women handed him another piece of bread, he noted pustules on their hands. The women noticed his staring and hid

29

their hands behind their aprons. Isabelle pressed on. "Did you bring the pox with you? How long have you been around our village?" It seemed to be getting easier to understand them.

"No, listen. I am going back to my teammates. I want to go home." Paxton clutched his belt and tried to stand. He succeeded but wobbled as he moved forward. He had to look down as he threaded his belt through the loops of his pants. "You've been very kind. I've received a gift from you girls. My life. It would be ungrateful of me to throw your effort back at you. Excuse me; I will try to go home now."

The twins were not ready to see this very strange stranger leave. "My name is Elizabeth. This is my sister Isabelle."

"I am Paxton. Goodbye." As he got into the field, he felt something squishy under foot. "Damn cow pasture." He paused to sense the direction of the sound of the church bell and moved away from it. Paxton drew a bead on where he figured he fell out of the wormhole.

"Paxton, stop!"

He looked back to the twins but kept moving. "No, I'm going home!"

"Paxton, please look out! Stop!"

Sudden pain. Electric fire raced up his spine and exploded out his temples. He felt himself floating, flying in a cocoon of pain. *I must be disintegrating. Atomic structure unstable. Side effect of wormhole? I'm dying. Why does it have to be so painful?* Then blackness.

NINE A.M. THE DAY AFTER THE EVENT

Albert, Isaac, and Marie stood outside of Paxton's apartment door. Albert was doing what he always did when agitated: taking apart, cleaning, and putting his pipe back together. "All right people, when the constable arrives, don't say more than necessary. Maybe we can find something useful here."

Marie confronted him. "You mean a suicide note."

"I mean anything."

Isaac interrupted. "Albert, it's not too late to get in the pool."

"Isaac, it's amazing how fast you can put a betting pool together. You'd bet on your own mother."

"Well, that would depend on the odds."

"You've got the thumb drive?" Marie asked.

Isaac pulled a flash drive out of his pocket, the size, and colour of his thumb. "If there's a hard drive in his apartment with power, and a USB port, I'm in."

Brisk footsteps ascended the stairs. They turned to see a constable, holding a small packet of mail, approach them.

"I'm Constable Peel."

Albert made introductions. "When Paxton didn't report for work this morning I called, but there was no answer. We came to see if we could find out why he wasn't at work, or why he didn't call in. The landlady refused to let us in without a police presence, so I called for a constable."

"Right she was. It appears Mr. Frost didn't pick up yesterday's post." Constable Peel put the passkey in the lock. "Does Mr. Frost do this sort of thing often?"

"No, he was always diligent in his work."

The constable opened the door. "Mr. Frost, this is the police. We're coming in."

The apartment was as austere, clean, and neat as a model apartment put up for show. Isaac went to the TV. He picked up the remote and hit the ON button. A local channel came up. This remote had preset buttons. He punched button one. The on screen display asked, "Would you like to set this channel as preset one?" Pressing presets two, three and four yielded the same results. "It looks like he didn't watch much TV." Isaac turned it off. His eyes swept the room. They slid to a stop at the Stevenson Prize, framed, and hung on a wall. "I've never actually seen one." Isaac traced the prize with his fingertips. "Albert, is this why he got the God's Room assignment?"

"I've watched him since he won the prize."

Isaac walked to a laptop on a small desk. After making eye contact with Albert, Isaac looked at the laptop, then the constable.

Albert slipped up beside him. "Marie and I will distract the constable. Be discreet and quick." Albert spoke louder. "Constable, may we look at the rest of the apartment?"

"Right sir. I find you can tell a lot about a person by how he keeps his kitchen. Most of all, his refrigerator." Constable Peel marched ahead to the kitchen and opened the refrigerator.

Albert smiled, "Well that doesn't tell us much." Inside were two bottles of generic cola: One diet, one regular, and one tub of generic margarine.

With a look of frustration, constable Peel opened the freezer door. "Well, we seem to have quite the gourmand here." In two neat columns were generic frozen microwave meals. There was one column of breakfast meals, and one column of dinners, separated by a container of generic vanilla ice cream. "There is one less breakfast than dinner. It would appear Mr. Frost never made it back yesterday."

The constable was about to close the freezer door when Marie spoke up. "You're missing something."

Constable Peel swung the door back open to peer inside the freezer. The look on his face showed he didn't get it.

"The meals were arranged alphabetically." Eggs and bacon were on top of eggs and sausage and so on. The same pattern held with the dinners. Albert opened the door beneath the sink and took out the trash bin. Inside lay an empty package of breakfast burritos.

"Could we see the bathroom?" Marie asked.

"A woman would be interested in the state of the bathroom constable," said Albert.

With Marie in the lead, the three of them inspected it, a bathroom as bland as the kitchen. Plain white towels draped a rack attached to a white wall. Marie opened the door of the cabinet beneath the sink. "It appears Paxton did enjoy some creature comforts," said Marie. Beneath the sink was an open package of a premium toilet paper.

"I guess that leaves the bedroom, constable," said Albert.

"Where is the other gentleman?" Constable Peel burst back into the living room. "Stop what you are doing sir." His voice was crisp with authority.

Isaac, who had worked quickly, palmed the thumb drive. "There's nothing on his laptop, Albert. No music, no porn, no sports. Some work-related files and some emails about the travel plans from his last holiday."

"Sir, I'll have to ask you to stay in my sight from now on."

Albert spoke up to defuse the situation. "I believe we were all going to the bedroom, constable."

Isaac said, "I heard what you said about kitchens and bathrooms. I say if you want to know what a man is like, you look in his underwear drawer. There's a reason it's a cliché. Because it's true."

They all crowded into the bedroom, Constable Peel in the rear. A crisp, white bedspread was neatly in place. Marie pulled back a corner to reveal white pillowcases on a white blanket and sheet. A small cross hung on the wall above the headboard. On the left side of the dresser rested a faded photograph.

The framed photo was a portrait of a young woman. Dark hair parted in the middle draped over the woman's shoulders. Her face had the energy and vibrancy of youth. The woman watched the bed's occupant from the photo. The frame's upper right corner had a black ribbon taped to it.

Constable Peel picked up the photo. "Might this woman be a spouse or girlfriend?"

Albert shook his head. "Paxton was younger than the woman in this picture. It's probably his mother."

Isaac pulled open the top dresser drawer. Black socks were on the left. White socks were on the right. White underwear was in the middle. He plunged his hand beneath the underwear and pulled out a plastic bag bulging with herb-like matter. Tearing open its plastic zipper, he pushed his nose in and inhaled. "I don't think this is the Colonel's secret blend of herbs and spices."

"I'm afraid I'll have to take that, sir." Constable Peel looked around and opened the closet door. Long sleeved shirts were on the left, short-sleeved shirts on the right. Ties in the middle.

Again, Marie noticed the pattern first. "The shirts and ties are organized according to the visible region of the electromagnetic spectrum, from red to violet."

Looking down they noticed the shoes: black dress shoes, a space, and white sneakers.

"What colour shoes was Mr. Frost wearing when you last saw him?"

No one could remember.

Isaac pulled open another dresser drawer. His jaw dropped open. "Oh, God, Mary Jane was right." He pulled out a neatly folded blue teddy.

Constable Peel said, "I think I have a good picture of Mr. Frost. A well-organized aesthetic," he looked at the teddy, "with one or two unusual habits."

Marie shook her head. "You don't get it." She had a look of pensive disdain.

"Let me explain, constable," Albert interrupted. "The female neural cortex is wired different than a man's. Go ahead Marie, what do you see that we're missing?"

"Paxton was tightly organized on the outside because he was afraid of coming undone on the inside."

"The reason he is becoming undone is this?" Constable Peel held up the bag of pot.

"No. Keeping such tight control must have been exhausting. That was how he self-medicated."

"And what of the blue teddy?" snickered Isaac.

"Use your imagination." Marie glared back at him.

"You got all that from his apartment?" asked the constable.

"No. I also talked with his girlfriend."

"Well then, has anyone inquired of her where Mr. Frost may be?"

Albert explained about Mary Jane being a ventriloquist dummy.

Turning back to Marie, Constable Peel asked, "Was Mr. Frost present when you had this conversation with his girlfriend?"

"Of course, Constable."

"Well there is one more thing I noticed about Mr. Frost. It seems to have escaped the attention of the lot of you. You're all talking about Mr. Frost in the past tense."

The pain woke Paxton up; the smoky ceiling above him whirled. Lips, tongue, mouth all puckered with thirst. When he became more conscious, other sensations flooded him: the smell of earth and wood, the smell of urine at his crotch, the touch of a coarse blanket covering him, a ringing dizziness in his head. Most of all, he felt pain and thirst.

A wooden creaking sound turned his attention to a table with two benches. There in the deep shadowed half-light a spectral figure of uncertain shape arose. It silently approached, and observed him. Paxton could barely make out the outline of a face. The figure turned, shuffled to the door, and left as quietly as it arrived.

His need for water forced Paxton to a sitting position. Two figures floated toward and above him. *Angels?* His eyes adjusted to the dim light. No. They were the two young women he met before. "May I have something to drink?" One of the women brought a jar and a bowl that had water in it. He drank without caring that some of it spilled.

Something seemed to be in the water—medicine? He hoped that's all it was. *Close your eyes and swallow fast.* She poured more and he drank again, trusting that it was all right. He stopped drinking when he heard moaning. A woman knelt by a bed which was against another wall. On the bed lay a small figure.

The large woman rose from her bedside vigil. She turned and advanced toward Paxton. She leaned down and over him. In the deep shadows, he imagined that her scowl was as foul as her breath. *Be polite.* "Thank you again."

"What do you mean, again?"

From behind her, Paxton could see one of the young women shaking her head.

"For letting me in your house, and now for the water."

Two people entered. Sunlight illuminated a small patch of the cottage. One was a man he saw before. He was shorter than average but solidly built. It was the same man who'd run him out of the village.

The new figure was a monk. He was a head taller than the first man, and thin with bony features. His unbleached cassock made him appear like a specter made flesh. He spoke. "Dominus vobiscum." (*God be with you.*)

Paxton replied. "Et cum Spiritu tuo." (*And with your spirit.*)

"I was told you claim to be a man of some learning. I am Stephan, abbot of the Cistercian monastery in this village. You are in the home of good man Jonah."

"I am Paxton Frost. What happened to me?"

"You came between a bull and a heifer of his interest. The twins were able to beat him away. They persuaded their stepfather, and some other men, to bring you into their home. Jonah then sent for me."

36

"Thank you. May I have something to eat?"

"We will first examine you."

"I don't think there is anything your physicians can do for me."

The silence that followed was all enveloping. Paxton checked the hearth. Even the fire lost its crackle.

"This is not to be an examination of your body." Abbot Stephan's stolid voice put Paxton on alert. "It is an examination of your soul. You are to stand trial for witchcraft."

Chapter 4

To Paxton the room seemed to tilt on its side. He put a hand on the bulrush-covered floor to stop his fall. A sour taste rose in his mouth. "Look, I'd like to stay but I have to find my friends." Paxton staggered trying to get up. "I have to go." He stumbled getting to the door, only to find two men and Jonah blocking his exit.

Abbot Stephan stepped back to stare at Paxton. He hesitated before grabbing Paxton's pinstriped, oxford shirt. "Warlock's garments," he hissed. "We will use the other door." He turned to a door, which opened to a croft. Paxton followed the abbot.

Outside, three monks waited. Two positioned themselves on either side of Paxton; the third moved behind him. They bowed their heads and pulled up their hoods, and tucked their hands into the sleeves of their cassocks. They didn't look like people, more like living ghosts.

It doesn't look like I have a choice.

Close to the cottage, various herbs clumped together; some tall with narrow leaves, others short and wide, most with seed heads showing. The path into the croft led downhill, dividing the garden in two. Then four perpendicular paths divided the croft again. Passing out of the field, the procession turned right on to a wider path.

They kicked up dust with every step. The wide dirt path separated a fallow field from the village. Behind every cottage was a large croft, each growing its own mix of vegetables. The years Paxton had lived with his mother in undeveloped countries had taught him to recognize the artichokes, and the dark-headed stems of asparagus. He saw beans, cabbage, lettuce, and the leaves of various root vegetables. When a breeze blew out from the village, the fresh herbs smelled good. Paxton fingered the box that held his last couple of joints. An idea sprouted in his fertile imagination.

The sound of metal striking wood—one clear *thwack!*—drew Paxton's attention. Next to a cottage stood a man wearing bland expression, and holding a headless speckle-feathered chicken by its feet. The peasant was patient as he waited for the bird's mad flapping to stop. The breeze changed directions. It told him of other smells—the waste of chickens, pigs, and humans.

The procession didn't walk straight for the church, but took an indirect route that continued on a downslope. It leveled out as it circled the village. Judging by the colour of the dirt, Paxton guessed it hadn't rained in quite a while. Dry grass and thorny weeds crept towards the path, looking for moisture. Tiny insects flew up, annoyed by the passing of these two-legged beasts.

Looking at the setting sun, Paxton realized almost the entire day had passed. That God-awful bell continued its dirge. The church and the monastery were the tallest buildings. He had no trouble getting oriented. They turned to the east, to go back into the village. He then saw the reason for this route: Ahead was the lowest point of land and a giblet. It was not like the hanging trees in the model medieval villages he'd seen. Those were clean, smooth sided affairs with a preservative painted on them. This one smelled of green, fresh wood. It was rough-hewn with threads of rope dangling from its crossbeam. *Nice touch. All we need is a raven perched on the upright.* Weeds flourished underneath the gallows.

Paxton's throat was as dry as the dirt path. "What will happen now?"

Abbot Stephan looked at the sky. "It is getting late. I have changed my mind. You will take your evening meal with us."

Food. Thank God. Thank God, they didn't bring a rope and ladder. They didn't bring a rope and ladder! This bastard is playing head games with me. The bastard. I'm left with two choices, fight back or die.

Paxton slowed his pace to let the distance between him and the abbot open up. When Paxton got underneath the gibbet, he planted his feet like roots seeking moisture in the parched earth. He stiffened his back before the monk behind oomphed into him. The other monks took two more steps before they saw their prisoner was not keeping pace. One monk looked like he was about to speak. Paxton spoke first.

"Abbot!"

Abbot Stephan looked around. Not seeing Paxton, he turned to where Paxton should be in the procession. He now looked further behind.

Paxton stood with his fists held out from his body. The sun was behind him. The abbot had to squint to see him.

The abbot was taller than Paxton. The advantage was with the Stephan. The monks on either side stepped away. The monk behind, stepped to the right. Paxton and the abbot faced off. They were Old West gunslingers in old, Medieval England.

Paxton refused to move. *It's my life. Make him respond to you.* The church bell repeated its dirge. *Read my mind. I'm not moving.*

"Understand. I am lost from my friends. A storm separated us. They are looking for me now."

There was no reaction from his adversary.

Paxton pushed harder. *I have nothing to lose, except my life.* He spoke with as much authority as he could muster. "I am nobility in my land. As a prince in the kingdom of Connecticut, only your king has authority over me."

"Where is this land?"

"Far over the Western sea. I, my friends and I, came to your country on a pilgrimage."

The abbot advanced toward Paxton. "You are not in your land now." His sinister voice trickled from his mouth.

"There will be trouble for you, if my friends find I have been harmed."

Abbot Stephan snorted. "You brought an army with you?"

"No, but I have influence in the king's court."

"The king is far away."

"How can I prove that I am not a warlock?" *Bad choice Paxton. They'll tie you up and throw you in a river. If you float, the river rejected you and you're a warlock. If you drown, the river accepted you and you're still dead.*

Abbot Stephan stood over Paxton. "It matters not." He slithered two callused fingers around Paxton's collar. The bruise from his belt now was in sharp contrast to Paxton's pale flesh. "It appears you tried to commit one of the sins of Judas. How did you escape your own condemnation?"

"Abbot Stephan, you have sinned against me. You have sinned against the rules of your order. The Bible commands you to give rest and sanctuary to the traveler. You have also sinned against God. 'Thou shalt neither vex a stranger, nor oppress him: for ye were strangers in the land of Egypt.'"

"Exodus 22:21. I have already stated that you will take your evening meal with us. I follow the rules of my order. Remember, 'Maleficos non patieris vivere.' Exodus 22:18. *(Wizards thou shalt not suffer to live.)* I will not be sinning against God." The abbot's shoulders slumped. "I tire of useless argument, and so should you. Lord Paxton." He delivered the last two words with as much indictment as that of being a warlock.

Abbot Stephan turned and continued his march to the village and the monastery. The other monks resumed their positions around Paxton. *You have to be alive to be hungry. You might as well eat.*

The village was as homespun as the serf's clothes Paxton saw earlier. Wattle-and daub-sided cottages, with thatched roofs, empty streets. The place was like a new, open grave, lying in wait for its lodgers. Wandering pigs appeared to be the village's only tenants. Long tendrils of shadows crept toward the church and walled monastery. As the procession continued, doors seemed to crack open of their own accord. From inside, an eye or two would rebuke him. The doors then shut in a verdict of guilty.

The monastery compound and the village church were the only permanent structures. They were large and made of stone with vaulted roofs. The tiny procession entered the monastery compound. Its door opened into a cloister of bare earth. A horizontal stone and iron sundial occupied the centre of the open space. A well was located in a corner of the cloister, near a building. This building was separate from the others. Paxton could see that the outside walls of other buildings formed the walls of the compound. The bell of the village church now changed its tempo, picking up speed.

"Why does the church bell always ring?"

Abbot Stephan's thin eyebrows furrowed. "The bell tolls for services and prayers."

"What services can you have all day?"

"Burials." The abbot's gaze fell to the ground. His worn, leather shoes matched his worn, leathered face. "The priests here in Alton were among the first to die of the pox. 'Percutiam pastorem et dispergentur oves gregis.' Zechariah 13:7. (*Strike the shepherd and the sheep will be*

42

scattered.) Until the bishop sends another priest, it is up to us brothers to do the shepherd's work."

A young man ran to the abbot. He stood by the abbot's side, waiting for instructions. In the late day, even the young man's shadow was sharply defined and handsome. He held a clay jug in his right hand. A linen towel was draped over the man's other arm. The jug and towel matched like a couple married thirty years. Stephan turned and held out his hands. The man poured water on them. As the abbot dried his hands, the man went to the other monks and repeated the ceremony.

Paxton held out his hands, and noticed the young man wore boots instead of sandals. He had to admire the quality of his footwear. The leather was a polished, cordovan colour. The boots were form-fitted to his legs. He noticed the man's sash like a dog alerted to a squirrel. It was a sash of vivid purple. It had intricate gold and silver threads woven in it. There was hand woven scrollwork, whose only purpose could be to delight the eye. As Paxton examined him, the young adult was likewise examining Paxton. He started with Paxton's brown, scuffed loafers, and worked his way up. Paxton smirked. *What would they have made of my Metallica tee shirt?*

The abbot's eyes went back and forth between the two young men like two pans of a scale. "This is Ignatius. He is a novice in our order. He will be your companion, and instruct you in the ways of our order. Ours is a small monastery. We have no prison cell, or a guesthouse. You may have a cell in the lay brothers' dormitory." Stephan shifted his eyes to glance at the sundial. The time was six o'clock. "It is time for Vespers. Ignatius, this is Paxton. He will conform to our order, the same as you."

The church Paxton saw was not the village church, but a smaller one in the monastery. One of its walls formed part of the back wall of the compound. In it was the humblest of interiors. It had plain, vaulted walls with a stone altar at one end. There were no pews or kneelers.

All this time Paxton remained silent. He mimicked the actions of Ignatius and the monks, kneeling and standing when they did. When it came time for chants, he became flooded, almost drowned. Memories—not just memories—emotions enveloped Paxton. He buried, forgot, and exiled these emotions. Childhood emotions, they were comforting in their simplistic security. In his fall into adulthood, they were frightening in their loss.

Now he stood in the monastery surrounded by Gregorian chants that were as new as the dawn. A blanket of peace for the soul, spread on the waves of music. Growing up was fearful. People moved on from childish comforts. For these men, time, in his cosmologist sense of the word, did not exist. The waves of a child's emotions slapped against the hard rock of reality. These men wrapped themselves in a Linus blanket of security, while disease and pestilence raged outside their walls. They had the comfort of knowing, 'It's God's will.' His mother lived and died in a walled compound of the heart, as impermeable as the monastery's stonewall. *Was it 'God's will' that my mother died of untreated uterine cancer, or was her death the result of her certainty of 'God's will?'*

Vespers services ended. Again, without words, Ignatius led Paxton to another building. The separate building Paxton saw earlier proved to be the kitchen. It was Ignatius's job to gather bowls and spoons for the monks. He took them to the refectory, and then went back to the kitchen for a heavy, steaming kettle. Paxton supported the kettle while Ignatius ladled out soup. They then went out of the compound by a side gate to the bake house. Here they gathered loaves of bread. He and Paxton distributed the loaves to the monks. They left for the buttery. They gathered up clay cups. The same potter that made the jug appeared to have made the cups. Ignatius gave a small cask to Paxton. In the refectory, they emptied ale from it into the monk's cups.

Great. I'm assistant to the chief, head gofer of this institution. Ignatius and Paxton ate, after they served the monks. They sat alone at a

44

small table, grey with age, like some of the monks. *I'd give my left nut—hell I'd give both nuts—if I could be sitting in the University's cafeteria right now. What did they call this stuff? Pottage.* Paxton stirred it with his spoon. *What was it?* Spooning it into his mouth, it had a homogenous flavor, look, and texture. Guidebook memories came back.

A thick soup or stew made from boiling grains and/or vegetables. They kept it over a fire for days. As people ate the pottage, the cooks added ingredients. *They have plenty of meat.*

After the meal, Ignatius performed his duties in reverse.

As mute as the Sphinx, Ignatius led Paxton to the dormitory. No one lit any candles or torches. Chill, darkness seeped through every opening in the building's walls.

The monk's part of the dormitory was closest to the church. Ignatius opened a bedroom door for Paxton and left. The room could hold a small bed—straw mattress and blanket—and no more. Paxton was going to have trouble stretching out. A small cross hung above the head of the bed. *Some things never change. I'd better try to get some sleep. I bet these people have a habit of rising early.*

Sleep did not come easily to Paxton, but when it did, he slept deeply.

"Brother Paxton. Brother Paxton, wake up."

It didn't seem as if he had gotten any sleep at all. "What time is it?"

"It is Compline."

"What time is that?" Paxton demanded.

A perplexed voice pierced the darkness. "It is Compline, the end of the day."

Paxton sat up and swayed his head from side to side. "What do you want?"

"We must go to church."

45

Paxton brushed his hand at Ignatius as if he were swatting away a mosquito. "Go, lead the way." Paxton shuffled behind Ignatius to the church. They said prayers, and returned to their cells.

Well, that should be it for tonight. Paxton fought to get back to sleep.

"Bother Paxton, Brother Paxton, please arise."

Paxton's head was swimming and he didn't even sit up. "Don't tell me, more prayers?" He breathed in deep, trying to get in more oxygen. "What time is it now?"

"Matins."

"Go." *I'm beginning to see a pattern here.* Paxton grabbed Ignatius's purple sash, and thrust his other arm out to touch the wall. *It's as black as the devil's heart at midnight, on a moonless night. Christ. It is midnight, last night was moonless.*

After prayers, Paxton walked with Ignatius back to their respective cells.

"O come, O come Emmanuel."

"What are you singing Paxton?"

"It is a song from my kingdom. My mother sang to me. It uses the same music as you do. Ignatius, are we going to do this again, in let's say three hours?"

"Of course, Lauds."

"But before then we go back to sleep. When do we get up and stay up?"

"Prime." Ignatius paused. "There are many strange things about you."

"My kith are different from yours. To me, you are strange. We all worship God."

"That is not what I have been told."

Paxton entered his cell and fell on the bed. The rope undercarriage screamed as if to break under the sudden weight. *These people are nuts.*

I'm supposed to go to sleep just to wake up in three hours, just to go back to sleep before waking up again. Hang me now.

Before Lauds, Paxton made a desperate attempt. He hit 999.

NO SIGNAL AVAILABLE

"Fuck."

FIFTEEN PERCENT POWER AVAILABLE

"Fuck." *Albert will get here and set up a transceiver. If I turn the phone off, he'll get no response. If I leave the phone on, I'll drain the battery.* Hands trembling, Paxton turned off the phone. *Now, where is Ignatius? Don't tell me he is sleeping in.*

Paxton opened the door to his cell only to see a pair of boots running away as fast as possible. "Ignatius. What are you doing?" A scowl crossed Paxton's face as he ran to overtake Ignatius. He grabbed Ignatius by his sash and dug both heels in the floor. "Ignatius, why are you running away?"

"You are a warlock." He was shaking so hard, he would make a perfect bartender for James Bond.

Ignatius's eyes went dinner-plate wide. Paxton smelled fear. It smelled as if he peed in his pants. "No, Ignatius, why do you say that? What have I done?"

"When I came to wake you up, I heard you. I heard you in your cell."

"You heard what?"

"I heard you calling forth your demon familiar by name." Ignatius wrestled his sash free from Paxton's grip. "I heard you calling your familiar by name, twice." He was backing away, loathing foaming from his mouth.

Paxton relaxed his stance. "Ignatius, did you hear me say fuck?"

"Yes." Ignatius spat his word at Paxton.

Paxton saw the opening. *Be calm, and casual.* "Ignatius, I knew you would be calling me to prayer. I knew I didn't have time for a full

47

prayer to God in my native language. When time is short, to say fuck is a short prayer to ask God for his blessings and protection. It is our quickest prayer."

Ignatius fidgeted in place. "You swear this is true?"

"'I say unto you, swear not at all; neither by heaven; for it is God's throne: nor by the earth; for it is his footstool: or by Jerusalem; for it is the city of the great King.' Matthew 5: 34, 35."

Ignatius shifted his weight from foot to foot, as if balancing a scale. "Forgive me, Brother Paxton."

"No problem. We will never mention it."

Chapter 5

Ignatius and Paxton repeated the routine of prayer and service. In the refectory, they noticed one small but significant change. Abbot Stephan was missing. Paxton continued to serve the other monks while Ignatius served the head table.

When Paxton sat at the rear table with Ignatius he whispered, "Where is Abbot Stephan?"

"Obey the Grand Silence," Ignatius whispered back.

After the morning meal, as dawn broke, Ignatius and Paxton took the bowls and spoons back to the kitchen. To go from the refectory to the kitchen they crossed the bare earth of the cloister, still wet with the morning dew. The dew turned the dirt from a light to a dark brown. Only now were birds starting their morning wake up calls.

When they were in the middle of the open ground, Ignatius whispered to Paxton, "I inquired as to the health of the abbot. The prior told me that after morning Mass, the abbot took his meal in the kitchen. He then told the steward to prepare a noon day meal for the abbot to take with him."

"Where did he go?"

"The prior didn't know."

"How long will he be gone?"

Ignatius shrugged.

"What is to become of me until he returns?"

"Ah. The prior said that his instructions are for you to stay here and serve."

"What does that mean?"

"He took that to mean you are to continue to assist me."

"What is your work here?"

"The monks must be given opportunity for prayer and the copying of books. It is up to the acolytes and novices to work with God's children outside of the monastery. I acted as almoner, receiving and giving alms, and ministered to the girls in the convent school." Ignatius shook his head. "Now the abbot has set me to do manual labor, even to repairing an oven in the bake house. The oven's fire broke through the chimney's mortar. That cracked some stones. We will repair it."

Leaving the barren cloister by a side gate, a path of trampled flora led to the maw of the bake house. The morning breeze brought them the nurturing scent of fresh bread.

Paxton noticed the bake house was over four metres high. There was a door centred in front. Two windows in each of the long sided walls let light into the building. Four ovens facing the door were more than half the height of the bake house. The ovens had vertical sides for half their height. The top half of each was a cylindrical dome. It was above the oven on the far left that Paxton noticed a blackened crack circling its chimney. At the base of the oven was a wooden trough, a bucket of limestone pebbles, another of sand, an empty bucket, some hand tools, and a few large stones.

Paxton looked at the damage. "How do you intend to make the repairs?"

Ignatius pointed at the fractured stones. "I'll clean out the old mortar, pull the damaged blocks, and give them to you. We'll reuse as many as we can. I've replacement stones if necessary. While I'm removing the cracked stones, you will crush the limestone into a powder." Ignatius scrambled up the arch of the oven. When he got to the oven's roof, he turned to Paxton. "Hand me a hammer and chisel."

Paxton tossed up the tools, and sitting on his heels, began his own work. *College entrance track in high school. Three AP courses: computer science, math, and physics. A doctorate in physics from Columbia. And now the only job I can get is busting rocks.* "Where do you come from Ignatius? You are not dressed quite as a monk, or any of the villagers."

"As you claim to be, I am of noble birth."

Paxton rubbed the stinging sensation on his cheek.

"I am the second born of Lord Despensers." Ignatius sat cross-legged on the oven's roof. The cloud-white plaster looked like a heavenly throne. He gazed away. "I was born on the wrong side of the blanket. My father did not acknowledge me until I came of age." Ignatius faced Paxton. His voice hardened. "The monks know me for my earthly nobility," he stroked his purple sash, "and allow me to continue to wear my favourite boots and sash." Ignatius became alert to what he had said, squirmed, then his shoulders dropped. "Forgive me Paxton. I suffer from the sins of ambition and vainglory."

"I do not believe the Pope has declared ambition one of the seven deadly sins." Paxton laughed. "Both of us are ambitious in our own ways. I forgive you your ambition if you forgive mine." Paxton hung his head. "I thought that men such as us, could not join the religious life."

"Anyone can be influenced and anything can be obtained, for the right kind of coins. What of your family, Lord Paxton?"

I'll need a careful weaving of fact and fiction here. My mother was a BAC."

"I do not understand?"

"I called her a BAC, Born Again Christian. She believed there was only one, strict way to worship God: her way. She believed everyone else was going to hell. Trying to look down on everyone became exhausting for me. The constant worrying that I could fall out of God's favour, or worse, my mother's favour, was too much. I could not look at her and say, 'I believe as you do.' The first chance I got I left Connecticut, for the new city of York. I studied at the University there. Then I came to England." Paxton rested his head against the side of the oven. "For years, I have been running from my mother. Life would be so much easier if I had something, or someone, to run to."

"So you have been banished."

"No. Mother has gone to her eternal reward. I can return any time." *Time. Don't break down now Paxton.*

"And what of your father?"

Paxton shrugged. "Never knew him. I don't even know if mother knew who he was." *Why did you discourage my questions, Mother?*

"And you still claim a title and land?"

"Like you, I struggle to make my own destiny."

"Will you be opposed by other nobles? Who rules in your absence?"

"Lord Albert rules among my nobles. I have faith in him."

"You should have faith in God, not men. You told the abbot a story of being lost in a storm."

"All true, a special kind of storm. We call it a wormhole. It's complicated. What of your half-brother? Does he still live at home?"

"Some years ago the future duke was sent to serve as seneschal in another noble's household. It puts my family in good favour with that noble's clan. It also gives my brother a chance to judge the desires and motives of other nobles. If that family should become important to mine, perhaps a lady of that house will catch his fancy."

"A marriage made of alliance more than love. I left my mother's house before something like that could happen."

Ignatius and Paxton continued their work in silence. At last, the quiet was broken by the monastery's bell. "This largest block I will recut up here," Ignatius said as he slid down the curve of the oven. The two men walked back to the monastery. The dew was gone, baked away by the morning sun. They brushed against dry grasses guarding the edge of the path. Insects now rose and flitted among the weeds.

Passing into the cloister again by the side gate, they kicked up powdered earth. It swirled about, and settled. Paxton noted the time on the sundial. *Nine. They call this Terce.* In the church, the familiar tone of the Gregorian chants filled Paxton with both awkwardness and peace.

After services, they walked back to the bake house. The birds of the field stopped their morning songs, and now were darting among the grasses and wild flowers, hunting bugs and seeds.

In the bake house Paxton boosted Ignatius back on top of the unused oven, and sat to pulverize limestone.

Ignatius had cleared most of the mortar around the largest stone. "Abbot Stephan will not be back until tomorrow's evening meal at the earliest. He has gone at least as far as Sandalburg. There is the castle of the Lady Wilhelmina."

"You said you didn't know how long he would be gone, or when he would be back."

"I still do not. If he went in any direction but north on the forest road, he would be able to get a noon day meal from a farm or village." Ignatius passed several small blocks down to Paxton.

"Then he may go north, eat his meal, and return by early evening."

"Why?"

Paxton stood up to take some small chimney stones from Ignatius.

Ignatius turned and scuttled back to work on the largest block. "If he goes no farther than the castle, he can return by tomorrow's evening meal."

"Why go to the castle?"

53

Ignatius chiseled mortar from the large stone on top of the chimney. "He may be reluctant to put to trial someone who claims noble birth. He may need to consult with the Lady."

First the execution, then the trial. "Off with his head!" Shouted the Queen of Hearts. "Who is the Lady Wilhelmina?"

Ignatius stopped his work to look wistfully in the distance beyond the bake house walls. "She is the widow of the late Duke of Northumbria. He gave her Sandalburg Castle and its estate as her Morning Dowry."

"What is a Morning Dowry?" Paxton paused at his own work.

"Your nobles do not practice the custom of giving the bride a Morning Dowry?"

"Perhaps we do. It may be that we call it by another name." Paxton tried to wipe the fine dry limestone dust out of his hair and off his face.

A pale pink blush started in Ignatius's earlobes. "The Morning Dowry is given to a noble's bride the morning after the consummation of their marriage." The blush now deepened and started to cover his cheeks. Ignatius pushed the stone block across the top of the oven. "It is given in appreciation for the gift that a woman can give only once." The blush now completely enveloped Ignatius's face.

"The duke gave her a castle and estate?"

"Yes. The duke, God rest his soul, was a most generous noble. Most nobles would give an ermine cape, or perhaps jewels. It is hers as long as she pays the taxes on the land to the new duke's clan."

"How large is the estate?" Paxton grasped the rock, now almost overhead.

"This village, Alton, and its farms are at the southern end. It is a day's walk to the castle. The castle is at the western end of the duke's lands. From her castle, its estate is a day's walk in all directions except west. It does not include church land."

"Of course." Paxton's cerebrum kicked into gear.

Area of a half-circle = $1/2r^2$

r=walking distance in one day≈30 km

$1/2 \times \pi \times (30km)^2 \approx 1414 \ km^2$

$1/2 \ 100ha=1km^2$

$100ha/km^2 \times 1414km^2 = 141,400ha$

"That's over 141,000 hectares! Minus church land."

Ignatius came down to examine the stones he gave Paxton.

A grinding noise caused Paxton to look up. The largest block tilted, hesitated, then slid down the oven's sloped side, above Ignatius's head. Paxton's cerebrum revved into high gear.

$\sqrt{(a \times 2d)} = V_f + V_i$

Where: a is gravitational acceleration of $9.8m/s^2$, d is the distance of about 2 m, V_f is the final velocity, and V_i is the initial velocity of 0m/s.

$V_f \approx 6.3m/s$

$t=d/v$

$t \approx .32s$

$a = (V_f - V_i)/t$

$a \approx 19.6m/s^2$

Finally,

$F=ma= (d \times v)a$

d = density of rock, $\approx 2500kg/m^3$, and v = volume of rock, $\approx 0.006m^3$, $a \approx 19.6m/s^2$

Ninety-four newtons are going to hurt.

If his brain went into high gear, his muscles went into overdrive, grabbing Ignatius by the hair and pulling him back.

The stone missed Ignatius's head by two millimetres and split in two.

"Oh brother." Paxton wheezed.

"Yes. Brother." Ignatius panted. "Cain slew his brother with a stone, but you have saved my life from a stone."

The work continued in rhythmic silence. Ignatius removed stones. Paxton cleaned them. Ignatius chiseled out the damaged mortar. Paxton smashed limestone into powder. The monastery's bell called for noon prayers.

As they left the bake house Paxton asked, "Is it possible I could get a bath. I have been to other lands and learned how to make something called soap. We will need animal fat, I see you have sheep, wood ash—"

"We also have olive oil, potash, soda, and white clay."

"You know about soap."

In the monastery, Ignatius showed Paxton a small room with a basin, pitcher, and a bowl with castile soap. Afterward they entered the cloister. Its quiet atmosphere seemed to grow even more still. Birds flew off their perches and over the monastery's wall. Monks walking to the church from the brew house, mill, library, or other buildings slowed their progress to engage in oblique curiosity about Paxton. Others clustered in small groups to exchange their own nonverbal communications. Ignatius looked around and changed his pace to move away from Paxton.

After noon Mass, Paxton and Ignatius resumed their service to the monks in the rectory. At the head table, Ignatius gazed at the prior and gave a small smile. The prior scowled in return. After their duties, Ignatius led Paxton to the farthest table. Paxton sat at one corner, Ignatius then sat at the corner diagonally opposite. He divided his food in half with a knife and pushed it back together, repeatedly. Finally, looking at the head table, Ignatius got up and sat next to Paxton.

Paxton and Ignatius spent the rest of the day, and all the next, in silence.

Late afternoon on the second day, just as Ignatius predicted, Abbot Stephan returned. At the head table was a new monk. This new/old monk wore a black cloak over his white habit. Paxton also noted a non-monk at the table. He had a short full beard. His build resembled a mature oak.

After dinner, Paxton broke his silence with Ignatius. "Who are those people?"

Ignatius straightened up and smiled. "The Dominican is the confessor to the Lady Wilhelmina. The other must be the smithy at the castle."

"How do you know this?"

"Did you not see the singe marks in his beard and tunic? How his right hand is more callused than the left? Did you not take note of the smell of smoke about him? What else could he be?"

"Why are they here?"

"To take you to the castle for trial. If a noble's permission is needed then you must be brought to the noble."

"When do you think they will try to take me to the Lady's castle?

"After the morning meal."

I'll stay awake and slip out between prayers. "Peace be with you, Ignatius." Paxton listened as Ignatius's footfalls faded away. Hearing nothing Paxton tried to open the door. *Bolted. It's bolted from the outside.* He lay down on the bed. *Stay awake and think of Plan B. Think of—*

"Wake up Paxton. It is Prime. Time for prayers."

"I don't give a damn about prayers." *I want to escape.* Paxton pulled his legs up to his chest.

Ignatius stepped back from Paxton. "There is nothing you can do for your body. Do not also abandon your soul."

The rest of the morning proceeded as the others, only with more coldness and distance between Paxton and Ignatius.

As they put the small ale casks away in the buttery after the morning meal Ignatius opened up. "I heard Abbot Stephan tell the steward to prepare three noon meals. I will ask God's blessing on you in your own tongue. Fuck you, Brother Paxton."

"Ignatius, no one has acted in a more Christlike manner than you."

Ignatius rocked side to side on his feet, and again his face started to flush.

Paxton swallowed hard. "Fuck you too, Ignatius."

"Thank you Paxton."

I'm going to hell.

Chapter 6

The door of the buttery creaked a warning. It resisted opening, to reveal who, or what, was on the other side. Nevertheless, it did open. Ignatius and Paxton saw three silhouettes backlit by the morning sun. The tall centre one entered. Removed from the sun's glare, Paxton saw it was the abbot. The silhouette on Stephan's right entered and resolved itself into the Dominican monk. He ran a hand through a balding head of grey hair before settling both hands on a stomach with the girth of an ale cask. The last silhouette entered and became the man Ignatius had identified as the smith.

Stephan turned a bit to his right. "This is Friar Bernard, the Lady Wilhelmina's confessor." The friar's lack of expression would have made any poker player proud. The abbot's tone was clipped and dry. Moving to his left, he said, "This is John, the smith in the Lady's castle." The smith smiled and rubbed his palms together like a sumo wrestler eager to enter the circle.

Looking back at Paxton, Stephan's voice dropped lower and slower. "You will accompany them to the castle of the Lady Wilhelmina, where you will meet your fate." Stepping back into the daylight, the abbot dissolved back into a silhouette. "Come Ignatius, your work here is done. Farewell, Prince Paxton of the house of Frost." The abbot's words dripped from his mouth with sarcasm and venom.

The friar watched the abbot scuttle across the cloister, the young Ignatius in tow. When they passed the sundial, Friar Bernard said, "We have no irons to restrain you," the friar opened his left arm to the smith, "and John would like to do mayhem to your body. You claim noble birth. Let there be peace between us. We will take you to our nobility, where you may have the comfort and rituals of the caste." The friar's voice sounded like shoes scuffling on a gravel path.

Looks like I have to continue my 'nobility' bluff. "We will take the road north. For such a journey I hope you have food for a noon meal."

The friar displayed no surprise at Paxton's knowledge of the particulars of what their trip would entail. He held up a large sling sack and put the sling over his left shoulder. Friar Bernard walked out of the buttery, and headed for the main gate. Paxton turned to the smith. John smiled. His smile was as steely as the iron with which he worked. John put his hands under Paxton's underarms. He lifted Paxton up and examined him on each side. Tiring of his new pet, John dropped Paxton.

Walking through the village, people stared at Paxton. Some showed an expression of relief. Others scowled in anger. *I've seen this play out on the news channels. 'Yankee go home.' I would like nothing more than that. OK. Plan A, slipping out in the middle of the night didn't work. Go to Plan B. What is Plan B? Wait until we are alone in the forest. When lunch is ready, smack down Johnny boy, grab the sling sack from Friar Tuck, and run like hell. Maybe then, I can get back to the point I popped out of the wormhole. After that, who knows?*

Turning north to the forest, they passed the cow pasture where Paxton first saw the twins. Far in the field, he saw a solitary male figure wearing a wide brimmed hat to guard against the sun. The twins with their golden waterfalls of hair cascading down their backs, were not present. *Why aren't they in the field? I want to wave good-bye to them.*

There was no abrupt line between pasture and forest; merely a gradual change from field to brush, from brush to seedlings, from seedlings to young trees, from young trees to mature growth. Animals flourished in this transition zone. Deer, hares, and squirrels sought edible vegetation. Foxes hunted the hares, and red squirrels. One fox stopped to judge the men. He resumed his prowl for meat, deciding that his position as a hunter didn't change to that of being the hunted. Men hunted them all, and other men.

The road wasn't a true road. It consisted of trampled vegetation and clods of earth by the hooves of livestock. The dappled sunlight darkened as old trees reached up with an ambition to blot out the sun. Time became difficult to measure with sunlight so diffused. The deeper they traveled into the forest, the more abysmal the forest stillness became.

After too long without a stop, Paxton thought he heard a waterfall. Sound scattered like sunlight in the forest. Breaking out into a clearing, Paxton saw that the makeshift road crossed a wide stream. To his left flowed a waterfall indeed, about three metres tall and fifteen metres wide. The water tumbled to its base only to spray back up almost two metres. Grey, flaked shale flanked both sides of watery cliff. The path entered the stream ten metres downstream from the falls.

The friar turned to Paxton and pointed to the falls. "There is a deep pool just downstream of the falls. The pool ends abruptly here." Bernard sat down and motioned for the smith to sit next to him. "Paxton, take off your shoes and roll up your trousers. We will put our shoes in the pack. We can cross here, where the stream is shallow, and have our meal on the other side."

As soon as you get out of the water, I'm going to knock Johnny smith into the deeper water, grab the sack, the shoes, and lunch, and run. There better not be any upsets. I don't have a Plan C.

The crossing was slippery but uneventful. Where they crossed, the water reached up to Paxton's mid-calf. He couldn't judge the depth of the water to his left. As the friar climbed out of the stream, Paxton turned and rushed John. Pushing against the smith, he fell to his knees, then heard Bernard laughing.

Paxton felt himself lifted out of the water and swung around like a human hammer in a bizarre hammer throw competition. Paxton arched up in the air and crashed down in the depth. Trying to rise to the surface, he felt a weight smashing down on him pushing him down into the stream. Now someone was walking up and down his body.

His brain screamed, *Get off, you're killing me!*

Now the weight walked off Paxton and he shot to the surface. The friar had led him to believe the water was deeper than the metre or so he found himself in. Paxton heard the smith laugh before seeing him, climbing up the bank. He now felt warmth trickling down his right leg. *Oh God no!* He thrust his right hand to his pants below his crotch. He felt the warmth of the phone's battery shorting out. *My last remote hope of contacting Albert is gone. My joints are soaked, too, dammit.* He shouted with all the vengeance he could muster, "You son of a bitch! I'm going to kill you!" Paxton charged the smith. As he hit the riverbank, the smith struck out with a foot to Paxton's chest and pushed him back into the water.

"Come, come now Lord Paxton. Did you not say yesterday that you wished to bathe? So now why do you wish to strike down the smith?"

This friar would make a good poker player. I'll kill them for losing me my phone.

Bernard had put out a spare set of dry monk's garb on the ground. Paxton climbed out, away from the smith, and gave him his shoes. The friar and smith set about studying Paxton's loafers.

"Everyone in my kingdom has shoes that fit like that."

"Change out of your wet clothing while I give thanks for our bread and cheese."

Giving thanks, Bernard used a knife to slice a small loaf of bread into three parts. Then he divided a round of cheese the same way.

Paxton took off his shirt and twisted the excess water out. *How am I going to get stuff out of my pockets without raising questions as to what everything is? What will they think of tighty-whiteys? I can take off the underwear with the pants, fold over the pants and start at the waist to roll up and squeeze out the water.*

A question rose in Paxton. "What did you say to John as you took off your shoes?"

"My dear Lord Paxton. If you wanted to escape us wouldn't this be the perfect spot." Friar Bernard made ticking noises with his tongue. His amusement showed with his eyes and tongue.

"You could be with the FBI, or the Mafia." Paxton snapped. The other men returned blank stares.

Paxton finished getting dressed and put his wet clothes in the sack. When the friar and the smith finished eating Bernard reclined on the ground. "We will wait for you."

"That won't be necessary." Paxton snatched the knife from the friar and cut two slices of bread from his share of the loaf. Making thin slices of cheese, he placed the cheese between the two slices of bread and cut it diagonally. "It's called a sandwich." Paxton stuffed one pointed end in his mouth and took a bite. Now Paxton slung the sack on his shoulder. "Let's go."

The next few hours passed without incident. For a while, they climbed uphill until Paxton could see a break in the forest. Stepping out of the oak forest, the small troop stood on the east side of a valley. The friar leaned against a tree and pawed a sweaty brow. He pointed across the narrow valley to the west. "There is the castle of the Lady Wilhelmina, and the town of Warren." Friar Bernard wheezed.

Paxton stepped forward to get a better look. "There, is that it?" He was stunned. Paxton expected knights in shining armor, jousting, and tournaments. He wanted to hear the music of musicians and minstrels. See pennants fluttering above embattlements, and stone towers. He strained to hear the laughter of ladies-in-waiting.

It's a dump. I've changed my mind. This was probably an arranged marriage, to cement relations between two noble households. The duke was stuck with a bargain basement, discount bin wife, an old crone with a hump, and a wart on her nose. Paxton could practically hear the duke. *'Honey, you go take care of your estate. I'll stay in Banburn, and dive into the pool of ladies-in-waiting.' When he found out she was coming back, he killed himself.*

A river ran farther west in the valley. The castle sat squat on a bend in the river. To the northeast of the castle lay a town.

Paxton noticed a moat that connected to the river, surrounded the castle. The river was choking the castle's moat with silt. *This must be one of those ancient motte and bailey castle complexes.* Beyond the moat, an earth bank rose maybe ten metres. A stone crenellated stockade ascended another three metres high. Spiked timbers on the top of the stockade stood guard. *I'll bet the bailey behind the stockade is barely big enough for the castle's servants to live and work.* Looking past the stockade Paxton saw the motte. The steep sided hill grew some twelve metres or more above the bailey. A wood palisade two metres high ringed its top. Crowning all that was the keep, a two-story wood affair.

Was the motte a cut-down hill? Maybe they used the earth dredged up for the moat to build up the motte. He looked at the colour of the wood. *The second story seems to be a recent addition.* Smoke that rose out of the centre of the keep provoked no interest in the smith or the friar.

Drawing near the castle, Paxton saw the exterior wall of the stockade wasn't stone, but whitewashed plaster. Like grapes drying into raisins, the plaster was crumbling off its wood backing.

Moat silting up, plaster over a wood wall, and a second floor addition. They're putting lipstick on a dead pig.

Walking toward the bridge over the moat, Paxton heard a voice call out. On the lintel, centred above the two massive, wrought-iron-bound, wood doors, was a small watchtower. A guard in the tower called to the people inside the castle. The two vertical lips opened wide and Paxton passed between them. Behind the doors, he saw an iron lattice gate above. Spikes like iron teeth were ready to descend and bite off any unwanted intruder.

Passing through the courtyard of the bailey, they went to the motte. Its stone base extended out about a metre. They passed through two smaller gate-lips and entered a covered stairway leading up to the keep. Paxton stumbled on the way up. The steps were irregular in height and depth so Paxton was always in danger of tripping. *Rank amateur workmanship.* After stumbling a few times, Paxton began to appreciate the design. *Any adversary trying to charge up the stairs would be in danger of tripping and falling clear down to the stone base.*

They exited the stairs to a walkway surrounding the keep. On the left side of the keep was an exterior stairway to the second floor. At the keep's door they were met by a pockmark faced man dressed in clothes like Ignatius's, down to the purple sash around his waist. Paxton looked at the man's boots. *They're as good as the ones Ignatius wears.*

Friar Bernard spoke. "Harold, this is Prince Paxton of the house of Frost. He comes from the kingdom of Connecticut."

Harold looked Paxton up and down. "A prince is in monk's garb?"

"These were given me when my clothes got wet."

"Where is Konectic?"

"Connecticut is beyond your Western sea."

Harold nodded and escorted the three men through a centre hallway. The door at the end of the hall, Paxton guessed, would lead them into the Great Hall of the keep.

Entering, he observed a ceremonial fire some three metres in diameter in the centre of the Hall. Four pillars supported the chimney that carried off the smoke and sparks. To the left of the fire were two rows of more than a dozen people, with the better dressed in the front row. Harold led Paxton and his two companions around the right side of the fire. Harold stopped Paxton just past the centre of the fire before he escorted the friar and the smith another quarter of the way around.

Harold spoke up. "My Lady Wilhelmina, I present to you Prince Paxton of the house of Frost. He is from the kingdom of Konectic. It is over the Western sea. Prince Paxton, I present you to the Lady Wilhelmina and her lady-in-waiting Sarah."

This place reminds me of those mansions where the lights are out so people can't see that the owners had to sell the furniture. A low dais ran the width of the Hall, about nine metres deep from the back. On the dais, only two wooden stools, a taller one for the Lady and a shorter one for the Lady's lady.

Both women rested their white, flat-soled shoes on the bottom rungs.

Their dresses, complimented each other, silk for Lady Wilhelmina, linen for Sarah. The dresses were tight at the waist and flared at the hem, which reached the floor. Each woman wore a gold sash that hung down on her left side. The dresses ran up to the neck, with long sleeves that flared out at the elbow to end at the wrist. Their left hands rested outstretched on their laps, with the right hand laid gently on top.

A white, cone shaped headdress crowned the Lady's head. Paxton guessed it was some thirty centimetres in length, raked back at about a thirty-degree angle. Its point let down a white gauze tassel of about the same length. A white wimple covering most of her face held the headdress in place. Sarah's headdress was similar, Paxton judged, at two-thirds the height and tassel length.

It was easy to describe Sarah: slender and small, with a heart-shaped face and a pixie nose. Her lips were full, and bow shaped.

Paxton found it harder to describe the Lady in physical terms. On a scale of one to ten, she broke the babe-o-metre.

Her lips didn't display the overt sensuousness of Sarah's, but to Paxton her face seemed to hold all manner of possibilities. Most of all it was her presence. She was a woman who could walk into a room and other women would huddle in small groups, cross their arms in front of them, and whisper among themselves, 'there's nothing special about her.' But in their hearts, they knew they were lying.

Turning her head to her chaplain and the smith she asked, "Do either of you have anything to say of this man?"

The smith bounded forward, snapping a look back at Paxton. He looked like eight-year old Timmy who ran to his mother to say he caught little Paxton and his sister playing doctor behind the garage. He jumped on the dais so his back was to Paxton.

The smith blocked Paxton's view of the Lady, but he saw Sarah lean to her left and tilt her head to the right to hear the smith's whisperings. Hearing them, Sarah's mouth formed an oval that made up a third of her face. Her eyes went as wide as if she found out she got a pony for Christmas. She buried her face in her hands and her whole body quaked.

She shook her head so hard that the tassel on her headdress whipped her shoulders. Then an eye peeked through her parted fingers at Paxton.

Paxton stepped forward to defend himself. He wanted to tell the Lady that no matter what the smith said, it was a lie. Turning his attention from Sarah to the Lady, Paxton saw that the smith seemed to have shriveled. The desiccated man backed off the dais, to his place next to the friar.

Paxton could see the muscles in the Lady's jaw tighten. Her eyes narrowed to an unblinking stare. Only her face moved to follow the smith back to his starting point. That look could bake an Easter ham.

Mentally, Paxton pumped his fist. *Another time, another place, but little Timmy is getting his.*

If her look was all fire, her voice was all ice. "Friar Bernard, have you learned anything of our hostage?"

Hostage? I can do hostage. You keep hostages alive. Hostage is good. Maybe my luck is changing.

The friar stood still, unaffected by the verbal frost that covered him.

"He does have some interesting meal habits. He calls it a sand-witch."

Now the Lady's rapier eyes turned to Paxton. "What do you know of witches in Konectic?"

"In Connecticut we pronounce the word with a b."

The statue of justice depicts a woman wearing a blindfold. If you were to take off the blindfold, you would see the eyes and face of Lady Wilhelmina.

"You come in the guise of a monk?" The Lady was judge and justice.

"My clothes are soaked from a fall in a river. These were provided to me by the good friar."

"Catherine." The Lady's authority was in inverse proportion to her whisper.

A woman from the back row, on the other side of the fire, stepped forward. She looked like the kind of woman who could shingle your roof, or field strip, repair, and reinstall a kitchen garbage disposal with no problem.

Lady Wilhelmina said, "Prepare a fire in the old minstrel's cottage, and bring Prince Paxton his evening meal."

Catherine looked at Paxton as if she would have preferred to be snaking out a floor drain, turned, and left.

The Lady issued another quiet command. "Sarah."

Sarah sat straight, and assumed a poise that was a pale imitation of the Lady's.

"Please escort Lord Paxton to the old minstrel's cottage. We will talk at our morning meal."

Sarah hopped off her seat and hurried around the fire. Approaching Paxton, she flipped a wrist to indicate he should follow. Bowing to the Lady, Paxton turned to fall in behind Sarah.

Following close behind Catherine, Paxton saw her exit the keep and turn right. Sarah started for the stairs when Paxton stopped her. "Catherine went this way." He went back to follow her and turned a corner of the concourse. Paxton stopped when he saw Catherine climb a break in the top of the spiked timbers and jump. Wide-eyed Paxton rushed for the palisade. Looking between the spikes Paxton saw Catherine slide down the motte. She dug one foot then another into small protrusions or soft spots in the earth. Her constant braking made for a controlled, slow descent to the bottom.

Paxton felt a hand on his shoulder. "Catherine has her own way of going up and down." Sarah turned back to the stairs. The descent out of the covered stairway was slower than going up.

"Sarah, I will have to apologize to the minstrel for intruding on him."

"Geoffrey has passed on to his eternal reward."

Paxton hesitated. "Did he die of the pox?"

"No. The old man departed for God in his sleep."

"Good. I mean it is good he didn't suffer. Have you lived here long?"

"Since the death of my Lady's husband, the Duke of Northumbria, in his castle at Banburn."

"How long ago was that?"

"One night less than a score."

"Why did the Lady leave her late husband's castle in Banburn?"

Sarah remained silent.

Okay. There is more here than meets the eye. Let me try another track. "When will you return to Banburn?"

"When the Lady Wilhelmina decides."

They passed out of the stairway, into the open bailey, and turned right. Dusk was already blanketing the earth and sky. They headed for a cottage that had smoke rising from a chimney. Entering the cottage, Catherine rose from in front of the hearth.

Paxton interlaced his fingers and pressed his palms together. "Sarah. I wish to speak to you in private."

She turned to Catherine. "Wait outside."

When Catherine closed the door behind her, Paxton turned to Sarah. "Sarah I must know what the smith said. I must show the Lady the he is wrong."

Her face contorted so much Paxton feared it might tear off. "You must show her?" Sarah's voice squeaked out. She hid her face in her hands.

"I know the smith is no friend to me" Paxton's voice rose.

Stifled wails came from Sarah's body. Paxton realized they were laughter.

She straightened up while sputtering noises came from her chest. Trying to regain control over her face, Sarah raised her right hand to her face. She held out her thumb and index finger about five centimetres apart. "He said," she sputtered and tried again. "He said he knows nothing of the size of the Kingdom of Konectic, but that your personal kingdom is quite small." Giggling, she ran for the door.

70

It took Paxton a few seconds to recover. In three large strides, he was out of the cottage. He used a few fast steps to give momentum to his words. "Oh… YEAH! Well, well it's big enough for Saaaraaah!"

The ponytail tassel sashayed side to side as Sarah turned a corner and ran up the stairway.

What else can go wrong? Paxton turned and stopped when he saw Catherine insolently leaning against the cottage. "Get my meal."

Catherine gave a quick, smirking glance at his crotch and hurried off.

Paxton stormed into the cottage, slamming the door shut. Flinging the bag of wet clothes by the fire, he flattened himself against a back wall. *All right, if all the antimatter was used up, it may take as long as two weeks to get more from CERN. Albert can run simulations until then and get a good idea of where and when to look for me. I've lived longer than that in the boon docks. They'll come for me.*

Sitting at the break room's table, Max divided his time between monitoring the telly, and working Mary Jane's pulleys and levers. Isaac and Cecilia joined him and slumped into chairs on the opposite side of the table. Cecilia finished reading the article in the newspaper she brought with her. "Well, at least our names weren't mentioned in any of the papers."

"Everyone's done a good job of covering up the details of The Event," said Max.

"Do you think that will make any difference?" Isaac scowled. "This was supposed to be Noble Prize stuff. We'll be lucky to hold on to our positions here. Anything new on the telly, Max?"

Max had Mary Jane on his lap and moved her head to face Isaac and Cecilia. "The story appears to be moving farther down the news cycle."

Isaac put an elbow on the table and his head in the palm of his hand. "Max, I can still see your lips moving."

"Quit playing with that damn doll," Cecilia shouted. She slapped Mary Jane with the newspaper so hard M J's head spun completely around. When it stopped, M J's eyebrow's had tightened into a V and her fangs were bared, ready to clamp on Cecilia's hand. Cecilia dropped the paper on the table and stormed out.

YORKSHIRE EVENING POST

Ruling on American scientist's disappearance from U. of Y.

The coroner has ruled on the disappearance of an American scientist, Dr. Paxton Frost. He declared that a police investigation led him to conclude Dr. Frost died in a boating accident, and the manner of death as drowning, in Loch Lomond. Police have discontinued attempts to recover the body.

Dr. Frost was part of a team working to validate M theory at the University of Yorkshire's European High Energy Collider. Dr. Wesley will hold a memorial service at the University Chapel. Dr. Frost had no living relatives.

Chapter 7

Paxton took stock of his miserable surroundings: pallet, straw mattress, a rag filled pillow, and blanket. A cross hung on the wall over the bed. A chair, a table with a bowl, cup, an empty pitcher, and a candle in a candlestick, completed the furnishings.

He picked up the sling bag with his wet clothes and possessions. A fire flickered in the hearth. *I might as well get busy.* He tipped the table on its side with the legs facing the fire and the tabletop angled to the door. *Clothes over the table, underwear out of sight. Joints closest to the fire, followed by the wallet's contents. Laser pointer?* Pressing the button revealed the pointer worked. He removed the battery and put it in backward. *I don't want you to cause any mischief.* He laid the phone next to the table. *One brick, useless. The rest everything else goes between the fire and the table.*

There came a loud kick at the door. Bracing his knee against the door, he cracked it open. Catherine stood there, one hand holding a bread trencher covered with a meat stew, and the other a pitcher of ale. She thrust the food at him, looking at him like a lab specimen.

Paxton took the food. "Catherine?" he whispered.

"Yes?" She looked at him.

Paxton kicked the door shut in her face.

Paxton, wh wh why do you do dumb things like that?

The night passed without incident until the sound of birds in the thatch roof woke Paxton. Low chirp, high chirp, low chirp, followed by four quick chirps. *It's still dark.* The bird song continued until he could see dawn through the cracks in the roof. That was when the cock started crowing.

Might as well get up. He shuffled to the hearth to check on his belongings. "Son of a bitch." *I am going to die and everything up to now has only been in preparation for a slow death.* He held his hands out with palms up, and looked to the ceiling. *A thatch roof.* Paxton observed the roof. *A thatch roof in need of repair.* He followed the trail of pot crumbs to a group of field mice, asleep, smiling little mouse smiles He fumed, "I hope you all die of the munchies."

There were a series of loud kicks at the door. *Gee, I wonder who that could be.* Paxton opened the door to find Catherine there. Matted, stringy haired, long faced, both figuratively and literally, Catherine.

"Mass."

"You are as beautiful as you are eloquent."

The chapel was at the back end of the bailey, a two-minute walk from his cottage.

They sure do pack the buildings in tight in here.

After Mass, Friar Bernard hooked an arm around Paxton's arm. "Walk with me."

"Friar, you appear to be walking slower today."

"The only thing worse than the blessing of old age, is not to receive the blessing of old age. See how the others walk ahead. We may make use of that to talk in private." The friar looked at Paxton. "You have nothing to confess?"

"I confess that I want to get back to my own time." *Did the friar catch that?*

75

"You said you became separated from your companions in a storm. This is the one that caused you to lose your possessions?"

"Is this some sort of trial?"

The friar stopped for a moment. "If you wish it to be. When was this storm?"

"Six days ago, before I met the twins' stepfather, Jonah."

"There have been no storms here in months." He looked up at the empty sky. "People say that this is like the time of Elijah, when God shut up his Heaven."

"What do you say, friar?"

"I say you lie, Prince Paxton." The assertion could have been a prosecutor's closing statement.

"If I would tell you anything else, you would call me mad."

"You would rather be called a warlock than mad? A most interesting choice."

"My choice would be my freedom. Everything else is a nightmare. Why does the Lady call me a hostage?"

"You were told the late duke gave her Sandalburg castle and its estate as her Morning Dowry."

"Yes." Paxton nodded.

"Now, if the duke rules the Sandalburg estate directly from Banburn, the taxes he collects go in his purse. If his Lady rules the estate from her castle, the taxes she collects go in her purse, but as man and wife, one is as good as the other. It is the same household."

"Okay, so he gets the taxes if the money goes in his pocket or his wife's."

"Okay?" The old monk raised his eyebrows at Paxton.

"It means I agree or I accept."

Having traveled the length of the bailey they now turned to go up the stairs.

"Take my hand, Lord Paxton, to help me up the stairs. With the death of the duke, Northumbria goes to the Lady's uncle. Now the taxes the Lady collects still go to her purse, but she must pay taxes to the new Duke of Northumbria. The Sandalburg estate is still part of Northumbria. The Lady's uncle wants the Lady out of Sandalburg and back in Banburn. To do this he will tax the Sandalburg estate more and more. If she can't pay, he will force her back to Banburn castle and rule Sandalburg himself."

"And directly collect the taxes for himself," Paxton snorted. "A real piece of work he is."

Climbing the stairs, they reached that height where the stairs were rough and uneven. "The King's battles on the continent claimed the lives of the new duke's sons and he has but one daughter left. As a dowry to a husband, he may then give Sandalburg castle to a son-in-law."

"So, he squeezes the Lady off her property, collects the tax from the peasants, and gets a castle to give as a dowry. He will then be able to tax his son-in-law on the estate, and in effect gets the dowry price back. This guy is not just a piece of work; he is a brilliant piece of work."

"I know not your words but your voice tells me you do not approve. 'Viduae et pupillo non nocebitis.' Exodus 22:22." *(You shall not hurt a widow or an orphan.)*

"So the Lady hopes by holding me for ransom she can raise the tax money."

"That would seem to depend on the value of your life."

Paxton shrugged. "Whatever money the Lady needs she may have double."

"Can you produce such an amount?"

"Not now."

They had entered the Great Hall where trestle tables were set up.

"We will sit on the dais with the Lady, Sarah, and Harold."

"Bernard, there don't seem to be enough servants for this castle."

"The Lady left Banburn in some haste. She took only her retinue. If she brings in serfs, there will not be enough people to work the land. To maintain the castle and her private fields in this time of disease and drought is not easy. We must all do more than enough, including hostages."

They almost reached the dais. Paxton whispered one last question. "Why won't anyone say how the Lady's husband died?"

"You refuse to speak the truth of your appearance. Like you, I will not speak. Unlike you I will not lie."

The lady sat at the centre of the table. Sarah sat to her left. Harold, then Friar Bernard, then Paxton sat to her right. The friar gave a blessing and they ate a light meal of eggs, white bread, and ale, stronger than water, but weaker than Bud lite.

Harold turned to his right with a grin. "Friar. What do you think of our hostage?"

"I'm afraid he makes a very poor hostage,"

The others at the table slowed their eating to listen to the verbal sword fight.

"Should we send him back to Stephan?" Harold thrust.

"Not yet. Being a noble, he may have some value." The monk parried.

"You recognize my nobility, Friar?" Hope lifted Paxton's voice.

"Climbing the stairs, I took your hand in mine. I noticed how soft it is. Likewise, I noticed the soles of your feet, after your fall in the river; I could see they were uncallused. They are as soft as a noble lady's."

"And what do you know of a noble lady's feet?" Harold sniggered.

"My dear Harold. I was not born a monk, nor have I lived my whole life as one."

The Lady announced, "If you are good for nothing else, I will put you to work under Catherine, repairing roofs."

Paxton grimaced. *Not Catherine.* "I would make an excellent tutor." With some changes, he told them of his university studies in the new city of York. He spoke of learning under Neil Tyson the Moor, and Michio Kaku the ancient Nipponese.

"Can you sing, and play an instrument?" Harold laughed. "With such stories you would make a good replacement for old Geoffrey. Perhaps you are a warlock and his spirit haunts you."

The Lady swept imaginary crumbs and arguments off the table, "We have a tutor in the friar."

Bernard turned to Paxton. "I will be leaving in a few days with Abbot Stephan and the priests of Warren for Banburn. We will petition the bishop to assign priests to Alton."

"Friar, I will give you a letter. You will ask the bishop if any foreign nobles have been looking for our hostage. If no one has looked for him, have the bishop send my letter to the archbishop in London." The Lady now set her eyes on Paxton. "When I mentioned Catherine's name I saw how your heart did leap."

Sarah coughed, suppressing a laugh.

The Lady Wilhelmina glared at Sarah, who now tightened the muscles around her mouth. "You will learn useful tasks: you will learn to be my valet des chambre under Harold; perhaps from the chaplain, how to be my brewer; or even under Catherine, how to repair roofs." The Lady gave a sideways glare at Sarah.

Paxton stared down at his plate. *I gain time.* "How far is it to Banburn?"

"Two days' travel by foot," replied Friar Bernard.

"And you leave when?"

"Early next week."

Paxton wiped his itching palms on his lap. *This is all about taxes.* "Lady Wilhelmina, how can I be of use to you? Your smith, John, can he do fine work?"

"Yes," was the guarded reply.

"I will need enough silver for…"

Harold tittered. "Our hostage wishes us to pay ransom to him."

"You will have none." The Lady's tone was a dead weight.

Paxton raised his voice. "You will get all the silver back."

"No."

That was definite. "May I have steel?"

"How much?" Her tone breathed a little life.

Paxton picked up and stared at a spoon. "Enough for five spoons."

"We have spoons," she said.

"I don't wish him to make spoons. I have knowledge from my land; it may be of use to you, with the smith's help."

The Lady waivered. "What do you want the smith to do?"

"Fine work that I will instruct him on. I will also need parchment, quill, inkpot, a spoon,"—*now let's nail this door shut*—"and the services of Catherine."

"Harold, tell John he is to work for Lord Paxton. Sarah, tell Catherine to go to the smithy, and obey Lord Paxton's words."

"Thank you Lady Wilhelmina, for allowing me to be of service to you. I hope the smith, Catherine, and I will be finished before Friar Bernard leaves for Banburn."

The Lady rose, indicating the meal was finished. Harold and Paxton went to find the smith. Harold found John, and gave him the Lady's orders.

As they left the keep, John turned to Paxton. "What is the nature of the work to be done?"

"Do you have steel such as for making knives and spoons?"

"There is plenty of chain mail. Do you want your steel poured or forged?"

"Explain what is involved in each."

"If it is to be forged, I can take a single piece of steel and shape it as you wish. Before I can pour molten steel, I must first make a mold. Then I can make many copies."

"I will make two drawings. One drawing will show you looking down on it. The other will show you looking at its side. You decide how to make five of them as quickly as possible."

Paxton laid a parchment on the table and used the spoon to make his measurements. He made two drawings: one of a top view and one of a side view. He gave the drawings to John. "Can you make this?"

The smith stroked his sooted beard. "Five times? Most of the time to be used will be in making the mold."

"Can it be done before the friar leaves?"

The smith looked at Harold, and jerked his head to Paxton.

"I believe the Lady wants you to work for Lord Paxton before any other duties."

The smith took a hammer, chisel, a piece of sandstone, and set them on the table. "Then I should get to work."

Paxton turned to watch Harold leave and saw Catherine leaning on the door, pouting. "Catherine, how nice it is to see you. We will be working together." He walked up to her, and grabbed the free end of her sash. "I need you to make something for me. It must be the same material as your belt. It should be about so long." His fingers ran out about thirty centimetres. They stopped at one corner on the belt's free end. "What is this?"

Catherine curled her fingers around the sash and pulled hard. Paxton crushed the sash in his hands and pulled back. "Stop!" *Um... please?* Always watching Catherine, Paxton's fingers moved back to the belt's corner. Catherine's countenance could light the coals in the smith's furnace. He looked at the corner. It was the same material and colour as the belt, hidden in the folds. An embroidered capital C. "You know how to spell?"

With all her might, Catherine pulled back. "I know something of your letters."

"How did you learn?"

"I look. I think. I remember."

"Catherine, you learned some spelling by seeing and remembering? I'm proud of you. Now tell me if enough cloth is available for what I want done."

Catherine stayed as still as a fox watching a hare.

"The Lady has plenty of fine cloth. Not just woolens, but linen and fine silks." She gestured to the second floor of the keep. "All her valuables are in her private apartment."

"I don't know if the Lady will let me use silk. Linen is good enough if you have it in the colour of her sash."

Catherine grunted in agreement.

"Is there perhaps red thread for you to do embroidery work?"

More grunts.

"Catherine, you're becoming lovelier with every word you don't speak. What I need you to make is the same width as your sash. It is to be about thirty centimetres long, with five pairs of loops inside, and an embroidered letter *W* in red thread in one corner. Then get two red coloured cords to bind it when it is rolled up."

"Do you have permission of the seneschal to use the Lady's cloth?"

"Seneschal?" Paxton racked his brain. "Who is the seneschal?"

"Harold."

"I have the Lady's permission."

"If you have nothing more to say, I must leave. I have duties to the Lady to perform." She walked out of the blacksmith's shop as she spoke.

"Please have your duty to me finished by the end of the day." *Speaking of Harold,* Paxton turned to the smith. "Where did Harold go?"

The smith pointed with his hammer. "The stable."

"Okay." *I'll just follow my nose. What did the Lady say? Some sort of valet. An indoor job would be nice.* Paxton trotted to the stable and stuck his head in. He allowed his eyes to adjust to the darker conditions. "Harold?"

"Over here." Harold was whispering with another man. Leaning on a long bow, he grinned at Paxton. "Good Lord Paxton, I do not believe you have met Gunther."

Paxton walked deeper into the shadows. "How I could have missed him?"

Gunther hobbled over. "Your Lordship."

"Gunther is the chief of the Lady's guard, her gamekeeper, and her bailiff."

"The Lady keeps you quite busy. Well you have broad shoulders." Paxton looked up at the man. *Figuratively speaking.* Paxton turned back to Harold. "The Lady mentioned that you may have duties for me to learn."

"Not now, Prince Paxton. Gunther and I were just about to go on a hunt." He paused, and raised a finger. "I have an idea. Why don't you join us?"

"Uh. I don't hunt."

Harold turned back to Gunther. His grin threatened to split his face in two. "Didn't I say this prince would bring as much mirth as old Geoffrey?" He moved nearer Paxton. "You hunt now."

"Are you not afraid I might try to escape?"

Harold shrugged. "The horse we'll give you is old and slow. I must warn you, Gunther's arrow is fast and sure."

"Um, I don't ride horses either."

Harold's jaw could have dropped to his knees. "My dear Lord, even if your ransom is paid we may still keep you."

"In my land we ride in coaches." Paxton allowed a little bit of irritation to show.

"Gunther, prepare a horse for the prince." Harold thrust the bow at Paxton. When he took it, Harold gave him the quiver of arrows. "I wish you a good hunt."

"Aren't you afraid I'll use this on you?"

"And why should you. Should there not be peace between Konectic…"

"Connecticut, C-o-n-n-e-c-t-i-c-u-t."

"Yes, and Northumbria? I will get another bow and quiver."

Harold ran into the tack room. While Paxton waited, Gunther led two horses out into the yard. Harold bolted from the tack room and into the sunlight as if he was running to buy the last ticket to a World Cup match. Paxton cantered behind him. Harold took the reins of both horses; Gunther went back into the stable.

What do I know about horses? Mount and dismount on the left. That's it.

"Here, let me take your weapon, Prince Paxton."

"Harold. You will treat me with the respect a noble hostage deserves. Do you understand? I don't know how secure you believe your position is here…"

"I can only be relieved of my position by the Lady, or by my family who has appointed me to her." Harold was formal in both his stance and his tone. He gave the reins of one horse to Paxton.

"The Lady said I may have the position of her valet in the castle."

"If you are to have a position in the Lady's service then you should have some knowledge of the Lady's estate." Harold let the reins drop.

Gunther led two more horses from the stable.

"Who is the other horse for?" Paxton asked.

"My dear Lord, you really do know nothing of hunting? How do you propose we bring back any boar or stag?"

84

Paxton looped one rein to the other side of the horse's head. Putting his left foot in the stirrup Paxton tried to mount the horse. Pushing on the stirrup the horse kept moving to its right. This caused Paxton to hop on his right foot trying to keep up with the horse's right turn.

Paxton stopped and turned to Harold. "Well, I guess this means I'm not going hunting with you guys."

Harold held out a hand to Gunther as if pleading with him. "Gunther."

Gunther walked up to the horse's right side and pulled down on the saddle's right side. "You are pushing into the horse. Push down on the stirrup."

Pushing as straight down as he could with his left leg, Paxton lifted himself up. The leather creaked as he swung his right leg over. After he settled in the saddle, Harold approached.

"Your bow and quiver, Prince Paxton. Try not to fall off. That would get me removed from the Lady's service."

"Um. How do I steer? Where's the brake? Harold!"

"Just do as we do." Harold sighed like a steam engine giving up its ghost.

Halfway to town Gunther spoke to Harold. "I brought noon day meals for you and me, but I did not take into account Lord Paxton."

Harold turned around in his saddle to look past Paxton back to the castle. "We may stop in town to buy something."

Gunther laughed. "I have enough coins. Let's leave our horses in the care of the widow Beatrice. Perhaps she will give him a meal and dessert."

Harold laughed as well. "Her dessert has become expensive." A pause. "So I have heard."

Trotting into town, Paxton's crotch slapped the saddle in time with the horse's pace. *I'm going to bruise them before I've have a chance to use them. And the smell. I can't tell difference between the horse and me. Neither of us has had a bath lately.*

The small parade moved through Warren. Townspeople stepped out of their way. The men doffed their hats. Others stared at Paxton, who guided his horse like a drunk trying to ride a straight line.

Leaving Warren, Paxton saw more serfs' cottages similar to the ones in Alton. Past the cottages and their crofts, he viewed the grain fields. Swiveling his head, like a pigeon wary of a hawk, he was ever alert for the presence of a gibbet.

Gunther and Harold led the way, conferring quietly. One would lean to the other and whisper. He'd straighten up and the other would then pendulum in. Back and forth, they whispered like this.

I don't know what you two are doing, but I'm sure you're not just exchanging recipes for game. Every stride the horse took caused the saddle to creak. Every few strides Paxton had to shift his weight to put some feeling in his buttocks.

Gunther led the hunting party through a small, muddy stream to cottages that were even more ramshackle. All except one cottage. Paxton noticed the roof was in better repair than the others were, and much better than his cottage. Stopping there, Harold looked back at Paxton. "We will leave three horses here. I'll tell the widow to tend to them until we return."

God, don't turn me into an ass falling off the horse. When you're on water, you get seasick. Flying, you get airsick. Here I guess it's called horsesick.

Paxton helped Gunther hobble the horses. Harold entered the cottage, Paxton heard him speaking, but couldn't make out the words.

Paxton picked a stalk of wild grass to play with. "Gunther, how far do you think we'll have to go into the forest?"

"My dear noble, you truly know nothing of hunting. We hunt best early in the morning, right after Mass. Early or late, we find the best game near the forest edge."

Harold emerged from the cottage, spotted something in the grass, and whispered to Paxton, "Look, we've not left Beatrice's croft, and we've found game, a nice, fat hare. Go on Lord Paxton. You may have the honor of the first kill."

What am I supposed to do, argue with him? Maybe if I delay long enough the rabbit will hop away. This bow and arrow thingy is like a limp set of chopsticks.

"Lord Paxton," Harold whispered. "May I make a suggestion? Lay the arrow on the right side of the bow. Now put the arrow's nock on the midpoint of the bow string."

Gunther and Harold stepped back. Still Gunther whispered loud enough for Paxton to hear. "This is as amusing as his riding."

"I wonder if Beatrice will find him as amusing," said Harold.

The hare turned to face Paxton. It crouched and thumped its right hind leg, acting like a mini bull getting ready to charge.

Is this animal dumb, or is it mocking me?

Range, about ten metres. Speed of arrow, about thirty metres per second. Flight time to target, .33 seconds. Height above target, 1.8 metres.

Distance arrow drops, $d=.5gt^2$, where

$$d=.5 \times 9.81 metres/sec^2 \times .33 sec^2 \approx .54\ metres$$

Aim arrow 2.34 metres above centre of target.

Paxton let loose the arrow.

Gunther let out a whoop. "Well done Lord Paxton. You hit the tree in the flank. Now quickly, let loose another arrow before it gets away."

Chapter 8

The hare sat back on its haunches chewing a piece of clover. Now it swiveled its exclamation-point ears forward. Sensing Paxton's intent, it leapt ninety degrees to its left. Bounding fast for the brush, it was on its fourth bounce when Gunther's arrow struck amidships. The arrow tip exited the rabbit's left side and flung the body to the ground.

The three men walked to the still body. The large, black marble eye told Paxton nothing. Was the animal alive, or dead, or something in between? Gunther pulled out his arrow and slit the hare's underbelly from throat to anus.

Definitely dead, thought Paxton. The animal's heart was the size and the colour of an oversized, ripe strawberry—a strawberry with a hole through its centre. *First horsesick, now rabbit sick.*

"The widow will delight in having some meat for her pottage." Gunther said. "She'll treasure this more than coins."

"The townsmen give her plenty of meat. Men from Warren, and Alton, and travelers from Banburn and other places." Harold leered as he took the carcass to the cottage.

"And the women of the town do their best to stop their men from feeding her." Gunther shot his words like arrows back to Harold.

Gunther and Paxton marched through the dry croft at the edge of the forest. The woods stopped at the valley floor, and trees marched like soldiers up the wall. Small, scurrying animals stopped to listen to the chattering of the two-legged beasts. Halfway up the valley wall they turned north before continuing their ascent.

"Is this woman an outcast?" asked Paxton.

"She is and she isn't," Gunther replied. "Other women look down on her. As all women are soulless beings, how is one more worthy than another? Men? They also condemn her, when they are in church."

"You speak about your serfs and women in ways that are foreign to me."

Gunther looked over his shoulder. A half smile came to his lips. "If you truly do not understand, Beatrice is more than capable of explaining to you. We'll wait here near the top of the ridge for Harold." Gunther pointed his bow down the hillside. "See, even now he hurries to join us."

Harold walking ahead of the packhorse pulled its reins hard, encouraging the animal for more speed. "Why didn't you wait for me?"

"The longer we wait, the later it gets. Even now, we've lost the best time for hunting. Tie the horse here and we'll go over the crest."

As they crossed over the ridge, Paxton stopped to admire a small inlet of the valley floor. A grove of apple trees looked like waves splashing almost to the forest.

Gravestone stumps of oaks wove among the victorious apple trees. The two groups of trees stood apart like armies about to engage in more combat, apple vs. oak. A thin line of defeated oak lay crumpled at the forest's shoreline.

The hunters settled in. Gunther sat and rubbed his back against a stump. He laid his weapon by his right side. Reaching to his left hip, he pulled up a wineskin. He squirted a drink into his mouth, and then passed the wineskin to Harold. Harold put his head against a tree trunk facing Gunther, and took the wineskin for a drink. Paxton lay on his right side facing Harold and Gunther. He took the skin when Harold passed it.

This must be one of those male bonding things. Harold folded his hands on his lap to take a nap. *No one's expecting any action soon.* Paxton got back up. "I have to make water." He turned to walk into the forest when an arrow zipped between his legs and thwacked into a tree.

"Not too far Lord Paxton." Gunther lay back down.

Later, Paxton watched as the shadows meandered toward the sun. After noon, they gave way to the east. The dark, warped shapes pointed to the late afternoon.

"The trail has been spoiled by poachers." Harold rolled onto his stomach.

"There are no more poachers." Gunther held an arrow straight up.

"Then why is there no game?"

"How much longer do we wait?" Paxton whispered and shifted his weight. *I hope I don't sound whiny.*

Gunther said quietly, "We won't have to wait at all." He crept forward, commando-style.

Harold rolled to a crouch and moved behind Gunther and to his right.

Paxton squatted behind the branches of the fallen oak.

A yearling buck, its antlers just nubs, emerged from the forest and went straight for the orchard. Once it was in the copse, a doe appeared. She crossed the clearing between the opposing trees and disappeared into the orchard.

Gunther grinned. "Now see the older buck, at thirty yards, inside the woods," He whispered. "He sends the yearling and the doe first, to make sure the way is clear." Gunther set an arrow in his bow and drew back the string. He centred the arrow on his target. Suddenly Harold reached forward with his bow and flicked Gunther's trigger fingers away. The errant arrow slithered to the ground like an angry, blind snake.

Harold lay on his side, holding his stomach, and kicking his legs in uproarious, silent laughter. When the crimson colour of glee faded, he looked through wet eyes at Gunther.

The arrows were now not in Gunther's bow, but shooting from his eyes. Gunther pointed at Harold, then at the buck.

Harold got into a firing position. He took aim, and then checked that no one was in position to return his favour.

Paxton kept learning more about animal anatomy than he wanted to know. He avoided the dressing of the stag by volunteering to bring the packhorse. Still, the results of gutting the stag confronted him.

Paxton and Harold tied the disemboweled carcass to the horse. The hunters started to return the way they came.

"Why didn't we bring all the horses?"

Gunther stared at Paxton. "Has confidence in your ridership increased that much?"

Paxton's silence spoke more than words.

Harold piped up. "Lord Paxton am I not the greatest hunter of our number?"

Paxton cocked his head at Harold. "What gives you that distinction?"

"Have I not brought down the largest game?"

"If greatness is measured by size, Lord Paxton would be the best. He has struck a tree."

"No Gunther." Paxton said. "You are the best. It is harder to hit a small target than a large one, and your target was bouncing."

Returning to the horses Gunther and Harold discussed whether to stop and eat the food they brought, or press on back to the castle.

"We should not deny Lord Paxton his dessert. I have already given the widow Beatrice the meat of the hare in payment." Turning to

Paxton, Harold continued. "Go and enjoy yourself. We will dine here and wait for you."

Paxton headed for the cottage door. *Never pass up a free meal in this place. Maybe if... WHEN... someone from the team finds me he'll bring a Big Mac and a large Coke.* Arriving at the cottage door, he raised his hand to knock. *Stop.* Paxton snatched back his hand. *They don't knock because they believe you are calling out some wood god.*

Paxton pushed open the door and shuffled a bit along the wall to make some noise. He closed the door with his left foot. This gave his eyes time to adjust to the decrease in light. He scanned the room. *Not many personal belongings. The few items here she's organized well. Kitchen utensils set in a frame by the hearth. Clothing folded on a table. A bed put in a far corner. A blanket lay straight and even across the bed. It looks like a model cottage in the recreated tourist villages.* He drew in a deep breath. *It's not antiseptic like a model cottage.* Paxton sniffed and sniffed again. *But not foul. More like clean earth and wood smells. Even the dirt floor looks, well, it looks swept.* He looked harder. *It is swept. You can see the lines from a broom.* Paxton relaxed. *It's like a camping version of my apartment.* He grated his teeth. *I still hate camping, with a vengeance.*

He approached the hearth. Because she was directly between the fire and him, Paxton saw her in silhouette. Nearby, a frame stretched a rabbit skin. It reflected light back to the pot and its owner. Feeling confident, he moved forward to the woman stirring the pot. "Excuse me Widow Beatrice. My name is Paxton. I was told I could have something to eat."

She didn't answer but moved toward the table in the centre of the room. When she reached it, firelight illuminated her in a glorious swath from head to foot. Paxton drew in a breath in surprise. His heart gripped his throat. For the first time the potential for joy came to Paxton. *The hair. Her hair. The cherry, cheery, glossy hair of Roseann. The colour of her hair and the colour of her name are the same. Roseann. Somehow, in the warping of space-time she came back to me. I can rescue you. You're here, alive and—.* The woman looked at Paxton. *It's not her. The hair's the same, but the face, it's not her.* He watched her pick up a bowl from the table. Walking back to the pot she ladled out a bowl of pottage with meat. She shuffled back to the table, then set the bowl next to a spoon, and dragged herself to the bed. Paxton eased down on the bench next to the table. His mouth told him he was hungry. The sight of pottage knotted his stomach. Staring at the food, he stirred it, then lifted some to his mouth. *Roseann.* He turned the spoon upside down letting the pottage fall out. *Not Roseann.*

Who are you to taunt me like this? He stalked her with his eyes and his heart. *The first thing I'll do is eat your food.* Paxton shoveled in a few spoonfuls of pottage. *Analyze the woman logically.* Paxton smiled. *I'll be like an owl. The wisest of all raptors. Beatrice is sitting at the middle of the bed, on its edge. Her forearms are crossed on her knees. Her feet are parted. She's staring at a spot on the floor between them. She could be a few years older than me. Just like Roseann. However, Roseann wasn't this... run down.* More pottage went down his gullet. *Her hair is clean, and combed, and Roseann's. Her skin is washed, thin, and sunken. I'll bet she's slowly starving. Well, that's no concern of mine. Nobody's very healthy here, with all the dying going on.* Paxton finished his bowl. *She might as well be a sixty-thousand-mile tire with seventy-five thousand miles on it.*

Paxton looked up. Beatrice's roof was solid and in good repair. He turned his head around, not as much as an owl, but enough. *My apartment has more food.* "They said you could provide me with some dessert." The cottage was so quiet, he was aware of his heart beating slowly, one, two, three, four. Beatrice bent to her ankles and grabbed the hem of her tunic. She pulled it up to her waist and lay on her back. She bent her knees and moved her feet apart.

He whipped around to see the door. If his eyes had heat vision, the door would have burst into flames. *You two are laughing at me, aren't you? Memo to self. Throw Gunther and Harold under bus. Second memo. Invent bus.* Without thought, Paxton got up. He swayed like a drunken robot to the bed and sat on its edge, at Beatrice's waist. He looked, stared at her. He tried to force his vision through her body and into her spirit. *Who are you?*

Beatrice shut her eyes tight. When nothing happened, she opened her eyes. She turned Paxton's face away.

I get it. Don't stare. Well, can we talk? He looked around for something to say. "Nice roof," he stuttered. "The, the roof in my cottage isn't as nice. In fact, it's terrible. Have you hired someone from the village?" Beatrice said nothing, again. Paxton held a sideways glance so as not to look at her. "Or did your husband do it before he died?"

Now it was Beatrice's turn to stare. *She's looking at me as if I'm the village idiot. Maybe I am.* Paxton turned back to face her. "Are you capable of speech? Can you talk?" his stuttering voice demanded. *Maybe she can't.*

"I repaired the roof myself." The statement was as plain as her face.

Paxton looked back at the roof. "That could be dangerous. I'm glad you weren't hurt." He angled his body to see Beatrice. "Has your husband been dead long?"

She turned away. "Too long."

Paxton gazed at her, trying to comprehend her. "You have no children?"

"They are dead also."

"Dying… dying seems to be a popular pastime around here. I won't be here long. I'm staying at the castle of the Lady. I expect my friends to come looking for me soon. If any strangers come through, send them to the castle. I'm sure they will reward you."

94

She was as responsive to his words as the hare Gunther had killed that morning. Paxton glanced past her waist to her hips. He pulled her tunic down past her crotch.

Christ. She's all skin and bones. What am I supposed to do with that?

You're supposed to do her, do her, do her, and do her.

The voice struck his whole body. It was like falling into an icy pond, in January, in a blizzard. Like a searchlight looking for an escaped prisoner, he scanned the room.

"Mary Jane?" *First visions of Roseann, now this?*

What? Were you expecting Albert or Cecilia?

He walked to the centre of the room and whispered. "I was hoping for Albert or even Cecilia. How did you get here?"

Remember what I told you in the Bottle Room. 'I am you.'

"So I am going mad."

That's what she's going to think if you keep talking aloud.

"I don't care what she thinks." Paxton fell silent. *What are you doing here?*

Stiffening your spine so you can stiffen something else.

I don't know her. I don't want an old whore. I want something. Paxton paused, collecting his thoughts. *I want someone more.*

Look at her. She's not that much older than you. Beggars can't be choosers. You knew Roseann for what? A little more than two hours?

I was scared. What else could I do?

All right Paxie. You're willing to run away. So what are you going to do while you're running?

I don't understand.

Who else is going to give you a tumble? Catherine? One of the ladies? You'd love that wouldn't you? You have to work with what you've got, or are capable of getting.

What do you suggest I do?

Talk with her, not to her. Talk with her without expecting anything in return. Women notice that.

I'm not here to develop a relationship. I'm here to survive until help arrives.

It's possible that will be a long time. How does the rest of your life sound?

No!

Well, if you don't think you'll be here long enough to have a woman for a friend.

Paxton interrupted. *I have Marie for a friend.*

She's friendly, not a friend. One's an adverb, and the other's a noun. Paxton you can have whatever you want. A friend. A friend with benefits. Paxton glanced at Beatrice. *Benefits without a friend. Get it in gear and choose something.*

Paxton glanced at Beatrice's face. Sitting up, she slunk into the corner.

She can tell something's going on with me

He reeled to the door.

I don't believe you. The voice rose in pitch. *Paxton, you gutless wonder!*

Get thee behind me Satan. Matthew 16:23.

Oooo. Getting all olde tyme religion are we? Our faux nobility is getting all faux noble. Let me clue you into something Paxie. This isn't a woman's voice you're rebuking. This's your voice, or part of your anatomy speaking. What are you going to tell Gunther and Harold?

I'll tell them, gentlemen never speak of their conquests.

What about Beatrice?

What do I care about her?

96

Chapter 9

Come on. Get going. Paxton used his heels to spur his mount. *If you were moving any slower, you'd be going in reverse.*

The hunting party entered the bailey. Harold and the packhorse trotted to the kitchen. Paxton followed Gunther to the stable. After he dismounted, Paxton turned to Gunther. "I must see if the smith has completed his work for me."

Gunther ordered Paxton as if he were a common villager. "First, care for the horse." He led his steed inside.

Paxton used the halter to pull the horse's ear close to him. "Let him come to my castle sometime." Paxton led the old mare in. "I'd take him to an amusement park." He examined the animal front to back. "Gunther, how do you undress this thing?" Again whispering to the horse, "I'd take him and Harold on a roller coaster ride." Paxton tied the reins to a post and managed to get the saddle and blanket off.

Gunther untied the reins and backed the mare into a stall. "I'll do the rest if you have other duties to perform. I'm sorry we couldn't bring your kill back to the castle."

"Right now, no one is more sore-y than I am." Paxton stepped into the courtyard and looked around. Guards were pushing gates shut. They would throw a bar across the wood and iron vertical lips, and then drop the iron-toothed gate behind it. *The world's largest chastity belt.* Someone else emerged from the chicken coop. He heard pigs grunting in a pen, in a far corner of the courtyard. Paxton sniffed. *I hate pig shit.*

Paxton saw Catherine on a ladder rethatching one of the roofs that needed repair. *It's like putting pasties on a sixty-five-year-old stripper.* "Catherine," Paxton called. "Catherine!" Stopping, she twisted to see him from the roof. "Have you done what I asked of you?" She dropped behind the roof like an enemy periscope beneath the waves.

The plinking of metal on metal drew Paxton into the smithy. Ash, fire, and smoke were the first sensations to hit him as he entered. "John?" The metallic plinking stopped.

The smith looked up from his work and put his tools down. He walked to the table Paxton and he had occupied in the morning. Paxton came to the table to see the final products. Picking them up one by one Paxton compared them to his drawings. "You do good work, John." Also on the table lay a gold silk cloth wrapping and two red cords. Opening the casing flat, he saw the loops sewn in. One loop was above another. There were five pairs. The pairs of loops were evenly spaced along the wrapping's length. The capital letter *W* was embroidered in red thread, in the centre of the cloth scroll. "This is good."

Paxton became aware of another presence in the foundry and looked up. "Catherine, you do good work." He rubbed the letter *W* between a thumb and forefinger. "I'm sure the Lady will be pleased." Paxton smiled at Catherine. "You're smart. May I teach you more?"

He put a sample of the smith's work under the pair of loops closest to the embroidered *W*. "Excellent." Paxton shifted his gaze between Catherine and John. "Have either one of you mentioned what was being done?"

"I asked Sarah for the material you requested. I told her it was at your command." Catherine put emphasis the word your. "I'm sure she informed the Lady."

John spoke up. "The friar came in. He picked up one of your tools, examined it, and left."

"No one else?" They shook their heads.

"Well. It won't be a surprise, or not a complete surprise, but I think the Lady will be pleased. Do either one of you know what meat will be served at the evening meal?" *Please don't tell me venison.*

Catherine leaned to the side to peer out of a window. "I see the friar heading for the keep. Perhaps he knows."

Paxton grinned. "Thank you Catherine."

Catherine smiled and went to work. "I will bind these up while you ask Friar Bernard."

"Thanks again." Paxton ran to catch up with the friar.

"Catherine. You know we're having mutton. Why didn't you tell him?"

"I have my reasons." She began putting the items in the wrapping.

"Why do you seek to rile him?" The smith went back to his work.

"I'm curious. Have you never baited an animal to see if it hides or fights?" Catherine rolled the cloth scroll up.

"I know many have suffered from their curiosity, both men and animals." The smith used a pair of tongs held in his left hand to pull a piece of iron from the fire.

"I'm bored John. I want more. This noble," Catherine wrinkled her nose on the word noble, "can provide some entertainment."

The smith used the hammer in his right hand to emphasize his words. "You poke in books and letters too much. Someday..." The smith held the hot iron up with the tongs. "This is your curiosity." He laid the iron flat on his anvil. "This will be its result for you." Several blows of the hammer sent waves of sparks scattering in all directions. "Any questions?"

"Where is it?" Paxton's voice came from the door.

Catherine and John fell silent. "There it is." Paxton strode to the table. "This is going to be so simple and yet so profound."

Catherine picked up the cloth. "I rolled them in the cloth and used one cord near the tops. The other cord ties the wrapping at the middle."

Paxton felt the cloth. "Yes. I am glad the Lady gave you silk to use."

"When you unroll this do you want the tops facing you and the bottoms facing the Lady?" An interior light shone in Catherine's face.

"Yes."

"Then I have done well."

"Catherine, you and John have done better than well." Paxton leaned forward. "I'll make sure the Lady knows of your contribution."

The smith's hammer pounded furiously at the iron.

The trestle table was set up on the dais for the evening meal. The Lady sat at the centre, with Sarah on her left, and Harold and Friar Bernard on her right. Paxton asked that his plate be set across from the Lady. His smile threatened to split his face in twain as sure as any broadsword.

The mutton platters arrived and Paxton waved for Catherine and John to come forward. "My lady, let me present John and Catherine who did the work according to my rules."

Paxton placed the wrapped cloth on the table. "Consider, my lady which is more valuable, silver metal or silver coin?"

"I told you, no silver."

"I have not used any silver, my lady. I only wish to say that any material worked is more valuable than in its natural state. Silver coins are worth more than silver nuggets. Is not a silver cup worth more than silver coins? The same amount of material, iron, silver, or gold, when worked into something useful, is more valuable. My lady, I present a gift to you, which we in Connecticut find most useful." Paxton opened the cloth with a flourish. Everyone seated at the table leaned forward.

Sarah brushed her hair back. "They look like tiny pitchforks."

"We almost call them that. We simply say forks."

Sarah again spoke up. "Why is there the letter *M* embroidered on the cloth?"

Paxton looked down. With the forks pointed at him, the cloth was turned around one hundred and eighty degrees. To everyone seated opposite him the letter *W* looked like the letter *M*. Paxton whirled back at Catherine. She studied a blank spot on the ceiling as if it was the most interesting thing in the world.

Paxton sat back facing the Lady. "Allow me to demonstrate." He pulled the forks out of their loop enclosures and gave one to everyone seated at the table. "Please follow along. "With the fork in your left hand, spear a large piece of meat." Paxton did so with the Lady's fork.

"You dare serve yourself before me!"

The Lady's voice sounded like langrel fired at Paxton.

"I was presenting this piece to you, my lady."

He placed the mutton on her plate. "Everyone do the same."

Sarah, Bernard, and Harold each chose a piece of meat from the platter. Last, Paxton choose a piece with his fork. "Now fix the meat down with your fork." The assembly pushed down on the meat. "My lady, don't wrap your fist around the fork. Look. Place one finger on a flat side." Paxton checked them off one by one. "No, Lady Wilhelmina, turn the fork the other way. It should curve to you." Paxton got up and around the table to stand behind her. "Now with the fork holding the meat down draw your knife across the meat to cut it." Paxton went to Sarah. "No, my lady. It is easier if you cut a small piece. Take the fork out. Transfer the fork to your right hand. No. Hold the meat down with the knife and pull out the fork."

Like a man trying to keep spinning plates balanced on wood dowels Paxton ran from noble to religious and back. *Don't tell. Show.* "Here let me show you." To another, "No, do this, not that." He sprinted back to the Lady Wilhelmina. "That's good, you got it." The Lady was cutting a piece just right for her mouth. From the side Paxton could see her eyes widen in hope. He turned his attention elsewhere. "Sarah stop. Don't cut so fast."

Screech! The sound of a knife hitting a pewter plate caused everyone to stop. The Lady's perfect piece flew off the table, bounced off the dais, and hit the lower floor.

Anyone who saw the Lady's face also felt his own soul grow as cold as an Inuit's nose.

What followed next Paxton recalled as the battle of Muttonshire. "The Lady curled her fist around the fork's handle and slammed it into the hapless mutton. The knife cut in directions I didn't think possible. Muttonshirens were pinned in place, cut down and up mercilessly. All the others at the table now joined in the blood lust for destruction of the inhabitants of Muttonshire. Small factions of survivors tried to flee to the outer edges of the plates. The forks found them, and picked them off, one by one. They were defenseless against this new weapon. Soon the battle was over." Paxton sighed. "All that remained was the poet's song, 'that once there was a piece of meat, for one brief shining moment that was known as Muttonshire.'"

I guess Emily Post wasn't written in a day.

Chapter 10

Paxton looked east, musing on the battle of Muttonshire, which had been two days ago. The morning sun stared back, painting the clouds a pale orange. Paxton, Harold, and the Lady walked the palisade. "I'm glad you found the forks useful." Paxton said. "I know you worry about being able to pay your taxes to the duke." Earlier, the lady had showed him an oak case. In it, Sarah had embroidered the silk lining with the Lady's family crest. Two silver forks lay inside.

"Harold will take it as payment of my tallage to the duke."

Paxton asked, "If the duke is pleased, will you return to Banburn?"

The Lady clasped her stomach and hustled to the spiked walls of the palisade. She placed her head between two wood spikes, and hurled her morning meal over the wall. She wiped her mouth with a handkerchief. "That's all I have to give to Banburn."

Okay, change the subject. "What of the letters to the duke and bishop about me?"

"Do not let your impatience show, Prince Frost. I will collect my ransom as soon as your nobles can be found."

I've been here over a week. It will be another week before Bernard and Harold return. I'll be gone before then. "I am not worried. Yet I am concerned. I remember how difficult it was for the friar to climb these steps." Paxton gazed at the stone stairs leading to the bailey. "It took him days to recover from the trip to Alton and back."

"Yes. He is old, but this trip will be easier. Father Casimir here in Warren has a cart as well as a horse. He will drive to Banburn."

"So Bernard and Harold will be cart pooling."

"Your English is strange Prince Paxton. By your smile I sense a jest." The Lady leaned to Paxton. "They will be accompanied by Abbot Stephan."

Paxton stopped. "Is he here? When did he arrive? Where is he?"

"He arrived in Warren before sundown. Abbot Stephan, and others stayed the evening with Friar Bernard. Do you think he has forgotten you? He talked in the evening with Father Casimir and Friar Bernard. This morning he talked with my servants."

"About me?"

Sarah tells me he asked about many things, including my late husband. The church in Alton still needs priests." The Lady paused. "The abbot still wants the duke and bishop to allow you to stand trial." The Lady paused in her words and steps again. "Do not fear Prince Paxton. You are under my protection. For now."

"I thank you Lady Wilhelmina. For now."

Paxton stopped to watch the last of the morning fog burn off. The castle's iron gate, in the up position, strained against the locking pins. The heavy wooden doors swung inward. A spear of sunlight pierced the courtyard. Whether in the half shadow of waning night, or in the light, the castle stirred with lethargic movement. *No rat race here. A slow, deliberate pace of activity.* The castle was the queen. All of the human subjects attend to her needs. The clink, clank of iron being forged came from the smithy. A servant expelled the waste products of chickens, horses, and pigs from the castle. Another servant applied new plaster to the stockade as if mending broken bones.

From here, Paxton could see the road into Warren. On its far side ran a small muddy stream. A few cottages dotted its opposite bank. *Beyond the stream, one cottage has a roof in better repair than the others do.* "My lady, when can Catherine repair my roof? Last night it finally rained. I moved my bed twice to get out from under the leaks."

"Catherine will first take care of my needs, then the needs of my castle, then the needs of my household. When there is time and material, your needs will be met."

"I am part of your household. You put me to work as a brewer for Bernard, and a clerk for Harold. In my time… uhm, place, we call that multitasking. Don't I qualify as a member of your household?"

Harold stepped between the Lady and Paxton. "My lady, this foreigner," Harold slurred the word contemptuously, "challenged my keeping of your accounts."

"I tried to show Harold a different, a better way to keep your books."

"First forks, now bookkeeping?" Harold sneered down on Paxton.

"I mean no disrespect to your bookkeeping." Paxton now positioned himself between the Lady and Harold. "These diaries that Harold keeps, record what you have at the end of the day, or week, or month in Roman numerals."

"As it has always been done." Harold spoke from behind Paxton.

Paxton continued. "I use Arabic numerals. One through nine, plus zero."

"Zero?" The Lady raised her eyebrows.

"It is a place keeper. The point is this." Paxton drew a breath. "Let us say that Harold records that you have LXIX silver coins. You use XVII silver coins to make two forks." Now Paxton pointed at the Lady. "How many silver coins are left?"

The Lady held out both hands. She repeatedly stuck out her fingers and thumbs, then curled fingers and thumbs back in.

Paxton pulled a piece of folded parchment from a drawstring purse. "The friar gave me this purse. Harold allowed me to have parchment. Here is a copy of what I gave to Harold." The Lady unfolded the parchment. Paxton stood beside the Lady to point to what he had written. "Here are Arabic numerals and Roman numerals above them. You will notice there is no Roman numeral that means the same as zero." Paxton drew a finger to the bottom half of the page. "This is what we call double entry bookkeeping. One column we call silver coins. Another column we call silver forks."

"We do not call any such thing." Harold wrestled to regain control of the conversation.

The Lady raised a hand to silence Harold.

Paxton continued. "In the left column you have 69 silver coins. In the right column you have 0, meaning no, silver forks." He indicated the next line down. "Now, to make the forks you used 17 coins, so I take 17 from 69 which leaves you with 52 coins." Paxton looked up to Harold. "That's LII for you Harold. Now in the second column you had no forks, which is marked with a zero. The second line down shows 2, for two forks. Using double entry I can show you not just your raw wealth, but where it is coming from, and where it is going. I can show how fast, or slow, your wealth is increasing or decreasing."

The Lady bit her lower lip thinking, calculating.

Paxton whispered, "This gives you control. It lets you see what is happening to your wealth as it is happening."

Harold shook his head. "Witchcraft."

Paxton returned Harold's sneer. "'Thou has ordered all things in measure, and number, and weight.' Wisdom 11:21."

"In my childhood, I survived the pox. I am not afraid of the curse you brought to Alton. You pile one trouble after another on yourself. Do not try to bring the Lady down with you."

Paxton's voice became a silk thread that wound around the Lady's ears. "I can do for your accounts what I have done for your table. If only you will give me someone to repair my roof."

The Lady faced Paxton, her head held high, and her shoulders back. "At the midday meal will you kneel and swear true faith and allegiance only to me?"

"As a prince, I should have my own servant. If a servant could be had to fix the sieve on my cottage." Paxton paused. "Afterward, I could release my servant for duties to you."

The Lady folded the parchment and tucked it in between her sash and waist. "Where would you find such a person? You will not take from service anyone in my household, neither any townsperson, nor any serf."

"A man clever enough to give you forks should be able to find someone." *On the other side of Warren is one cottage with a roof in better repair than the rest.*

"I see Father Casimir's cart approaching." The Lady now surveyed the bailey. "There is much work to be done here. I will decide later. Harold it is time for you to leave."

Paxton tracked the Lady's view of the bailey. He gritted his teeth. *Into every pastoral scene a little pigshit must fall.* There in the bailey, speaking to Catherine, stood a tall, thin figure dressed in the black cassock of a Cistercian monk. *Stephan. Damn him.* Paxton traced a line from Stephan's position up to the palisade. *He's almost directly under the break in the woodwork that Catherine uses to exit the palisade. He has his back to me. The motte slopes at about a forty-five-degree angle.* Paxton went to the break in the top of the wall.

"Prince Frost," the Lady rebuked. "What are you doing?"

"There is Abbot Stephan, and I am going to descend on him like an avenging angel." Paxton balanced himself on the wall. He leaped. He landed. He lost control. He was going down, too fast.

N=mg, where N is the normal force, m is my mass, g is 9.8m/sec^2,
Determine mg sine θ and mg cos θ,
The coefficient of kinetic friction is U_K=F_k/F_n,
The coefficient of friction is… the coefficient of friction is…
HIT THE BRAKES STUPID!

Paxton dug heels, calves, buttocks, back, the palms of his hands, head, and everything else he could, into the earth. His feet hit the metre-wide ring of stone at the base of the motte. His vertical velocity stopped, but his horizontal velocity was unimpeded. This velocity threw him forward, so he barely missed breaking his head on stone. Instead, it hit muddy ground. Paxton rolled to his back and covered his face with his hands. Burning pain coursed up his heels, through his legs, to his spine and swirled around inside his braincase. "Fuck!"

"Hear how he prays to God in his native tongue."

The pain was still there, undiminished, but now reasoned thought interwove with it. *There is only one man who interprets 'fuck' that way.* When Paxton decided he could move his head he rolled it to his left. There in front of him was a pair of polished cordovan leather boots.

"Ignatius?"

Ignatius bent to Paxton and pulled him to his feet.

"What are you doing in that outfit?" Paxton asked. "I thought you were—"

"For my work, I have been ordained. I am eager to tell my brother."

"That's great. I'm sure you will raise high on your own merits." Paxton wobbled in and lowered his voice. "Please be careful about calling me your brother. It could be dangerous."

An uncomfortable smile crossed Ignatius's face. "Paxton, you are my friend, but not my brother. Harold is my brother."

"Oh!" *Switch gears.* "Where is the abbot?"

"He is with Friar Bernard in the chapel." Ignatius wetted his lips. "He hasn't forgotten about you."

Paxton felt confident enough to be able to stand on his own. He took a few steps to determine that nothing was broken. He brushed off his pants. "So I've been told."

"Abbot Stephan brings other charges against you."

"What else?"

"In practicing witchcraft you brought the pox on Alton."

"Been there, done that."

Ignatius tilted his head at Paxton's non-English, English.

"You would commit the sin of Judas, casting your soul to perdition."

"That was, uhm, an accident."

"You tempt other souls to the devil. You inflicted them with the pox and encouraged them to denounce Jesus to save their mortal lives."

"Others? Others who? I've been in the care and feeding of you monks, or the Lady the entire time I've been here. Who else is there?"

Ignatius stepped toward the castle's chapel. Bernard, Stephan and two others walked out it.

"Oh no! Not them!" Paxton's voice rose. Thin faces were lightly freckled beneath curious blue eyes, and there was that hair again, the beautiful hair that absorbed the sun's light and his attention. Long, straight, streams of gold held in place with broad leather headbands.

The abbot started to call out to Ignatius. Recognizing Paxton, he stopped. The abbot spoke to the friar. Bernard nodded and Stephan advanced on Ignatius and Paxton. With his cassock sweeping the ground, he seemed to glide towards them.

All he needs is Darth Vader music. thought Paxton.

Still facing Stephan, Ignatius asked Paxton, "You know these women?"

Paxton squirmed. "I met them at their cottage."

"They tell a different story."

"I may have passed them in a cow pasture. Yes, when I was looking for my friends. I see they still carry their staffs."

Ignatius rubbed his forehead. "Yes. I found it impossible to relieve them of their instruments. They are a most stubborn pair. A trait that magnifies their troubles."

Stephan stopped about two metres in front of Ignatius and Paxton, watching them like a vulture. The morning sun transformed him into a silhouette of death. "It appears my work is never done. The twins have told me many things."

When the lady entered the bailey, Catherine abandon Ignatius.

"Under the influence of the devil they refuse to admit even more," Ignatius responded.

The abbot had circled behind them. Paxton turned to keep Stephan in view.

"You who claim noble blood will not rise in this world or the next." A vein on the right side of Stephan's forehead grew prominent. "'Sic et vos a foris quidem paretis mominibus iusti intus autem pleni estis hypocrisi et iniquitate.' Matthew 23:28." (*You appear outwardly righteous to men, but inwardly are full of hypocrisy and lawlessness.*) The vein throbbed.

Catherine and the Lady hurried over to Bernard and the twins. Bernard and the Lady withdrew a short distance from the three women and spoke in whispers. The Lady returned to the twins, spoke to them, and advanced to Stephan.

"I claim the twins as servants for me. I need a laundress and scullion."

Stephan paced a slow circle around the Lady. "I want the bishop, and the duke, to hear their confessions."

"Friar Bernard will make my arguments and theirs," the Lady murmured without moving to face the abbot. Stephan had to lean forward to hear her. "You will make your own arguments."

The creaking of the wagon drew the Lady's attention. She stepped forward until she was alongside the driver. "Father Casimir, when the

Alton monks are seated, go to the chapel for my friar." The Lady walked away in a deliberate, measured pace. She stopped and without looking back, said, "Prince Paxton, come with me."

Paxton protested, "I need to move my bed again. I climbed the roof to repair it and put two more holes in it."

The Lady started moving. "I said come with me."

Chapter 11

The new Duke of Banburn sat with a plate of roast goose on his lap, stabbing the meat with the fork.

"No, my lord." His honored guest stopped him. The duke pressed down on the goose with his knife, and pulled out the fork. The guest took the plate and set it on his lap. He pierced the goose's breast with the fork and demonstrated. "Then cut a piece of flesh, and pull the fork out when you have gripped the meat with your teeth. Your hands will not become greasy from the goose, and you can better grip the knife and spoon." He and the other members of the party from Sandalburg had practiced with the forks on their trip.

"What's wrong with grease? It makes your fingers tasty."

The duke and his guest sat in the duke's private garderobe. It was bigger than the one at Sandalburg. Still the guest felt confined. The duke sat too close. The Lord of Banburn leaned closer. "Have you seen your cousin yet?"

"Upon our arrival at Banburn I suggested we go to the cathedral to give thanks for our safe arrival." The guest used the fork again. "I didn't expect the bishop to be able to meet us then. I talked in private with his secretary. We will see the bishop tomorrow."

The duke took back his plate, knife, and new fork. He wiped the knife and fork on the front of his tunic. "I hear intrigue grows in Sandalburg like weeds in a field."

"It is more the pity. Some of these weeds are not of our own planting. I am distressed. Abbot Stephan's curiosity is aroused. He asked many questions on the way here."

"Idle heads are the devil's stage." The duke stuck the fork in the goose. Using his hands, he ripped out a leg. He opened his mouth and sank his teeth into the flesh.

"There is nothing idle about the abbot's head. In your own castle he talks to servants and other nobles."

The duke stopped chewing. With feigned casualness he asked, "What does he say?"

"It is not what he says. It is what he asks."

"Do not be coy with me. You are my ears where I cannot go," the duke whispered.

"My lord, you pay me to assist in your ambitions." He held out a hand.

The duke pulled a leather purse from under his cloak. Opening it, he took out two coins, and waved them under his guest's nose. "You owe me for eating my goose." The duke put the coins in a pocket and gave his guest the purse.

"Some of the weeds on the Lady's estate are a nuisance. Some are harmful to our effort. Some can perhaps be made useful." The guest counted out the coins.

"You are talking of the strange noble, Prince Paxton, held hostage by *that woman*." The duke looked into his guest's eyes. "No one comes to Banburn from Warren or Alton without replying to my inquiries. I ask about *that woman*. I even ask about you."

"You say, '*that woman*.' Do you hate or fear the Lady Wilhelmina that much? You cannot say her name."

"It is one thing to be held hostage by another. It is another for your fears to hold you hostage. Are you implying I fear something? What are you afraid of?"

"This is what I fear my lord. By 'making inquiries' you cultivate weeds in others heads. The abbot is an example. On his own, he has become suspicious of the young duke's death. He quizzed the Lady's servants, even the lady-in-waiting Sarah. Now he is in Banburn, where he may feast his mind on a never-ending banquet of mistrust. He asks questions about you, and me."

"Ha!" The duke tore off the goose's other leg. Shaking the leg like a sword at the man's nose, he smiled. "Now we learn of your true concern." The duke put the plate to the side of the bench and stood to pull up his leggings. "You thought you were discreet."

"I am discreet." The guest leaned in. "My lord, we are losing sight of our difficulties."

The duke wiped his hands on his breeches. "Such as?"

"Have you read the copy of the document I made? The parchment that Prince Paxton, of the house of Frost, gave the Lady."

"Yes. It appears that this noble knows of Venetian bookkeeping."

"If the Lady gives him permission to audit her wealth… he may find discrepances."

The duke laughed so hard he farted. "*That woman* and the abbot are like two starving dogs, growling over a bone, and you are the one who is in danger."

"And you may lose the crown jewel of your assets."

"Not my only jewel. Very well, I agree. The abbot must meet with some fatal difficulty. When and where?"

"Before he meets with the bishop. I will tell you what I have learned of his routine for tomorrow."

The abbot stood against the crenelated wall of the castle's north tower. He could understand why the Lady's husband had favoured rising early in the morning and climbing to this place. The cold, dewy air was like the taste of a crisp, tart apple. *There's freshness in the air that one does not find on the ground.* Cool night sounds started to fade. Already birds were awake, their nestlings calling for food. The males began proclaiming their territory. The abbot looked up. Heavy clouds shrouded the sky. *If God doesn't open his heavens, I will come up here later. I've heard one can see the lands of the lairds of the north from here.* Abbot Stephan patted the top of the wall. *Banburn serves as a gate. It can keep the northern lairds out, or it can let them in.* He looked west. *Sandalwood is the key to the gate.* The abbot meandered along the wall. He stopped to take in the calm silhouette of the cathedral. All the buildings in Banburn lay prostrate before the castle and the cathedral.

The abbot turned around to take in Banburn and all its lands, and sucked in his breath. A figure rose from the hole in the floor. "Oh, it's you." He recovered himself. "What are you doing up so early?" Abbot Stephan's question was like a fencer's balestra.

"I followed you up." The figure finished climbing the stairs to the open tower's floor, turned, and kicked a pebble down the spiraling stairs. "I remember, in our youth, you beat me in our fencing lessons." The other person's voice parried. "Now, like you, I seek the truth."

"The truth may condemn you to perdition." A riposte.

"Abbot, 'Circumdedit me in negatione Ephraim et in dolo domus Israhel.' Hosea 11:12. *(Ephraim hath compassed me about with denials, and the house of Israel with deceit.)* What is it that concerns you?" Parry and reprise.

"I have many concerns." A lunge from Stephan.

"Many concerns did not bring you here. Are you interested in the death of the young duke?" Parry and cut-over.

"Was the Lady in the habit of rising with the duke?" A reprise from Stephan.

"How would I know that?" A retreat.

"Perhaps your cousin spoke of their marriage." Another reprise by the abbot.

"I know the Lady was still learning the habits of her husband." A parry.

"I will ask the servants the morning habits of the duke and Lady Wilhelmina." Another riposte by Abbot Stephan.

"Abbot, I questioned them yesterday." Parry and reprise.

"What have you learned?" A feint.

"Let me show you what I know of the young duke's death." A final thrust.

Chapter 12

What is happening? Paxton sat up. He ran a hand over his flat mattress. *How do they manage to get so many rocks in so flat a mattress? What is not happening? These people have no concept of real time. Harold and the others have been gone three weeks.* Paxton peered through the tattered roof.

Epsilon Ursae Majoris.
Surface temperature, 10,800 K.
Mass, 5.788E30 kg. (2.91 Solar Mass).
Radius, 2,921,000km. (4.2 Solar Radius).
Magnitude, 1.76.
Constellation, Ursa Major.

He looked down at the bed. *How many times have I moved this thing to keep out of the rain? There's no good reason for Albert to take this long. What if I'm stuck here? I can feel my brain turning to Brussels sprouts. Steamed Brussels sprouts.*

He sighed at the roof. *In my time, I was a king of stars. Here, I'm trying to convince people I'm a jack of diamonds, and they treat me like a two of dung. I can't even do double entry bookkeeping right.*

Paxton grabbed the candle on the table, and shuffled to the hearth. Kneeling, he blew on the wood coals to wake a few. Touching the candle's wick to a coal, he blew hard. Paxton got a flame on the wick. Placing it back on the table, he sat on the bed to confront the candle.

"I'm trying to use the scientific method."

The candle flame winked back. *It is certain.*

"I ask a question. How fast is the Lady's wealth diminishing?"

The flame spun and stopped. *Cannot predict now.*

"I've done basic research. Sarah worked with me. She translated Harold's diaries on the Lady's income and expenses."

The flame bowed and shot up. *It is decidedly so.*

"I've constructed a hypothesis. The Lady is running out of money."

Sparks flew from the wick. *Don't count on it.*

"I've tested my hypothesis by doing an experiment. I've done double entry bookkeeping on the Lady's wealth."

The candle flickered and flickered again. *Without a doubt.*

"I've analyzed my data."

The flame turned and turned back. *Reply hazy, try again.*

"My conclusion is … the Lady's wealth is increasing."

The flame stood still. *Yes.*

"Why? How?"

The flame crouched low. *Concentrate and ask again.*

"Someone is adding coins to her treasure box."

The flame changed colour. *Most likely.*

"Money they're not supposed to have. Money if found on them would raise questions of where, or from whom they got it.

The flame swayed. *You may rely on it.*

"Like in the story, The Purloined Letter."

The flame twitched. *As I see it, yes.*

"Who?"

The flame waved. *Ask again later.*

Paxton wiped his palms on his pants and went in for the big one. "Will I live again in my own time?"

The flame cut its size in half. Then it cut it in half again. *Better not tell you now.*

Paxton blew out the impertinent candle, then opened the door to lean against its frame. Rubbing his arms was like trying to start a fire with popsicle sticks. His chattering teeth tapped out the temperature in Morse code. Purple morning light challenged the cold evening stars. He could see evening frost on vegetation. Soon it will become morning dew. With enough sun, it will fade away. Paxton looked up at the roof, and the new holes he created, trying to fix it. *That sieve isn't retaining what heat the fire gives.*

Paxton glanced at the keep. The Lady had become withdrawn. She took her meals in private, only Sarah attended her. *The strain of waiting for a reply is getting to her.*

Paxton persuaded Sarah to give the twins enough cloth to make two sashes. With a bit of praise, he got Catherine to show the twins how to embroider a capital letter E on one sash, and a capital letter I on the other. The twins also sewed the other letters of the alphabet, and their names in the cloths. *Now I can tell them apart. Unless they switch sashes.* Paxton scratched himself through a pants pocket, and pulled out the modern coins he had with him. He bounced the pence and pound coins in his hand. *I'm going to talk with Sarah.*

One of the town's young priests said morning prayers in the chapel. As usual, the Lady attended prayers, then went to her second floor sanctuary in the keep. Paxton waited until Sarah served the Lady, then they had their morning meal in the Great Hall.

"Sarah, I need to have a new roof, or be moved to another cottage."

"Every day the Lady feels better, and she expects to resume all of her duties shortly. Thank you for your concern Lord Paxton."

"Yes, that's nice, but what about me, now?"

"Are all the nobles of your land so rude?"

"The nobles of my land aren't threatened with using their beds as gondolas, and singing O Sole Mio."

After the morning meal, Paxton tramped to the stable. "Gunther," he shouted. Finding the mare he rode, he opened its stall.

Gunther climbed down the ladder from the loft. He approached Paxton like a man needing to clean up a mess he didn't make. "Lord Paxton?"

"I'm going into town. Help me harness this animal."

"The Lady did not tell me you had permission to leave."

"Does the Lady tell you everything? If necessary, I'll harness it and drive myself, I'll walk if necessary."

"No."

"I'm sure you don't want me to pester the Lady. She would be annoyed to know you can't handle me by yourself. We can go out and be back before the midday meal. Aren't you curious why I need to go into town?"

Gunther hesitated. He walked to a wall where his bow and quiver of arrows hung from pegs. "I'll tell the Lady we went hunting."

Paxton led the way. He was like a hound following the scent of his prey. Through Warren and across the stream they rode. When they arrived at the cottage, Paxton dismounted.

"No! Walk in front of the horse, never behind." Gunther shook his head. "Ruttish, fool-born codpiece," he muttered.

Paxton rubbed his ass with both hands. "Wait here for me."

"I never interrupt a man taking his pleasure."

Paxton walked to the cottage door and cracked it open. "Good morrow?" No answer. He walked around the cottage. Beatrice was in the garden behind it. "Good morrow." She stopped hoeing, stood straight, and brushed the hair from her face. *Her hair is so much like Roseann's hair. Roseann's smile hid pain, the night before she was murdered. The night I could have saved her, but I chose not to. Beatrice's pain looks like Roseann's, without the smile.* Paxton noticed a bench next to the cottage wall. "May, may we sit and talk?" Beatrice said nothing. She did nothing. "When we first met, I remember you could talk." Paxton patted the bench seat.

Beatrice sauntered over and plopped on the bench. She looked at nothing in the distance. "I'm sorry for the deaths of your husband and children," Paxton began. "You have no other relatives?"

She faced him with dead eyes. "No."

"We are somewhat alike." He stuttered. "I also have no one." Paxton could see no response. "No one comes here except for, uhm, business?"

"One of the young priests in Warren came here. He told me to follow the example of Mary of Magdalene. I asked him, could the church agree whether or not women have souls? If women do not, what does it matter how I conduct my life? If women do have souls, isn't it his duty to forgive me seventy times seven times?" She continued staring at nothing. "Father Casimir comes here." At this, her voice gained some life. "He sometimes comes with grain for my chickens." She gestured to a small pen. "Then we sit and talk of the weather, or the crops. Other times he comes with some meat. Then we talk of my husband, or children." Beatrice shook her head. "Grain for weather. Meat for family."

Paxton put his hand in a pocket and pulled out some coins. "I don't have grain or meat. I wondered?" Seeing the coins, Beatrice's body stiffened. "I was wondering, I have some coins from my… place. If you don't mind, would you come to the castle and build a roof for me?"

Beatrice picked up a new pound coin and fingered the twelve-sided milled edge. "For this, all you want is a good roof?"

"Yes."

Beatrice looked at the castle in the distance. "Has the Lady who lives there given you permission to bring me in?"

121

Paxton smiled. "We have a saying in my land. Better to beg forgiveness than ask permission."

"No! You are a warped, beef-witted, lout. No!" The colour of Gunther's face grew as dark as his horse, seeing Paxton with Beatrice.

"Come on, Gunther. You wanted to know what kind of trophy we would return with." Paxton carried two bundles. The one made from bed sheets lay still. The other made from a blanket roiled like pasta boiling in a pot. Paxton joined the knotted bundles together with rope. He threw the still bundle over the side of Gunther's horse. "That bundle holds Beatrice's' possessions. The squawking bundle holds her chickens."

"Do you think you can bring *her* into the Lady's castle?"

"Gunther. You're bringing *her* into the Lady's castle, because you're a hero."

Gunther's stallion shied from the squirming bundle of the blanket-encased chickens. He pulled on the reins to steady the animal. "And what is it that makes me a hero?"

"Why, you saved Beatrice from a brazen band of brigands. You single handedly struggled with six scoundrels. You ran the ragged rascals round a rugged rock. How many different ways do I have to say it? After that you attacked a giant."

Gunther, his horse, even the chickens paused to absorb this story. "A giant," Gunther said.

"Yes. A giant, as tall as a windmill, and with four arms." Paxton drew his horse near a decaying tree stump. "Unfortunately the giant threw you from your horse before he ran off. You're not just a hero. You're a knight-errant." Paxton helped Beatrice mount his mare, then climbed up behind her. "Do you mind if we call you Dulcinea?" He smiled up at Beatrice. *Don Quixote hasn't been written yet.*

For the first time, Beatrice smiled.

Instead of going through Warren, Gunther took them to the east and south of the town. The three of them rode the path between the town and the grain fields. Paxton watched the wind rippling the grain stalks. *The bending grain stalks are a good analogy for the phase velocity of waves propagating in space. $V_P = \lambda/T$.* The sound of the wind carried with it the smell of the town. Now the wind carried Gunther's gruff voice to Paxton. "All right, but no giants."

The wind fluttered their clothing and blew locks of Beatrice's hair across Paxton's face. Paxton smiled. "No giants." He pulled the hair that slapped his face away to tuck it behind her neck. Beatrice grabbed her hair and turned her face to Paxton. "Whoa!" The mare stopped. Paxton pulled his hand back from Beatrice's hair, and laughed. "Your eyes are like flashing train crossing warning lights." Paxton kicked the horse into gear. "Gunther on our other hunting trip you said, 'there are no poachers.' Is that correct?"

"Yes," he grunted.

"How do you know that? Maybe they know not to be in the forest when the Lady's hunting party is out. Maybe you don't see them. If there are no poachers," Paxton pulled his mare closer to Gunther's stallion, "why did Harold notice a lack of game?"

Gunther glared at Paxton. He pulled his horse closer. "There are no poachers, because I say there are none."

Paxton kept his horse close to Gunther's horse. "When we first went hunting, you offered to pay for my visit with Beatrice. Where did you get the money?"

Gunther grabbed the bridle of Paxton's mare and stopped. "Watch your tongue young prince or you may lose what it takes to enjoy that woman's company."

Beatrice looked on as if she were judging a medieval tennis match.

Paxton leaned forward and to his right. "Is your name Beatrice, Dulcinea, or *that woman?*"

123

"As to where I get the money, I am the Lady's huntsman. From time to time she instructs me to sell game, or give it to the poor."

Paxton kicked his horse forward, out of Gunther's grip. "When you sell the game, who gets the money?"

Gunther prodded his stallion ahead of Paxton's mare. "I give the Lady the money and she gives me a portion."

The question is, do you earn money from the Lady, or poacher's bribes, or both? "You can't safely hold a candle when you're burning both ends. Let us be at peace. You say 'there are no poachers.' Now I say it." Paxton reined his mare to a slow walk. "I have noticed no gibbet in Warren."

"The hanging tree is north of the town. It serves as a warning to the lairds of the north."

"Have they been a danger to Sandalburg?"

"They covet this land."

"Are they a danger now?"

"They are always a danger." Gunther sat almost sidesaddle. "You planned to bring this woman to the castle before we left. Do you have a plan for when we return?"

Paxton looked at Beatrice as he answered Gunther. "I suggest you take Beatrice to Catherine. Have Catherine give her a cottage near the chapel. You protected Beatrice from brigands outside the castle. When the friar returns he can protect her from the brigands inside the castle." Paxton now turned to Gunther. "I will tell the Lady, or Sarah, of your heroics in rescuing Beatrice. She will earn her keep repairing roofs. She will start with mine."

"And when she's finished repairing roofs?"

"Her name is Beatrice, use it. The Lady is short-staffed. Before the twins arrived, Catherine was the only female servant for the Lady and Sarah. I hope the Lady will use good judgment. Gunther, your stomach growls as loud as your voice. We'll have to hurry to make the midday meal."

Nearing the castle, the horses picked up their pace. They knew they would be free from their burdens at the stables. John and Catherine approached them. John's voice was as heavy as his anvil. "The Lady is angry with you Lord Paxton."

"Already?"

"You escaped from the castle."

"I didn't escape. Gunther and I went hunting. We came across a band of brigands and rescued Beatrice. We brought her here for her own safety."

"What is *that woman*—"

"Her name is Beatrice. Use it."

Recognizing the name, Catherine sped to the keep's hill. A third of the way up, she left a dust trail that reached all the way to the base. Paxton watched her go higher, farther, faster. *You Roadrunner. Me Wile E. Coyote.* "John, Beatrice will occupy a cottage near the chapel. When the friar returns—"

"He is already back. He arrived after the morning meal. The Lady couldn't find you." John said to Gunther. "It's good you couldn't be found either. I see where you caught him."

"Friar Bernard must have left for the castle after Lord Paxton and I passed through town. I'll explain our absence to the Lady. John, will you put the horses away?"

"Gunther didn't catch me. We went hunting. Where is Friar Bernard?"

"He is in the chapel hearing confessions. So few souls, and yet so many sins. You have some unburdening of your own to make, Lord Paxton."

Paxton left almost as much dust in his wake as Catherine did. Running into the chapel, he passed Friar Bernard coming out. Paxton

125

was a metre past the friar before he could turn around. "Friar Bernard." He grabbed the friar's cloak. "What news do you bring from Banburn?"

The friar ran a hand through what was left of his hair. "There is much news from Banburn. Good Abbot Stephan is dead. He died at the bottom of the stairs of the north tower. People in the castle now call it the tower of dread."

"In his heart he believed he was God's servant. I pray God judges him as such. Did he talk to the bishop or the duke? What news of my people?"

"He was to talk with the bishop later that day. Ignatius made his case for him. Stephan seemed ready to talk about more than you, but he kept his own counsel."

Paxton leaned in. "Stephan's dead. Okay. What did Ignatius say about me?"

Bernard gave Paxton a weak smile. "I do not think he made an argument as strong as Stephan would. Both the bishop and the duke agree you should remain with the Lady."

Paxton clenched the friar's cassock in his fist. "What of news of my people?"

"There is none my son."

"I'm abandoned. Lost." Paxton's voice cracked. "There will be no rescue."

"Let go of my cassock. Do not despair. The king will receive the Lady's letter. If your subjects are in London, we may get a reply soon. Perhaps by spring of next year."

Paxton twisted the cassock. "Spring? Spring next year is not 'soon'!"

"Again, I ask you: Let go of my cassock." Paxton released it. "If you are abandoned, it is fitting for your sin of pride. Good Abbot Stephan is dead, and you think only of yourself."

Paxton folded his arms across his knees. "The dead have no troubles old man. I'm alive and stuck here."

Looking up he saw Sarah gliding toward him with Catherine skipping behind. Sarah attempted her best pale imitation of the Lady. "Gunther told the Lady Wilhelmina a certain woman was brought into her castle. She understands it is for her protection from those outside the castle. The Lady has decided she can remain to perform duties assigned to her. She will not be molested inside the castle."

Catherine leaned forward, soaking up every word like a thirsty camel in the desert.

"The Lady wishes her meaning to be known without delay." Sarah smashed her right fist into the palm of her left hand.

Catherine jackhammered her head up and down.

"Your meal must be delayed. You will assist Catherine in her duties."

Paxton stood up. "Sarah, tell the Lady Wilhelmina there's a new tutor in Sandalburg. Everyone who wants an education will get one: reading, writing, geometry, trigonometry, and all the natural sciences. Men, and women, common, and noble. I've shown the Lady forks, and double entry bookkeeping. That's nothing. If my people won't come for me, I'll bring my world here."

Head up, shoulders back, Sarah left them and headed to the keep.

Paxton, speaking to the friar, indicated Beatrice. "Please give Beatrice a cottage, and let her put her chickens in the coop. Give her a meal, and then put her to work." Paxton jabbed a thumb in his chest. "On my roof." He squared his body to face Catherine. "Wipe that silly ass-smile from your face Catherine. What have you got for me?"

"Today your duties consist of working with the pigs." Catherine skipped to the rear of the courtyard. Metal jangled from a pocket in her apron. Peering over her right shoulder, she made tiny circles with her right hand, pulling Paxton in like a fish.

All right, I get it. Men are pigs. Following Catherine, he made several rude gestures he learned in a number of countries.

Catherine climbed the fence and sat on the top rail. "Separate the female piglets and put them in the smaller pen with the sow."

Paxton hustled around, catching, inspecting, releasing, and dropping off piglets. "Hey, I don't like this any more than you do." Facing his too happy tormentor, he said "Now what?"

"Now you will help me castrate the males."

Chapter 13

The hour was close to Compline. A wind whipped salt-water spray to sting Lady Wilhelmina's face. Standing at the bow of her ship, she stared into the distance. *Is there a safe harbor near?* The wind threatened to tear the useless chart from her hands. This chart hinted at safe channels but did not warn of the possibility of hidden shoals. Birds screeching interrupted her thoughts. Storm petrels hung nearly motionless in the sky above her head. Facing her, wings outstretched, they screeched their warning of rough seas. Lady Wilhelmina could remain at sea, would remain at sea, until safe harbor could be found for her cargo.

The wind stinging her with debris, dirt, and small pebbles brought her out of her fantasy. Lady Wilhelmina stood in one of the rampart's corners. She searched the side of the hill the keep was built on. Half way up the soft earth, she found Sarah scrambling beetle-like up the hill.

Looking to the bailey's courtyard, she saw saffron tresses identifying the twins. Earlier Paxton roamed the castle and its grounds, ferreting out all spare rope. He tied the pieces together to make one long rope. One twin held her herding rod upright, as Paxton tied one end of the rope to it. He tied the other to the other twin's staff. Then this twin dragged a circle in the earth with her rod. The length of the rope determined the radius. Paxton was inside the circle governing the work.

From her vantage point, Wilhelmina could also make out Friar Bernard and Harold. Bernard stood to one side of the circle, hands clasped over his pork belly. Harold stood next to him, arms akimbo.

The hillside was too steep. Wilhelmina had to lean forward to keep Sarah in sight. A noisy murder of crows circled above and in front of her. The ancient rampart's wall was made of timbers with roots sunk deep in the earth. Sharp points crowned the timbers. More recently white plaster had been used to entomb the wall to give it the appearance of stone. Here a few wood spears had rotted away, leaving a small gap in the defense work.

Wilhelmina could no longer see Sarah. She could only hear the sounds of her progress. Loose earth rattled away below the gap. Heavy breathing followed. "Oomph, ump." Panting and more earth skittered downhill. A female hand made it to the top of the wall. "Oomph, ump." Its mate followed. "Rrrrr." Her face rose into view like an angry, rising sun. The strain on her face matched the croaking in her throat. "Rrrrr, argh, ump." She wiggled through the opening. The Lady laughed. Sarah's efforts made up for the lack of a jester in her court.

"Sarah, why didn't you use the stairs?"

Sarah caught her breath before replying. "This looked quicker, and shorter."

"If you are going to scramble down and up the hillside you should watch how Catherine does it."

Sarah pulled her mangled hair back from her face. With her skinned hands, she brushed off her soiled clothes. "I am a lady. I do not need instructions from a serf."

The circle with a twenty-metre radius was complete. Paxton untied the rope from the outer rod. He looped it around the outer staff and tied

130

the free end to the centre staff. Now the twin scraped a concentric circle in the earth. The radius of the new circle was half the radius of the first circle.

The Lady and Sarah stood on the rampart, their capes furling and unfurling in the wind. They noticed Paxton waving for them to come.

"See how Paxton beckons us. Let's see what lesson he wishes to tutor now."

"Wait. You sent me down the hill to find out what he was doing. I climb back up. Now you say we are going down. We then go back up to retire for the evening!" Sarah's voice rose in pitch with every sentence.

"This time we will use the stairs. While we are descending you will tell me what you learned."

"One thing I learned is that before you sent me down, Ignatius gave you a letter from your aunt."

"I wanted to read the letter in private first." Wilhelmina gave the letter to Sarah. The seal of the new Duchess of Northumbria was broken.

Sarah read the letter. She looked up, joyful. "She says you are missed at court. Oh, she prays for your return! I would love to go to Mass in the cathedral again, with her and everyone else I'm so pleased. Tonight we will offer up prayers for our safe return. May we start on the morrow?"

"We are not returning."

"But why? I do wish to enjoy the music and the dancing."

"My aunt says nothing of the whispering and the whisperers. Of how I was the first to find my husband dead at the bottom of the stairs? Might I also have been the last one to see him alive at the top of the stairs?"

"She says nothing of the whispers because there is nothing to say."

"Then let her declare, there is nothing to say. My uncle and his wife said nothing as the whispers grew. Let them say something now."

131

"Send me back to court. If you have nothing to fear, I will send a letter saying, the apples are plentiful this year. If I see reason for you to stay away, I will say the apples are poor this year."

"What if I get a letter saying you have fallen ill and beg me to come back before you perish?"

Softly, Sarah broached the subject. "You are too young to spend your life mourning the duke."

Wilhelmina looked up. The crows fled. "My husband was like the great stag of the forest. My uncle wants nothing more than to be the great cur of the castle."

"What of the northern lairds your aunt mentioned? Especially Red Ahearn."

"Yes, her letter contains both honey and vinegar."

Sarah watched the preparations going on in the bailey. "When Paxton was gathering his ropes, I overheard your confessor ask Lord Paxton if he was trying to avoid the church's justice again."

"Again?"

Sarah nodded.

"Strange. Neither one said anything to me."

"Perhaps it was said in confession."

"You appear to need to make your own confession."

"Yesterday I went with Father Casimir to Alton where Paxton was first seen." Sarah cleared her throat. "The villagers say the pox left when Paxton left. Before then, the twins' stepfather put them in the convent school. Their mother then gave birth to a healthy boy and their brother Thomas recovered from his illness. They say the foreigner is in league with the devil and the twins are his familiars. My lady, it does not matter whether it is true or not. People believe it is true. Let us return home."

"Ignatius just returned from there. He states the pox has moved to Banburn."

"The castle can be locked, my lady."

"Castle walls can keep out armies. They cannot keep out death."

"Then we are doomed. The lairds will be on us if we stay. The pox will be on us if we return."

"Let us lighten our minds Sarah, and learn what our foreign tutor has for us."

Paxton asked the twins to stand outside the circles. "Good evening ladies." he said to Wilhelmina and Sarah. "Are these all who wish learning something now?" Paxton saw others hanging back by the buildings, careful as deer who know hunters are in the forest. "Tonight we will learn astronomy, logic, and how to use your imagination. Imagination is what puts the colours of the rainbow in your thoughts."

Paxton took one of the herding staffs and touched the centre of the concentric circles. "Let us imagine this centre is the Sun." Paxton held an arm out to Lady Wilhelmina. "Will you be my Sun?" He drew a line from the centre to the smaller circle. "Friar Bernard, will you stand on the smaller circle? We will call you Earth." At a ninety-degree angle to his first line, he traced a line to the outer circle. "Harold, will you stand on the larger circle? We will call you Mars. Friar how is it that Mars moves back and forth in the sky?"

"Mars travels around the Earth in a circle and also revolves around a smaller circle called the Epicycle."

"Does this hold true for the other planets, such as Venus?"

"Yes." His response was as measured as a rabbit sensing a snare.

"Now both of you walk at a normal pace this way." Paxton indicated a counter-clockwise circle. After they walked sixty degrees of arc, Paxton cried, "Stop." Both men stopped. "Earth, has Mars, appeared to have moved in front of you?"

"Yes," was the cautious reply.

"Continue your orbits please." They walked another sixty degrees around Wilhelmina, the Sun, and Paxton again called "Stop. Earth, where is Mars, now?"

"He is behind me."

"Continue your orbits." When the Friar walked half way through his orbit Paxton shouted, "Stop. Has Mars, moved forward?"

"Yes."

"Now will you, Earth, stand on the outer circle? Harold, stand on the inner circle. We will call you Venus." Derisive laughter came from those standing in back.

Harold spun around trying to identify the impudent servants. Some tried to slink around behind someone else. Others looked at the stars turning on their dim lights. Only the smith, his feet rooted in the ground returned Harold's look, stare for stare.

"Now Earth and Venus, resume your orbits at a constant speed. As they orbit, everyone will notice the same back and forth motion."

The twin wearing the sash embroidered with an I exclaimed. "Venus appears to move back and forth more quickly than Mars did!"

"That is because Venus is on the inside, faster orbit," said her older twin.

"This is what happens when you allow women to speak," muttered Harold. "Next they will demand a seat at council."

Friar Bernard stopped his orbit. "Paxton, son of Frost, are you saying…"

Paxton interrupted, "I am not saying anything. I ask that you use your imagination. In my land, we have a principle of simplicity called Occam's razor. It is named after William of Ockham."

"Entia non sunt multiplicanda sine necessitates. *(Plurality must never be posited without necessity.)* I am familiar with this Franciscan." Bernard's riposte was unexpected.

"I point out a logical explanation."

"Learn from the Bible. 'Devitans profanas vocum novitates et oppositiones falsi nominis scientiae.' First Timothy 6: 20." *(Avoiding the profane novelties of words and oppositions of knowledge falsely so called.)*

"Forgive me Friar. I accept your rebuke." *As Galileo will say 'But it still moves.'*

Wilhelmina stepped toward the two men. "It will soon be Compline. We must now go to chapel." She turned to lead the procession.

Sarah walked with her lady. "Even if he is not a warlock, he will get us in trouble."

"Do not be so sure. Have you noticed what everyone is doing? Everyone, even Friar Bernard, is looking at the stars. What would happen if I were in trouble? If I am loyal to Prince Paxton, maybe I can sail my ship to his land for sanctuary."

"You have no ship."

"Use your imagination."

Friar Bernard and Paxton brought up the rear. "Paxton of the house of Frost, I see you value logic and praise reason. You are at heart are a good man. May I ask a question?"

"I feel this is the same praise the Pharisees gave Jesus, before trying to trap Him."

"Are you comparing yourself to our Lord and Savior?"

"No. Neither do I compare you to the Pharisees."

"I ask if one man is burned at the stake as a heretic, and another burned at the stake as a warlock, what the difference is."

"There is no difference. They are both dead."

Chapter 14

Whooosh! Thwack!

Beatrice washed the wood boards' fronts and backs. She put the borrowed pail and cloth aside to make a clear area for her work. Her eyes swept left to right, top to bottom. She cleaned every crevice of every letter carved into them.

Paxton sat on his heels, off to the side. *She's a perfectionist.*

Finding an unwanted piece of debris, she frowned and tossed it away. She used her hands efficiently to level the area. She looked over her shoulder. "Thank you for bringing me here."

Paxton scanned the leaden sky. The chill air felt as heavy as the clouds looked. "No problem, if this is where you want to be. You worked hard at your lessons."

Beatrice went back to her labors. "The numbers come easy to me. The letters," she crinkled her nose, "not so much. Still." She ran her fingers on the names on the grave markers. "Knowing their meanings keeps me close to them."

"No one finds learning to read easy."

I did it! I said something nice to a woman in a social setting.

Beatrice did her best to smooth out everything. "Catherine finds letters and words easy."

136

"She's been working at it longer. By herself. I have to admit she's a clever girl." She scrubbed one marker after another. There were perhaps twenty in the small churchyard.

"Beatrice. Why does she hate me?"

She poured a little water from the wash pail wherever she found flowers growing. "She doesn't hate you. She hates me. She finds you attractive."

"God help the man she becomes pissed off at."

Beatrice stood still as she translated his words into her English, by examining his tone.

"She knows there can be no union between noble and common." Beatrice wiped her forehead with a hand. "So she pushes you from her and her from you, by being rude."

"That's dumb. Why does she hate you?"

"She senses between you and me what she wants for herself." She wrung out her wash rag.

"What's that?"

"Are all the nobles of Konectic like you?"

"Connecticut, C-o-n-n-e-c-t-i-c-u-t. Do you mean easy to talk with, not aloof?"

"Yes."

Paxton sighed. "Even I am not like that. Tell Catherine, if she can control the urges of her loins, I'll be nice to her."

"I'll tell her you desire peace between the house of Frost and her." Completing her corporal duties, Beatrice folded her hands in prayer at the foot of her husband's and children's graves. "I would like to go into the church now."

"Okay." Paxton picked up the empty pail and cloth. "Gunther, we're going into the church."

Gunther stopped pulling the arrows out of the tree he'd been using for target practice, and nodded at Paxton.

"I think that will be my next big invention. I will introduce the word 'okay' into common usage."

Paxton saw Beatrice adjust the bra underneath her tunic. "How does it fit?"

"It is almost as uncomfortable as learning to read."

"All I can offer is a theoretical knowledge."

"What is a te-o-radical?"

"Theoretical. It means I haven't touched you. You have to do the work yourself. Please tell that to the Lady and Sarah when we get back. If Catherine finds out first, she'll want to treat me like one of her piglets."

"I have the Lady's confidence, as she has mine. You have been as proper to me as a monk." Beatrice's face turned to stone. "As a monk should be, and one is not."

"Before we left the castle, I noticed some men staring at you."

"Yes. They know something is different about me. They don't know what."

"Are you saying you know what men think?"

"Men are simple." She pulled a hair back from her face. "Except for you Lord Paxton." Her voice rose a little.

"I'll take that as a compliment. What about women?"

"The women in the town see what is different. They don't know how it was done."

"Once again, you'll have to tell the Lady and Sarah."

"Yes, the Lady will need this." Beatrice again adjusted the cloth.

"What about Sarah?"

The corners of Beatrice's mouth turned up, as she made up her mind. "Yes, little Sarah could benefit."

Paxton looked around like a thief. "And Catherine?"

Beatrice and Paxton snickered together like schoolchildren. "Yes, Catherine most of all."

"Very much so. Beatrice, what about the twins?"

"Is it not queer, that the women, whose duties consist of herding cows, should not need these breast sacs?"

Beatrice and Paxton entered the church together. The church's wood floor croaked, announcing their entrance.

Father Casimir rose from his prayers. "Why is a noble in the peasant's church and not his chapel?" He approached and saw Beatrice next to Paxton. "Beatrice it is nice to see you in God's house, whether common man's or noble's chapel."

Beatrice sat in the back of the church, to continue her prayers.

Paxton led Father Casimir by the arm to the front of the church. "Father Casimir. This is the first I have seen of you, in the weeks since your return."

Father Casimir limped forward. "But this is not the first I have heard of you since my return."

"How is my friend Ignatius?"

"Since our return from that dreadful trip to Banburn I seldom see him, though the bishop set him under me. He went with my two subordinate priests to their new parish, in Alton, and informed the prior of his commission, as the new abbot." Father Casimir sat on a front bench, and plopped his hands on his lap. "I have given him my horse. He seems always to take letters from Sandalburg to Banburn and back."

"Does he ever talk about these letters?"

"They always arrive with the seals unbroken." Father Casimir paused. "He speaks with his brother, and me." Another pause came from the priest. "Friar Bernard and I speak also."

"What does Friar Bernard have to say?"

"He says you yearn to return to Konectic."

"I can't return. If I could, I would. You don't know how... lonely I am. I used to tell Mary Jane I was alone, not lonely. It was a lie."

"Mary Jane, is she your betrothed?"

"No." Paxton wiped his hands. "She's complicated."

"So you told Friar Bernard you're bringing your world here."

"Everything I can tutor about my world."

"'Ex his enim sunt qui penetrant domos et captivas ducunt mulierculas oneratas peccatis quae ducuntur variis desideriis.' 2 Timothy 3:6" *(For of these sort are they who creep into houses and lead captive silly women laden with sins, who are led away with divers desires)*

Paxton fired back, 'This is good and acceptable in the sight of God, our Savior, who desires all to come to the knowledge of the truth.' 1 Timothy 2: 3, 4. I can match you quote for quote."

"So you act to bring much of your world here. To make Sandalburg, Warren, and Alton as much like your land as you can. Perhaps even Banburn? Tell me, lost prince, 'Quid enim proderit homini si lucretur mundum totum et detrimentum faciat animae suae?' Mark 8:36." *(For what shall it profit a man, if he gain the whole world and suffer the loss of his soul?)*

A clear, young voice broke in, "My friend does not desire the whole world, only the part called Connecticut."

Paxton jumped off the bench. "Speak of the… Ignatius! I didn't hear you arrive."

"I know how to avoid the creaking boards. Father Casimir tells you only part of the reason for my trips to Banburn. I have found the most talented cobbler there." Ignatius raised up his robe. "Forgive me, both of you. This is one of the few vanities I have."

"Boots with Connecticut-style soles. Have I been a bad influence on you?"

"Do not fear for your soul or mine, or for your influence on me, Paxton."

AT THE SAME TIME IN BANBURN

"Take your place beside me, Bishop." The duke sat on his throne at the far end of the Grand Hall. The bishop stood to the right of the Duke of Banburn. "Tell me of the meeting between you and the laird's confessor." The duke set about cleaning his fingernails with one of his new forks.

"Safe passage was arranged for the laird and his escort, and accepted by you." The bishop bowed to the duke.

"Tell me what I don't know, bishop," the duke snapped. "What is he like?"

The bishop smiled. "He is full of the earnestness of youth. Perhaps he desires your surrender of Banburn."

The duke jabbed at the bishop with his fork. "I have a jester for such foolish talk. While God is divine, you are flesh and blood. If you have learned nothing, leave and I will conduct my own dealings with the," the duke waved the fork, as though to stab the right word out of the air, "clotpole."

"In all, he has less than a dozen knights and an equal number of men-at-arms with him. He appears full of confidence for whatever negotiation you have brought him here."

Trumpeters ended their discussion. A herald cried out, "My Lord, Duke Alphonso of Banburn, I present to you Laird Ahearn."

The duke placed two rows of men-at-arms from the entrance to the throne, and dry washed his hands. "Laird Ahearn, I thank you for coming."

The laird looked back down the Hall. "It was a bit of a walk you just put me through. It does make a man thirsty."

"Bishop, get wine for my guest and me. Sit next to me, laird." The duke gestured to an empty chair, shorter than his own.

"No, thank you, I'll stand," the laird said, now towering over the duke. "Can your authority over the church be so strong?" The laird gestured at the bishop. "Perhaps the bishop is only so weak."

"There are certain matters upon which the church and I are in agreement."

"You want me to be in agreement also?"

The bishop returned with a silver cup for the duke, who passed it to the laird. The bishop gave a second cup to the duke. "This is my finest wine, laird."

"I drink wine when a deal is reached, not before."

"Bishop, you are dismissed." The duke waited, then leaned forward, propping his forearms on his knees. "I propose a chevauchée, by you, of Warren. Then you capture Sandalburg and hold its nobles hostage."

"I've heard you can't control your women."

The duke squirmed like a man that hadn't visited the garderobe for three days. "Your advantages are these." The duke counted on his fingers. "The spoils from Warren, a ransom for the Sandalburg nobles, and an increase in your stature with the lairds."

The laird countered, "What strength lies in Sandalburg? Two, why should you hold up your end, when you could fight me off later? Three, you could then keep your money, and increase your stature with your nobles."

The duke took a sip of wine and paused to collect his thoughts. "*She has only her personal retinue. Less than ten men trained in war. Too high a ransom from you, and it would be cheaper to fight. I have a tongue in Sandalburg who will speak to discourage resistance by the woman. The only nobles there are the woman, her lady-in-waiting, and Harold, a noble of another family. The rest, treat them as you will the town of Warren." The duke drew a finger across his throat.

"What of the foreign noble?"

The duke winced. *Where are you getting your information?*

"He is of no concern to me. From what I hear, he is more trouble to the woman than his value as a hostage." The duke leaned back and flicked his free hand. "Do what you want with him."

Ahearn glanced into his wine cup. "If we can agree on a price for the three nobles, I'll drink your wine."

Chapter 15

Rain: cold, miserable rain had lashed the forest all day. It stopped before nightfall. Water continued dripping from branches, keeping the men in misery.

"Welcome the cold, the wet, and the night critters." Red Ahearn's eyes searched the forest floor. "These things bring pain to the body. Pain makes a soul humble. Humility breeds anger. Anger gives birth to violence." He raised his voice. "Violence fosters sweet victory!"

"Huzza! Huzza! Huzza!" Three times his men thrust axes, maces, and swords into the air.

Ahearn paced from one rough lean-to to another. "If a thousand men can defeat a hundred men, who will hear of it?" His gaze challenged each man sitting in his shelter. "If a hundred men can defeat a hundred men, who will boast of it?" Ahearn licked the upturned corners of his mouth. "But if less than twenty men burn a town, and carry off its harvest, take its wealth, and hold the castle nobles for ransom?" He stopped and raised his mace. "Who will deny this is sweet victory?"

"Huzza! Huzza! Huzza!" Bloodthirsty fists throttled the night sky.

"As is my custom, one will be left alive. The one who I identify as the duke's agent." Ahearn laughed. "We need someone to deliver the demand, and return with the ransom."

Another man spoke up. "Pretty words match a pretty face."

Ahearn froze. "I am like a child, who did all that was demanded of him." He faced his accuser. "He is about to go play." Now Ahearn spread his arms wide. "Only to have his mother say, he has another duty to perform." The laughter of his men topped the trees. "Why do I tolerate you old Gilchrist?"

"Will a young and pretty man boast of a victory over an old priest?"

The camp's laughter rose to the stars.

Gilchrist, scarred of face and grimly voiced, stepped away from the campfire. "When did we become the war dogs of the English? Do we feed off the scraps the Duke of Banburn throws us?" He paused in his words and his steps. "Ahearn goes to Warren and Sandalburg, not for his triumph, but for the English's bidding."

The men grew quiet.

The priest wandered among the men. "Do we raid Warren for our own treasure, or to strengthen the duke? We lay waste to towns, and leave one survivor to tell the tale, because we desire it. Do we need Duke Alphonso to glorify Ahearn?" The priest spat on the ground. "Ahearn is a fearless laird. He finds the enemy commander and strikes for him. Everyone he hunts scatters like voles from a hungry cat." The priest stopped his meandering and let his words sink in. "What of the pox? It has stricken Alton. Now it creeps into Banburn. Do we know it isn't in Warren? Can Ahearn defeat the pox? Maybe the duke pays Ahearn to ruin a dying town. Ahearn is fearless. The duke may be clever. Sack a diseased town and maybe take the pox back to our own land."

Ahearn sensed uncertainty rise in his men. He walked in a circle around Gilchrist. "I have met the duke. He covets the land the young

145

duke gave the Lady Wilhelmina as her Morning Dowry. He rides his passion like a man who rides a horse, with neither saddle, nor reins." He stopped and offered his hand to the priest. "Gilchrist is right. I am fearless. When I go to Warren, it is because I desire it. The town is a ripe apple, waiting to be batted from the tree. When I lay siege to Sandalburg and hold its nobles hostage, it is because I desire it." Ahearn pointed his mace at Gilchrist. "Is there pox in Warren? You are afraid of what you don't know. What I don't know, I have no reason to fear." He walked around the campfire between the priest and his men. "I will go south and defile Sandalburg's estate or be taken hostage myself. Those who are children may go north on the morrow. Those who are men, stiffen your spine." Ahearn grabbed his crotch. "And stiffen your middle leg as well, and follow me."

"Huzzah! Huzzah! Huzzah!' The deep-throated roars reached for the valley.

Not just the nights were chilly now. After the rains, the air retained its dampness. The Lady sat in the blacksmith's shop near the forge, and drew her cape close.

Paxton told her, "I was in Warren with Gunther and Beatrice, and we passed the cheese maker's shop. I've been trying to explain to John, that we get a cheese press. John can make a mold for each letter. Small. Small letters. He pours lead into each mold." Paxton tried to pantomime his expectations. The Lady's retinue returned vacant stares. "We build a plate with tracks on it, and then we can slip the molded letters in the tracks to make whatever document you want printed. Ink is rolled on the letters." Paxton made a rolling motion with one arm. The stares grew hollower. "Put it on the bottom of the top half of the press. The press is squeezed down." He made a rotating pantomime.

"On the cheese," John interrupted.

"No. On paper which is laid over the bottom half of the press."

"The paper is on top of the cheese." Sarah brightened with enlightenment.

"There is no cheese." Paxton's voice strained.

"He may have a chill," the Lady whispered to Sarah.

"I have no chill."

"Perhaps a fever." The Lady directed her words to Paxton.

"I think he ate some bad cheese," John cut in.

"Friar Bernard." Paxton reached out with his hands and his voice.

The friar noticed Harold entering the blacksmith's shop. "Perhaps Harold has something to say."

Everyone turned to see Harold in the doorway. "A letter from the duke has arrived." He handed it to the Lady. She broke its seal and unfolded it.

Everyone watched. "The duke writes that he met with Laird Ahearn to propose peace between him and the lairds of the north."

Lady Wilhelmina said. "He does not believe Ahearn desires peace and assumes the laird will strike south into Sandalburg valley. He wants me to retire to Banburn for my own safety." The Lady tossed the letter into the flames. "I will not leave."

Sarah leaned down and placed a hand on her lady's shoulder. "My lady, by staying you may risk the inheritance your husband gave you."

"I know what my uncle wants. If I go back to Banburn, my uncle will seize my estate." The Lady rose and paced the humble workshop. "Whispers will again rise about my husband's death. My uncle will silence the whispers if I give up my claim to Sandalburg." She paused, gazing into the glowing orange forge. Then she met Harold's eyes. Her face went through several shades of red. "I once said my uncle has the nose of a hunting dog. He also has the manners of a dog, spraying on every tree to mark his territory. If I stay, or go, Red Ahearn will chevauchée my estate. I will stay. Let Alphonso pay for my freedom and inherit a ruined land. Friar, I will pray in the chapel."

When she was out of earshot, Paxton grabbed Harold by an elbow. "Who is Red Ahearn and what is a chevauchée?"

Harold walked Paxton to the castle gate. "Red Ahearn is a laird of the north. Let me tell you of the man. He rides a chestnut red horse. When he found this horse, he had its sire and mare slain, then all others of its lineage. If he finds another chestnut one, he slays it and its entire lineage. No one on his land may have one like it. 'Et exivit alius equus rufus et qui sedebat super illum datum est ei ut sumeret pacem de terra.' Revelation 6:4." *(And there went out another horse that was red. And to him that sat thereon, it was given that he should take peace from the earth.)*

"What is this chevauchée?"

"The chevauchée is a manner of war. It is like the plague of locusts sent by God to punish the Egyptians."

"So that is why he is called Red Ahearn?"

Harold shrugged. "A chevauchée is a chevauchée. It is what happens after that gives him the title Red Ahearn."

"What else?"

"Ahearn burns all he cannot take back with him. He captures all who can be ransomed. The rest are slain—all but one, who is left to tell the tale. His men use all the females of age for their pleasure, before the women die. Except for Ahearn, who kills the women first, and then mounts their carcasses."

For Paxton, the past became the future, the future merged with the present, and he could not tell which time was which. "Then Warren must be evacuated into the castle."

"There is not room for all. Whom would you leave out? If the town camped here, there is only one way in, and the same way out. We would be like the Jews at Masada."

"Then we fight him before he gets to Warren."

"We are less than a dozen against twice that number of knights and men-at-arms."

"We enlist the town's men."

Harold spat. "Will nine give up their lives, so that one may kill a man-at-arms?" Will nineteen die so that maybe one may bring down a knight?"

"What will happen to the women in the castle?"

"The Lady, Sarah, and I will be ransomed. Perhaps Ahearn will choose you for ransom. Maybe you can entertain him with forks." Harold smiled grimly. "The common women, if they are lucky, will be chosen by Ahearn."

Paxton looked out of the gate, to the north end of the valley. "Will Ahearn come from the north, and take the road?"

"Of course."

"And the road follows the east bank of the river almost to Warren. Then it turns east to Warren, and continues to Banburn?"

"Except where it branches in Warren. The southeast branch goes to Alton."

"When I was first brought here the friar cut the corner and came straight to the castle." Paxton thought fast. "He has to take the road. The river is to his west, and fields are to his east. Right?"

"Yes."

"When will he arrive?"

Harold paused. "I think, sooner rather than later."

Paxton tried to swallow. *No spit.* "I can defeat him."

"Forgive my impertinence. 'Aut qui rex iturus committere bellum adversus alium regem non sedens prius cogitat si possit cum decem milibus occurrere ei qui cum viginti milibus venit ad se?' Luke 14: 31." *(What king, about to go to make war against another king, doth not first sit down and think whether he be able, with ten thousand, to meet him that, with twenty thousand, cometh against him?)* "Where is your army?"

Paxton started back for the chapel. "I won't need an army. I need effort from the town's people, knowledge of history, and a trick up my sleeve. I need the Lady. I need to be able to put the town's people to work, and I need someone to make the largest banner ever. If time is as short as you say, I need it done already. Go to the stable. Get horses for you, Gunther, and me. I'm going to the chapel."

Paxton stopped when he entered. He waited for his eyes to adjust to the dim candle light. Seeing the Lady at a kneeler, he went to a kneeler behind her. He leaned forward. "My lady." There was no reaction. "My lady, I need…"

"No." The Lady interrupted, not moving her head. "You need. Since I brought you here that's all I hear from you. 'I need.' No. People say I give in too much, too quickly." Her voice went husky. "No."

"My lady, I… you don't want your estate savaged. Red Ahearn can be stopped."

Paxton explained part of his plan.

"You speak like a young man hot to pluck a maiden's virtue. Ahearn will overwhelm you."

"Not if I… not if he is kept at bay. If he is kept far enough away, he can be defeated."

Paxton leaned so close, his lips almost touched the Lady's hair. "Your uncle and Ahearn have met. Perhaps Ahearn works for your uncle. If Ahearn is defeated, do you not also defeat your uncle?"

The Lady pivoted to Paxton. "Tell me. How many maidens have lost their virtue to that sweet tongue of yours?"

Paxton's face matched the scarlet colour of the maple leaves. He stammered. "A gentleman never tells."

He rushed out the chapel's door. "Gunther! I'm glad you're here. You got the horses, good. Harold, you, and I are going to Warren. We

150

will stay the night in Father Casimir's rectory." Paxton paced in a circle. "I need a large cloth, to make a banner, large enough to run across the road, and paint, red paint." The faster Paxton talked, the faster and tighter his circling. "I need…" Paxton saw the Lady exit the chapel. "The Lady needs two poles for the banner on, and she needs it all now."

Paxton took Gunther by the elbow away from the Lady. "You must gather all the poachers. They and all the castle's men who have bow and arrows will defend Warren."

"There are no poachers."

Paxton slapped him. "You've been taking money from every man who hunts illegally. If you deny it, I'm going to the Lady. Now I must go to my cottage."

"This is a lot of trouble for a few extra coppers."

Paxton hurried into his cottage. Then he slammed the bolt shut. Moving the table near a wall, he stopped, listening for anyone approaching. He put a chair on top of the table and stopped. His ears and nose were twitching. He climbed up the table, then the chair. He stopped and listened again. He dug his hand into the thatched roof where he hid the items of his past and future life. Finding what he wanted, he jumped off the chair, and put everything back in place.

Two nights later Paxton found himself in Father Casimir's rectory. He pushed the pottage of his evening meal around with his spoon.

"Lord Paxton please eat."

"Ignatius, you are my friend. Just call me Paxton." Paxton, Father Casimir, Harold, Gunther, and Ignatius sat around the table. "We don't know when Ahearn will arrive. Harold, we need the men from the castle into town now. Maybe put them up in the church. Gunther, after we eat I want to see how much land was plowed up."

"The serfs' plots run north and south, the length of the valley. They have plowed from east to west, destroying their furrows. Later, they will need to plow again, north and south for their private lands."

"If they don't plow deep enough, and far enough, their fucking lives will be spoiled."

"What is this fucking?" Gunther tilted his head.

Ignatius turned to Gunther. "A short prayer to God in his tongue."

"He is indeed a pious man. I've heard him pray like that often today." Harold said between mouthfuls of warm pottage, seasoned with basil.

Father Casimir shook a spoon at Ignatius. "You're never here. You're always asking for the reins to my horse. You go to Banburn, never saying when you'll be back. When you return, I have to feed the horse. His belly is always empty when you return."

"Harold, speaking of Banburn, our cousin got a letter from our father." Ignatius took the loaf of bread and cut a slice for himself. "Father wants to know why you haven't obeyed him and returned home."

"'Nemo servus potest duobus dominis servire.' Luke 16:13." *(No servant can serve two masters.)*

Paxton stopped spooning his pottage. "Why have you been recalled?"

Ignatius spoke first. "When the young duke died, the allure of a union with our family also died. Our cousin said father has obtained a place in a French noble's household. Imagine, Harold, all those French apples ripening, and no one to harvest them."

"Dear brother, 'filii huius saeculi prudentiores filiis lucis in generatione sua sunt' Luke 16:8." *(The children of this world are wiser in their generation than the children of light.)*

"Ignatius, while you're in Banburn, ask your cousin when he will assign another priest here," said Father Casimir.

152

Paxton took the bread. "Your cousin has influence in priest's assignments?"

Gunther toggled his spoon between Harold and Ignatius. "Their cousin is the bishop."

Paxton shoveled as much food as possible, to get finished quickly. "The furrows have to run from the road all the way to the forest. Has the banner I asked for been made? It must go across the road, south of the plowed up land. Father Casimir, we could use more rain. A little divine help would be appreciated."

"My bones tell me it will turn cold and wet," Father Casimir grumbled.

"Harold and Gunther, I want the men of the castle, and the town, to have target practice after tomorrow's morning service."

Paxton stood on the road to Warren. "I feel as weird as that looks." He pointed at the banner. This morning he wore a suit of armor that John had fetched from the castle. The armor, made for a smaller man, left as much of Paxton exposed as it covered. "Who made the banner, Elizabeth or Isabelle?"

John pushed a pole holding one end of the banner into the ground. "They're twins, who can tell? How do you know they painted it?"

Paxton forced air into his lungs. The undersized armor constricted his breathing. "That profile of a red horse's head looks like a cow." Paxton scanned the ragtag crowd. "Where's Harold?"

John walked to the other side of the road, with the other pole. "It seems last night he remembered Jesus's parable about a father asking his son to do a duty. He refuses, but on reflection decides to obey his father."

"Matthew 21: 28-29. So Harold bugged out on us." Paxton threw the helmet on the ground to be able to see the group of men in the field. "It's cold this morning. Let's get some practice and get back where it's

153

warm. Spread out in a line. Remember what I told you. You don't have to hit anyone. Shoot at the person farthest to the right. We want to keep them on the road. The road is at most, wide enough for two horses. Fire your arrows at a forty-five-degree angle upwards. That'll give you the longest reach." The men looked blank. *It's like trying to have a conversation with Lassie.* "A forty-five-degree angle is half way between straight up and level."

Paxton tried again to explain, then he heard it: singing and the rumble of bagpipes and drums. Horses and men strutted from the woods, forming a line perpendicular to the road. One man rode a chestnut horse, from one end of the line to the other.

Paxton turned to his mob. "All right," he said, with as much authority as he could muster. "We have no time to practice. Move to the right." The knight on the chestnut horse posted himself at the centre of the line. Paxton moved up the road to a pole holding up one end the banner. He kicked the pole over, waving for his opponent to come forward. "Come on you illiterate mother-of-fucking. You never heard of Thermopylae, Agincourt, or the Fulda Gap?" Paxton walked to the other pole and kicked down that one. Laird Ahearn accepted the emblematic challenge. It was like firing a starter's pistol. The knights surged forward. Mud fields bogged down horses. The furrows running crosswise to the advance made the horses stumble. The knights on the turf pulled left onto the road. *That's right come in a line. Come to me babies.* A ragged flight of arrows soared into the air. "Not now," Paxton shouted. "Wait until they get closer, guys!" A moment later Paxton looked back to give an order. "Guys?" They had scattered like dandelion seeds in a windstorm and were out of sight.

Paxton pulled out his laser pointer from his pouch. He pointed it at the ground to test it. *No light! Corrosion! Coming to Sandalwood, John threw me in the river. Water must have gotten in.* Paxton wiped his sweating hands on his pants beneath his armor. *Please God, let it be*

154

only a little rust on the battery. A corroded switch will kill me. He cracked open the base of the pointer and unscrewed it, pouring out the battery. *I forgot! I put it in backwards so no one could play with it. Be careful! Put battery in the right way. Screw in the base. Don't screw up, screwing in. Test it. It works!*

Paxton aimed the light at the lead charging horse. The laser light hit one of the horse's eyes. The animal bucked and threw its rider.

Range to closest target, approximately 50 metres.

Speed of knight on horseback approximately 25 kilometres per hour.

Number of targets, maybe 9.

Paxton's laser found another animal. Both the horse and rider went down.

Targets hit, ≤ 10 seconds.

25 kilometres per hour is about 6.94 metres per second.

50 metres divided by 6.94metres per second is about 7.20 seconds.

Paxton hit another horse's eye. *Six knights will overrun me. Please God, let me hold it together.*

Now the knight on the chestnut horse pulled alongside another, and with his mace smashed the other knight's shield. He forced another knight to give way. Now this rider rushed to the lead knight and forced him off the road. *The red horse!* Paxton aimed his laser at it. The laser hit, causing the horse to start and collapse on its left side. The rider heavy with armor, pulled his feet out of the stirrups and rolled on the horse's right side. His mount landed on its side, three metres from Paxton. The rider hit the ground feet first and managed to remain standing. He wobbled for a second, then charged Paxton. Paxton aimed for the eye slits. The scream was like nothing Paxton had ever heard. Laird Ahearn dropped to his knees, and flung away his mace, shield, and gauntlets. He pulled off his helmet, and mashed his fist into his eyes, two paces away from Paxton.

155

Paxton seized the heavy bronze mace. "Yield or you will be left alone to tell the tale, after your men die one by one. You will be alone, and blind in both eyes." Red Ahearn nodded vigorously. "Your Laird Ahearn yields." With that, the fight went out of the others. "The code of chivalry says you ransom nobles, and slay the commoner. I have a different code. After today, any noble who makes war on the Lady will be put to death. His common men-at-arms, who surrender will live." Past, present, futures were the same to Paxton. "You, Ahearn, slayer of women." He stuttered. "The justice you give to others will be given to you."

With the mace, Paxton wound up a perfect tennis overhead smash. With a wild grunt, he brought the heavy spiked club down on Red Ahearn's head. A loud crack and red, dark red, black-red blood and brain matter spurted up. He must have hit an artery, because the blood fountained higher than Paxton's own head. Blood, bone, and brain pelted him like heavy rain. Nothing was left of the top half of Ahearn's face. The mace's spikes had impaled themselves in the bottom half of his brain pan. "Lay down your arms and armor and go." It was a command and a prayer. Paxton studied the corpse held upright by the mace. "Do you want to go back north?" Paxton rotated the mace, and the remnants of Red Ahearn's head shook side-to-side. "Do you want to stay in the field as a warning to others?" He moved the mace again and the half-headed corpse nodded. Red Ahearn's men stood stunned in silent horror.

"God," said Paxton, "I'm so tired, and thirsty." He wiped the blood from his face, and looked at his fingers. *It's wet.* He licked the fluid from his hand. It tasted good.

In the Great Hall, the Lady sat on the same tall chair as when Paxton first saw her. A warm robe covered her. Paxton came forward and laid his trophy at her feet. In addition to the inhabitants of the castle, Father

Casimir and Brother Ignatius stood by. "Lady Wilhelmina, I give you the shield and mace of the late Laird Ahearn."

The Lady stared, petrified, at the weapons. "The rumor is true. You have indeed killed him." The pause became lengthy, then uncomfortable. Suddenly the Lady leaped to her feet. "You fool! You idiot. I wish I'd never laid my eyes on you." Her voice was like claws in Paxton's ears.

Paxton recovered himself. "But my lady, you've won."

"You vain, shard-borne, pignut! I could have ransomed him! I could have brokered a peace between us! I could counter my uncle, WITH HIM ALIVE! Now his clan will come against me in full force!" The Lady wrenched her hands as she stomped across the dais. Her speech grew increasingly frenzied. "Ignatius. I will write a letter to my uncle. I will bargain with him to take this poisonous, whoreson, toad off my hands. Perhaps the northern clans will accept him as a blood offering. You will take the letter to my uncle as soon as I finish writing." The Lady's dagger eyes stared at Paxton. Her voice was a panic-stricken mess. "Get out of my sight. Stay in your cottage. I never want to see you again." Her voice dropped an octave. "You warlock."

Chapter 16

The day was almost over. The tenants of the castle finished their Vespers prayers. Paxton stood in a corner of his cottage in the bailey, staring out the window. Twilight washed away what little colour that remained on the land. The only light in his room came from the dying glow in the fireplace.

I expect by the day after tomorrow, Brother Ignatius will return. He will have a letter for the Lady. Maybe it will be an order for my trial from the Bishop of Northumbria. Maybe it will make me a hostage to the duke. It's all over. What are the options: death by beheading, death by hanging, death by fire, death by the northern clans? The key word is death. He took stock of the meager objects in the room: a chair, a table with a water pitcher, bowl, and a cup, a nightstand with a candle, bed, the bed warmer Beatrice was using, and some wood for the fire. *Is this the total of my life?*

Beatrice held the long wood handle of the bed warmer, and slipped its brass pan filled with hot coals, between the blanket and the mattress. *I don't want it to end this way. If I'm going to die, I want to know what a woman is like.* Beatrice finished snaking the bed warmer up and down the bed and now returned it to the fireplace. Paxton circled behind her. *She's given herself to so many other men, why not me? Well, she's offered herself to me before.* Beatrice opened the bed warmer and dumped the wood coals in the hearth. *That would be nice. To lie under a blanket with a woman. She would be on her side in front of me. I would take my upper arm, wrap it around her, and draw her close. She would snuggle her buttocks closer to my groin. Perhaps use her upper leg to push between my legs. Get me to wrap my upper leg around her and draw me closer. That's the secret. To be vulnerable and safe at the same time.* Paxton smiled. *That's what makes it good.* Paxton shifted his weight from one foot to the other and back. Beatrice used the bed warmer's pan to bank the fire. *What if she has an STD? What if she has all the STDs? What if she gets pregnant?* Paxton frowned. *What do you care? You're dead meat.* Beatrice knocked the pan against the hearth and put it to the side. He opened and closed his fists, digging his nails deeper into his palms each time. *What are you waiting for, an invitation? You want this to end up like at Columbia?*

Without saying a word, he approached from behind. Putting his right hand around her waist Paxton drew Beatrice close. With his left hand, he brushed her hair from her neck. He softly kissed the spot where her neck met her shoulder.

"Stop that." Beatrice's voice was firm as she took a step forward.

"Why?"

"I'm leaving." Shoulders back, head up and staring forward, Beatrice walked to the door.

"You sold your," he stuttered, "your services, to other men. I can pay more."

Beatrice stopped, turned, and slapped Paxton. The blow almost dropped him to the floor. Tears streamed down her face as she ran for the door.

Paxton recovered and encircled her with his arms just before she reached it.

Beatrice screamed.

159

Paxton whipped her around. Breaking free, she grabbed the bed warmer, and smashed it into Paxton's head.

He went to the floor this time, dazed.

Holding the makeshift weapon in front of her, Beatrice backed to the door.

Paxton got up into a three-point stance and charged. Too quick for her, he got inside the arc of her swing. He squeezed her arm holding the weapon until she dropped it. With his other hand, he clutched her hair at the nape. Paxton turned her and forced her to the table. "I'm not afraid, I'm not afraid, this time, Roseann." He pushed her backward onto the table. "You don't understand," he said, as she looked up at him in bewilderment and rage. He lifted her skirt. "Ignatius is coming for me." Beatrice struggled, but Paxton overwhelmed her. "Tomorrow or the next day, the Lady will issue an order for my removal." He pushed his hands under the back of her knees and raised her feet to the table's edge. "Do you know what that means?" His arms cleared her skirt above her waist. He bent forward to keep her legs open as he worked at his pants. *There. Almost there.* "It means my death!"

Beatrice turned her face to the side, flat on the table, and crushed her eyes shut. Every muscle in her rebelled against what was about to happen. "If this is done again to me, I'll die," she said hoarsely, "a little bit more each day."

The realization hit Paxton. Blackness closed in on his vision, a coalmine of darkness. Indistinguishable sounds rumbled in his ears. The room swayed. He clutched the table to steady himself. "Oh, God." He staggered backward, like a ship foundering in a storm. He was no longer breathing, but gulping in air and vomiting it like salt water. He released Beatrice and retreated. His back touched the closed door. "Help me." The ragged words spewed from deep in his chest. Paxton pressed his hands against his temples. He slumped to the floor. "Mother, forgive me." Paxton sat, curled up on the floor, beating his chest. "O my God, O my God, I am wholeheartedly sorry for having offended thee."

Beatrice raised herself into a sitting position and straightened her clothing. Resting her fingertips on her temples, she cleared her thoughts. *Look at him. How he beseeches his mother, and God, for forgiveness of sins.* She sat puzzled for a moment, then found her voice. "You're a loggerheaded, beetle-brained, maggot-pie. You're a toad-spotted, qualling, foot-licker. Ask forgiveness of *me!*" She jumped off the table and charged at Paxton. She grabbed him by the back of his collar. "Come here." She half dragged, half pulled, all muscled Paxton to the fireplace.

Throwing him to one side of the hearth, Beatrice put two small logs on the fire. Their lengths were from front to back. Between them, she threw on straw, kindling, small branches, bark she ripped from larger branches. On top of the smaller branches, she placed two longer branches, lengthwise with the hearth. Beatrice bent low and blew air below the longer branches to wake up the fire. Flame flashed back to heat her face. The fire told her it was awake. Beatrice stood up to catch her breath. She looked down at the shriveled form that was Paxton. *This is too much.* She let out a long wail and dragged herself back to the nightstand with its pitcher of water and cup. Her shaking hands poured more water on the floor than in the cup. "You tried to violate my body. You were willing to violate my soul." As quick as a spark leaps from the fire, her mood changed. The anger in her face splashed into her abdomen and bent her over. She turned and hurled her words like jagged shards of black obsidian. "YOU! VIOLATED! MY! TRUST!"

Clutching the full cup, she stormed to the fireplace. She stood, taping one foot, facing Paxton. He drew his legs to his chest, tucked his head between his legs, and wrapped his arms around his legs to lock himself in. Even his feet pointed sideways to make himself as small as possible. *What is it about men that make them slaves to their passions?*

When they are babies, we wipe their arses. When they are small, we wipe their noses. When they are bigger, we wipe their tears. When they are men, they expect us to wipe their consciences. There will be no wiping here.

"You pill bug." Beatrice drank from the cup. The water renewed her body, if not her mood. *Control yourself. If you can't control yourself, others will control you.* Beatrice knelt in front of Paxton. She brushed the hair from her face, wiped her cheeks, and sat back on her ankles. She watched the smoke hanging low in the fireplace, as if unwilling to go up the chimney. As if it wanted to stay and see what happened next. Beatrice knew that when the smoke hangs low at night the dew would be heavy in the morning. She took another sip. Her throat wetted, her muscles opened up. Beatrice had to test her control. "Look at me." Her voice was firm and unemotional. *Good.*

She thrust the cup at him. Hands trembling, Paxton reached for it, but Beatrice pulled it back. "First, tell me about Roseann."

Paxton blinked. "I don't understand."

"You called me Roseann. You said, 'I'm not afraid this time, Roseann.'"

Paxton dropped his forehead to his knees. "I let her die." He let out a sigh it seemed he'd been holding forever. "I was a student at Columbia. That's a school. I spent all my free time in my studies. Other students went out to pubs in their free time."

"Pubs?"

"Public houses. Buildings where people pay to drink beer, and wine. Sing and have a good time. It was the evening after St. Sylvester's day. I had never been to a pub before. I was curious. I wanted to see what it was like. She was there. She came up to me and we started to talk. We had a few drinks and she invited me to spend the night with her. I had never been with a woman before."

Beatrice's eyes bulged in wonder. To her it seemed every boy half Paxton's age, when he felt his stirrings, found his way to her cottage. They would sneak in, sweaty palmed, knees quaking like aspen leaves, unsure how to ask for what they wanted. They would show her some coins, although she prized foodstuffs above money. When a boy produced the proper price, Beatrice would raise her tunic and the skirt under it and watch as the boy's eyes grew wide at the wonder of a woman. They needed little instruction. For the boys it was over too soon, and for Beatrice it wasn't over soon enough. Now here was Paxton telling her he may still be… She was tempted to ask the obvious question. She pondered other questions. *Was he awkward with women? Was he pious by nature? Was he awkward because he was pious? On the other hand, was he pious because he was awkward?*

"I was scared. What if," Paxton said, looking away, "she was like you? What if in nine months she came to my mother's house and said, "Goodwife Frost, here is your grandchild. What if she hired a highwayman to assault me, and steal my money? I could think of many frightening outcomes. I was too afraid to risk the one pleasant one. Two days later I found out someone killed her. She took someone else to her home. He murdered her, opening her head with a small statue. He confessed that he raped her dead body. I failed. If I hadn't been so afraid, she would still be alive." Paxton snorted, "She'd be alive, and I'd be happy. That's why I killed Red Ahearn as I did. So he couldn't do to you what happened to Roseann."

Beatrice dared to ask her question. "Were there any other women?"

"No. How can I say it? My mother was a missionary to the poorest and sickest of the world. She would say, 'There, you lay with a woman outside of marriage and this is what will happen to you. Sickness and death.' My mother died while I was still in the university. When I graduated, I got work in your country. I started seeing a psychologist…"

"What is that?"

"A doctor, for the soul. Like a doctor and confessor combined. Only without the piety. She said…"

"She?"

"Yes, women can be doctors where I live."

Why not? Paxton told me so many other fanciful things about his kith and kin, why not this?

"She said I have difficulties with women because I didn't have any normal emotional or social relationships with girls my age when I was growing up. She said I was looking for a teddy bear with benefits."

"This be-ne fat from a te-de bear will cure you?"

"No, teddy, one word. A teddy bear is a child's doll. It has soft stuffing inside and is about so tall." Paxton estimated with his hands to show her. "It's covered with fur and made to look like a friendly, smiling bear. A teddy bear with benefits. Benefits, not fats, it means, what men would like from women."

"Oh." Beatrice digested these words in her heart. She beat his head with her own words. "Women are not teddy bears." *Control yourself and you control your voice.*

Paxton ducked his head between his legs again. "Yeah, that's what she said." Paxton stood up straight and fixed his clothes. "Beatrice, with all the abuse you have received, I have never known you to act with malice. I fear I have closed the door between you and me. The one woman I know to be kind and gentle. I accept the results of my actions. No matter what happens to me, or where I go, I want you to know you are my polestar. You are a model of conduct I hope to emulate, if never achieve. Well I can start. Tomorrow I will go to the Lady Wilhelmina tell her what I have done. I will tell her what I tried to do. If I am to meet my death, then let it be for a sin I have committed, not for a false crime."

Beatrice rose and put the cup in his hands. "The cup is not yet empty." Looking at the hearth, the fire she started was burning out. "You will not talk to the Lady of this." She walked calmly to the door. "You will conduct yourself as you always have." Beatrice opened the door a little bit and turned to look back. Paxton had not moved. "However you will be watched." She stepped into the empty night and turned to the right. Not having any strength left she leaned against the wall. The door she left ajar. Swaying down the bailey, she used her fingertips to massage her aching temples. *Men.*

From the opposite corner of the cottage, a figure slithered forward. John made his way through the castle after Vespers. If anyone inquired, he would say he did his prayers best while walking. In reality, he went about seeing who stayed up. Who went late to bed? Who whispered or talked in their sleep? He learned a lot listening at doors. This night he happened to be at Paxton's door from the beginning of their quarrels. He thought for sure Paxton was going to know the real worth of this woman. Then the crying came. He heard the begging of forgiveness. Most shocking to him was the force of this woman. Of course, against that craven scut, it wasn't hard. Upon hearing her approach the door, he faded into the shadows where he lived. Now he stepped forward again, being careful to avoid the dagger of light that spilled out of the room. Listening again at the door, he could hear Paxton turning his stomach inside out. Going away, John whispered to himself. "She was right about one thing. Paxton will need watching." He paused, and thought about Paxton's and Beatrice's last whisperings. They were hard to make out. *Tomorrow I will ask the gamekeeper, has he ever hunted these te-de bears.*

Chapter 17

Paxton stared at the thatched roof. *The stars. There are no more stars. The roof closes off the stars. They were my worlds. I think it's closer to dawn than to dusk. Get up. Do what you know you are going to do. I don't owe Beatrice anything. I don't need to keep my word to her.*

Paxton rose from the bed.

The rooster will crow soon.

After morning Mass, Paxton grabbed Friar Bernard's elbow. "Tell the Lady that she is to have the ceremonial fire lit," he stuttered. "She is to dress in her finest outfit. Everyone in the castle is to attend. Harold has left. You will take over the duty of announcing me."

"By what authority do you issue orders?"

"All this will be done for the good of the Lady, and another," he stammered. For all the problems I have created, this is my final solution." Paxton swallowed. "'When thou wast young, thou girdedst thyself, and walkedst whither thou wouldest: but when thou shalt be old, thou shalt stretch forth thy hands, and another shall gird thee, and carry *thee* whither thou wouldest not.' John21:18."

Paxton finished his morning meal in the solitary confines of his cottage and waited. Then he waited some more. One of the servants called to him just outside the door. Paxton shuffled to the door and opened it. "My next invention will be to show you people there is nothing to be afraid of by knocking."

"The Lady Wilhelmina grants your request for an appearance before her."

They climbed the covered steps from the bailey to the keep. With each step, Paxton's legs grew heavier. At the entrance to the keep, Friar Bernard stood at the ready. The servant passed them to enter it.

Friar Bernard waited long enough for the servant to take his place in the Great Hall, and then turned to enter. In the Great Hall, the ceremonial fire blazed. The Lady's servants formed two rows to the left of the fire. Friar Bernard, with Paxton in tow, circled to the right of the pyre. The Lady and Sarah sat in their places on the dais. The shield and mace of Red Ahearn lay in front and to the right of the Lady. Red Ahearn's dried brains caked the mace's spikes. The Lady, in regal splendor, had wrapped herself in a pashmina cloak.

Friar Bernard again stopped Paxton half way around the fire. He proceeded another quarter way around before stopping.

"My Lady Wilhelmina," Friar Bernard intoned, "I present to you Prince Paxton, of the House of Frost. He comes to you from his land of Connecticut."

Paxton bowed to the Lady. "My lady, may I address Friar Bernard?"

The Lady gave a nod from her statue-of-justice visage.

"Good friar, does not the church teach that it is through the sin of Adam and Eve that we were separated from God? When God is offended, only God can provide payment for the offence. How can it be otherwise? Is this not why Jesus is True God and True Man?"

Paxton paused, and the friar spoke. "It is so."

"Did not Jesus say, 'If you are presenting your offering at the altar, and there remember that your brother has something against you, leave your offering there before the altar and go; first be reconciled to your brother, and then come and present your offering'? Matthew 5: 23-24."

Paxton turned to face the Lady. "My lady, there is offence between Laird Ahearn's clan and you. For peace you must give up a noble of your house to Ahearn's clan. May I approach the Lady?"

The Lady gave another nod.

Approaching the dais, Paxton knelt. "Make me that member of your house. My lady before Friar Bernard left to take your tallage to Duke Alphonso you asked me if I would swear true faith and allegiance to you. I now do so. I hereby declare, on oath, that I absolutely and entirely renounce and abjure all allegiance and fidelity to any foreign prince, potentate, state, or sovereignty; of whom or which I have heretofore been a subject or citizen. I, Paxton Frost, do swear that I will be faithful and bear true allegiance to Lady Wilhelmina, her heirs and successors, according to law, so help me God. My lady, I have no fortune. I do not have anyone who will give up fortune for me. All I can offer you is my life and my sacred honor."

John stepped forward out of the crowd. "My lady what sacred honor can this man have if he disobeys your order concerning the woman Beatrice?"

Paxton turned his head to face the crowd. "Yes, there is another matter. The lady commanded that no one should molest the widow Beatrice. Last night I attempted to lay with her. She refused. I offered to pay for her services and again she refused. I attempted to force myself on her and she still refused. Remember the story of Judah and Tamar in Genesis 38: 1-26. Others accused Tamar, Judah's daughter-in-law, of being a cult prostitute. Recall Judah's words, 'She is more righteous than I.'" He turned back to face Lady Wilhelmina. "I tell you this not to expose so much my faults, but to exalt Beatrice's virtue."

A wail came from the back row of the Lady's servants; an agonized sound such as a woman in labor might make. Beatrice was not quite standing. Elizabeth and Isabelle, on either side, held her up. She pressed her hands to her face to hold back the flood. Her body trembled like a death rattle.

With quiet serenity, the Lady dismounted her throne. She bent and grasped the mace with both hands. Walking in front of Paxton, she raised the mace above his head. He bowed his head and waited for—a blow? But she brought the weapon down slowly, tapping first his left shoulder with it, then his right. While doing this she chanted, "Paxton, of the house of Frost, rise as a noble of my family, noble in Sandalwood castle, and noble of its lands therein."

The Lady looked first at Friar Bernard, then to the assembly. "All the men save the noble Paxton and Gunther are dismissed. The women are to also stay." The Lady turned her back and walked to the rear entrance of the dais. Reaching the shield of Ahearn, she lay down the mace. She continued to walk back. When she was almost parallel to Sarah, she gave the slightest flick of her left hand. Sarah jumped off her chair and fell in line behind the Lady.

The rear door opened into a corridor to the back of the keep. At the end of the corridor were stairs to the Lady's rooms. Instead, the Lady turned to the first room on her right, her scriptorium. Picking up a blank sheet of parchment from a table, the Lady sat at the writing pedestal. Glancing back, she saw Sarah was behind and to her left. "Sarah, you are going to Banburn. You will take Catherine as your servant, and Gunther for your escort." She opened the inkwell, dipped in a quill, and started writing. "You will take clothing and whatever else you need for several days stay." The Lady paused, examined her words, and continued writing. "This letter is for Alphonso, Duke of Northumbria, in his castle in Banburn."

Sarah raised her eyebrows.

"This letter informs him of what I have done."

Sarah moved beside the Lady. "Will this letter save prince... noble Paxton?"

The Lady stopped to look at Sarah. "No. Paxton knows what he has done. This letter will only make sure that my uncle knows Paxton's blood will be on his hands. While Paxton is waiting his fate, I will make use of him." The Lady stopped writing. "It may be that Ignatius is on his way back with a reply to my first letter. If you find him, he must turn back and go to Banburn with you." The Lady powdered the letter to soak up the excess ink. "If he makes his way back without you seeing him, I will ignore the duke's reply. It is only a reply to this letter that I will consider."

The Lady blew away the powder and folded the letter. "If you do not see Ignatius on your way to Banburn, first go to the cathedral, he may still be at the rectory there. Try to enlist him as an ally. Find out from him what goes on in court."

The Lady pivoted in her chair to face Sarah. "When you are in court, be discreet. Say little, but listen a lot. By doing so, you will find who is loyal to me, and who is loyal to my uncle."

She placed her hands on her knees and leaned forward. "Sarah. Your head is as light as your heart." The Lady tapped Sarah's forehead with the feathered part of the quill. "Now you must keep up that appearance, but it must only be an appearance. Behind your pretty face must now beat the heart of a raptor."

The Lady dripped wax on the folded edge of the letter and put her seal to it. "My uncle will read this letter which tells him I have made Paxton my kin. Mark not his words but his countenance. A man's words whispers, but his face shouts."

Sarah put her hands behind her back. Smiling, she swayed and stepped to an imaginary rhythm. "If I am to keep up appearances, I would need to attend any dances there might be."

"Could you find a noble to dance with you?"

Sarah raised her arms high to smooth her hair behind her head. This caused her breasts to jut out. "The list of those who will not dance with me is shorter."

"Sarah. Your… private dances were not as discreet as you thought."

Sarah cocked her head and pouted. "If my dances were not discreet, noble boys tongues are less so. You *do* want to find out what goes on at court." Sarah lifted her head high. "What I do, I do for my lady." A puzzled look came to her face. "But my lady, who will attend your needs while I am gone?"

The Lady got up and handed Sarah the letter. "With Harold gone, I will instruct Paxton on his duties as my seneschal. Beatrice and the twins will attend to my personal needs."

"If they attend to you, they will find out."

"Then they will find out." The Lady pushed herself off the pedestal, left the scriptorium, and turned back to the Great Hall.

Clutching the letter, Sarah muttered. "It is only right. It takes three common women to do the work of one lady-in-waiting."

Chapter 18

The wall clock changed its numbers, five o'clock. The team gathered in the department's ground floor conference room. Lengthening shadows reflected the team's mood. Eight chairs sat around an oval table. A glass wall looked out on a parking lot. Max likened the conference room to a church. Those who arrived early sat closest to the door. Albert's chair, the pulpit, was closest to the window.

Niels asked no one in particular, "What do you think is going to happen?"

"Even I'm not taking bets on that." Isaac's voice was a combination of despair and resignation.

Cecilia asked, "Are you taking bets on who's getting blamed for this?"

"No." said Isaac.

Albert entered the room. "I could have waited until tomorrow to call this meeting." His sour face reflected his sour voice. "Then endure the calls through the night, from each of you. I decided not to wait. That is why I called for this meeting from the road. The University president and I just got back from London. We met with the new Oversight Board and representatives of the Defence Ministry. We will have enough funds, and time, for an orderly shutdown of the project. The departments or organizations that you came from will accept your return. There are contractual obligations to you that will be fulfilled. No one will suffer financially from this. The collider itself will continue to be used as a teaching tool for the various science departments."

"What will happen to you, Albert?" asked Marie.

"I've been offered a small position at Los Alamos."

"Their black projects department I assume."

"Yes."

"That's a nice way of keeping you quiet."

"Did you tell them about the advancements we've made in the months since the incident?" argued Max. "We've learned how to stabilize the wormhole. The wormhole is a sub space carrier wave whose power requirements are nil. This is Nobel Prize stuff."

Charles spoke up. "It's difficult to walk up to the stage in Stockholm over the body of a dead teammate." His sarcasm was palatable.

"It was an accident. Nobody wanted to kill Paxton," protested Cecilia.

"All right people," said Albert. "It will still be a long time before this project is wound up. There are experiments we started. Experiments need to be finished. We need to verify our data. All of this will take time and our *focused* attention. After that there are papers to submit for peer review. Then the University president and I will go back to the new Oversight Board for permission to shut this project down. It will be a long time before the money runs out."

He passed a hand over his face. "Our political minders, the OB, will arrive in a few days. We will give them a nice little dog and pony show. They will be here in the morning. We'll take them on a tour of the project and the facilities. That will finish up early in the afternoon."

"Marie, I've heard about an Historical Preservation site west of here," said Albert. "It just opened to the up to the public. Why don't you take them on a tour after the presentation? Hire a short bus to take them there. Arrange for a group tour. Bring them back for dinner at the University. They'll leave the next morning. You have a few days to prepare the entertainment. Be sure to keep all receipts to turn into the bean counters."

"So why is there always money for the high mucky-mucks?" asked Marie

"Because they are the high mucky-mucks. Meeting adjourned," answered Albert.

The morning of the visit began with problems. They all gathered in the department's auditorium. The conference room was too small, but the auditorium was too big. Albert's droning got lost in the huge space. Marie checked the various faces. The team yawned from the oversimplification. The Oversight Board members yawned from a lack of interest.

"Lights, please." Albert said at the end of the PowerPoint lullaby.

One of the board members asked, "Could one of the team go over the points you made, for those of us without a scientific background?"

Albert gave a light tone to his voice. "Marie, could you explain my explanation?"

"Thank you Albert." *Keep it simple, girl.* Marie abridged the brute force process they first used. That method used quantum gravity waves. Later how they discovered the natural state of the wormhole was a subspace carrier wave. This natural state used almost no energy to keep the wormhole open. She held up one of the two 'garage door openers' they built. "If someone was at the other end of the wormhole, he could open or close it with one of these."

"You've made another wormhole?" a woman with wire-rimmed glasses asked.

"No, this has all been computer simulations. Does anyone on stage have anything to add?" Marie looked up and down the table.

Niels looked like he was about to blow chunks of formulas.

Albert smiled. "Thank you Marie. Shall we move on to the EHEC itself?

Now she could leave to wait with the bus driver.

Marie understood why it made only page two of the third section of the Yorkshire Evening Post, for just one story. There wasn't much to see. It was a large area, but that was about it. The site consisted of a rise in elevation of the land here and there. Fencing separated the field teams from the tourists. The field teams scraped the topsoil away, exposing evidence of burnt wood. The plaques on various parts of the site showed what the motte and bailey castle might have looked like. Student volunteers, working the dig were more abundant than the visitors were. *This won't take long.*

Marie meandered over to the souvenir kiosk. She fondled overpriced coffee mugs and key chains, coasters, and T-shirts. Some items had a picture of a trowel and a brush and the words, "I dig archaeology." *Brother. First, they hit you with an entrance fee, then a donation box, then they sell this overpriced junk, and finally you exit through the gift shop.* Marie fingered, with no interest, the various knickknacks. She bought a keychain. It was the cheapest thing for sale. This keychain had a round fob with a logo on it. It seemed everything had one of several logos. "I dig archaeology," "Femina Wilhelmina," and "Princeps Gela," were three of them. Marie looked at the nametag of the pimple-faced girl at the cash register. The name "Anna" was on the top line, "Docent" on the bottom line.

Marie picked up a set of coasters. One coaster had the words Femina Wilhelmina on it. "Who was she?"

"She was supposed to have been banished to here for murdering her husband."

Marie pointed to the coaster with the words Princeps Gela. "What about this?"

"It's supposed to be the title and name of a wandering noble at this castle. He could be a work of fiction."

Marie grunted, and looked about. "What happened to this place?"

"It seems to have been abandoned all of a sudden."

"How come?"

"That's what we're hoping to find out. Many things could have, did go, wrong. There was a plague of smallpox about this time. Disease wiped out a lot of people and villages. There were private wars among various nobles. On the other hand, it could have simply been economically unsustainable, overtaken by history."

Marie fondled the coaster. Princeps Pax, Princeps Gela. "It's a funny name."

"He was supposed to be an odd duck, if he existed," said Anna. "He may have been Irish. The chroniclers say he claimed to come from across the western sea. So most likely he would have been Irish."

Marie was twirling the key chain on her right index finger. She did not need a key chain. She could use the coasters, but they were more expensive. On one side, one coaster read Princeps Pax on top, on the bottom Princeps Gela. "Could I trade back the key chain for the coaster set?"

"If you're willing to pay the difference."

"So that's what made him an odd duck? That he may have been Irish?"

"He kind of believed in women's lib. At least in educating women. Brought them into the castle and taught them liberal arts. That is another story. The church may have had him burned in the castle or hanged. They didn't like the idea of women getting uppity."

"Liberal arts?"

"Well, the medieval version of liberal arts. They called it the quadrivium: arithmetic, astronomy, geometry, and music. In addition, the trivium: grammar, logic, and rhetoric."

Marie had one eye on the parking lot. Her people were starting to get on the bus. She paid the difference for the coasters. "Thank you, Anna."

Marie counted her people to make sure everyone was aboard. *It wouldn't be nice to leave one of these high mucky-mucks behind. I'd like to leave them all behind.* She looked at the name on the coaster. *It doesn't seem Irish.* She finished counting noses. "OK driver everyone's aboard." While the driver cranked the engine, Marie pulled out her phone and fingered an app.

Irish to English.

Princeps. No translation.

Wait a minute. Pax is Latin.

Latin to English.

Princeps. Prince.

Of course. Back then, they were still writing a lot in Latin. The prince of peace. He must have been quite the megalomaniac. What about the other word?

Latin to English.

Gela. Frost.

Tears flooded Marie's face. *Prince Pax, Prince Frost.* Her throat tightened. *Breathe Marie. Try to breathe.* She grasped the overhead rails because her legs would not support her and twisted to face the driver. "STOP THIS HORNSWOGGLING BUS NOW!" She charged the door and beat it with her right foot. "OPEN UP! OPEN UP!"

Anna heard a commotion. The coaster woman was rushing headlong for her. *She is not going to be able to stop in time.*

Marie did, barely. She thrust the coasters to within a centimetre of Anna's nose.

"This guy. Was he real? Was he a prince?"

"We don't know."

"When was he?"

177

Anna's brain locked up. She stammered, "It's in your brochure."

A crowd gathered, but stayed back almost ten metres. No one wanted to tangle with this woman, as nutty as a granola bar.

Again, Marie whipped out her cell phone. "One more thing. Was he deformed? Or seemed to be injured in any way?"

"You mean like a hunchback?"

"I mean like his legs might have been broken. Like from a fall from a great height. Or was he paralyzed?"

Anna wanted to get rid of this crazy woman. "I don't know. It's all in your brochure."

Marie flipped through her contacts on her phone. She tried Albert once, twice, but didn't get through and she wasn't given the option of leaving a message. Marie squeezed the phone so hard the case threatened to shatter. She composed a quick text and sent it.

Albert hit the chrome button with his elbow. The air blew fast and hot. He rubbed his hands to get rid of the water. I *remember when the nozzles on these things used to be able to turn up. If you splashed water on your face, you could dry your face. When did they start getting cheap on these air dryers? Is it such a hassle to be able to make the nozzles swivel?* Albert exited the men's room and turned right in the corridor. He pulled out his cell phone for a quick check. Two missed calls and one new message. *That is why I turn off the phone when I am doing something important.* The calls and message were from Marie. Albert checked the time. *Probably wanted to tell me she is on the way back with her posse.* What Albert saw in the message froze him. He read the message three times: once to be sure of what he was reading, once to comprehend it, and once to believe it.

PAXTON IS ALIVE. I KNOW WHERE AND WHEN.

Chapter 19

The mood in the conference room was like a nerd version of rugby: a rugby game that had been going on for three and a half days. Cecilia, Charles, and Isaac formed one team. Marie, Max, and Niels formed the other. Albert held the unenviable position of referee.

"We have the chance to bring him back." Marie smoothed an imaginary ruffle on the wood conference table.

"For one thing," Cecilia said, "if it was him, and I emphasize if, he's been dead for hundreds of years."

"Excuse me; I'd like to hear from one side at a time." Albert stretched out the silence. "First we will hear the pros."

"If we have the chance, we have the obligation." Marie's eyes raked the opposition.

"Marie, I want to hear logical, rational discourse. I get too much passionate political polemics from the Oversight Board."

"That's good Albert. Can you say that three times fast?" Max covered Mary Jane's mouth with one hand. Mary Jane's hair had a reverse bob cut. She wore a tweed jacket with arm patches over a sweater vest, and white oxford shirt. Her pants matched the jacket. The black wingtip shoes harmonized with her socks, belt, and bow tie.

Charles droned. "Max got her a haircut." He faced Max. "You know that's never going to grow back." Returning to the group he said, "Somehow, that walnut head got an ID badge for the project."

"I told Personnel it was for a play." Max held up the badge. It had M J's picture, and the name **Mary Jane Frost, Ph.D.** on it. Embossed in the background was the Physics department faculty, special projects hologram. Embedded in the lower left corner was the QR code. "The neat thing is it works. You tap the card to the reader, hold her face to the biometric scanner, and she gets in the EHEC facilities."

Mary Jane nodded at Max. "The cheap bastards in Personnel won't put me on payroll. Look! My card says fa-cul-ty. Another thing... Chuck." Mary Jane spat at Charles, "Don't go calling Max a walnut head."

Cecilia sneered. "I have a hypothesis that the skill of ventriloquism is proportional to the wackiness of the ventriloquist."

"Cecilia, I believe I gave the floor to the pros. Max, do you have a logical argument you want to share?"

"Marie's and my argument flows from Niels's work. I'll defer to him."

"Thank you. Max. My work starts with our original Venn diagram that yielded a 4.78% chance of Paxton's exiting in a survival environment. My new data points are: the time period involved, and the mode of the topographical elevation surrounding Sandalburg Castle for a one-kilometre radius. Next, an assumption that Paxton could not survive a wormhole opening if the centre point of the wormhole was more than two metres below mode elevation, or survive without injury if the wormhole opened more than eight metres above mode elevation. Thank you, Marie, for having the presence of mind to get hold of a topographical map for the time period. We then overlay the original Venn diagram result on the new assumptions."

Charles barked, "Niels inhale. Cut to the chase."

Albert broke in. "The pros have the floor. What are the results?"

"If Paxton came out when and where we assume, it's 100% doable." Niels let the statement hang there.

"Thank you. Anyone else from the pros?"

"I'll go next." Max leaned in. "What we have is archeological evidence of a person of unknown origin. He claimed to come from 'over the Western Sea.' This would correspond with Paxton being an American. We have the name Gela which translates to Frost. We can tie the name Pax to this individual. This is prima facie evidence for Paxton's historical existence. Marie, your turn."

"We know how to manipulate the wormhole," she said. "The only way to prove or disprove the hypothesis is to try it. We project one end of the wormhole to just outside the castle for the time period. We open the wormhole, and send one person in. That person uses one of the garage door openers to reduce the wormhole to its subspace carrier wave state. He or she searches for Paxton for a maximum of two days. If he turns up, we grab him by the collar, open the wormhole with the clicker, and dash through to our end. The wormhole is then closed." Marie brushed her hands. "Wham. Bam. Thank you ma'am."

Isaac looked half asleep. Charles's fingers were drumming impatiently.

"Are the pros done?" Albert asked. "Let's hear from the cons."

Isaac opened one eye. "Take it… Chuck." He closed his eye and went back into sleep mode.

Charles flattened both hands on the tabletop. "The only thing that is prima facie is the illogical nature of the other side's arguments.

First, Niels is using the begging-the-question fallacy. He makes an argument that incorporates its own conclusion. We agree the Venn diagram shows a 4.78% chance of survival. You then construct parameters that conform to the original conclusion, and present that as evidence for Paxton's survival. The bottom line is that 100% of 4.78% is still 4.78%."

Objections from the other side caused a verbal exchange like a glove-dropping fight at a hockey game.

"People!" Albert shouted. "I gave the floor to the cons."

"Second," Charles continued, "Max is using the appealing-to-authority fallacy, claiming that because an authority says something is true, it must be true. The authority my colleague refers to is a trinket from a souvenir shop. The Royal Historical Society admits they can't confirm the reality of this myth. If someone should go through that wormhole, he might as well inquire about Beowulf, King Arthur, or Robin Hood." The others listened silently.

"Third, Marie is using the black-or-white, or false dilemma fallacy. She uses these alternatives as the only possibilities. We either go, or abandon Paxton. There is another way of looking at this. We have limited money, resources, and time. We should use them in the most efficient way possible. I say we go back to our original research. We present our papers on M theory for peer review. Then propose the hypothesis that Paxton may have lived in the past. Let the scientific community decide if this is an idea worth pursuing." Marie and Max exchanged glances.

"Finally. Assume an undergraduate student had presented a dissertation based on any of the pros' illogical fallacies. Who among us would not give that paper a failing grade? Damn it Marie I expect better of you."

The room was so quiet, Niels rubbed his fingers on the table just to have some noise. The cavernous silence lasted at least two minutes.

"Well, Albert, You're the boss. Do we fold, or play the hand we're dealt?" Marie asked quietly.

Albert took apart, cleaned, and put back together his pipe. "People are by nature about ninety percent emotional and ten percent logical. I would vote for going back, if possible. Not because it is logical, but because it is human."

Isaac opened one eye. "Are you saying we defy the Oversight Board?"

Albert cocked his head at Isaac. "What do you know about the OB?"

"I talked with a member of the Board. He said you approached them and informed them of these..." Isaac waved a hand around, as though to pull the right word out of the air, "concepts. That Paxton is, uhmm, was alive, and we should send someone to get him. Tell the team what the Board decided."

"What did your source say, Isaac?"

"They turned the proposal down."

"Albert! How long have you known this?" Cecilia fumed.

Isaac jumped in first. "Almost four days now. According to my friend."

"Albert. You said nothing about meeting with the Board." Cecilia's tone was harsh.

"Forgive me, but my logical side proved dominant in the decision: I wanted the debate on this matter to be free flowing, I didn't want any minor stimuli to create a bias. Last, you entertain a false idea as to the Board's influence on my decision."

"You regard the Board as a 'minor stimuli'?" Marie asked.

"I regard the Board as an unneeded, useless, and unwanted imposition. It is designed to politically protect the Home Office."

"I take back what I said about you. You da man Albert." Cecilia shot out her index fingers.

Marie leaned across the table. "If any of you feel uncomfortable, please, all we ask for is your silence." She faced Albert. "You won't have any problems granting anyone a leave of absence. Will you, Albert?"

"And leave you people to make a bloody muck of things?" Charles interjected. "Our reputation in academic, government, and scientific circles is already near absolute zero. In for a traffic ticket, in for the gallows, I always say."

"I don't recall you ever saying that, but we're grateful for the sentiment." Max turned to Isaac. "What about you Isaac?"

"You know me. You can't gamble if you're not in the pool."

Before Marie could talk to Cecilia Albert spoke up. "I'm sorry, people. No." Albert's voice was as cold as his decision.

"What do you mean, Albert?" Niels said. The atmosphere in the room went icy. "You led us to believe we could go after Paxton." The tight clock spring in Niels's head unwound unimpeded. "You bloody, grotty, old nutter. Are you off your trolley?"

Albert sat admiring his pipe. Raising his eyes, but not his head, he asked, "Finished, Niels? Then sit down."

Niels sat, like a boxer who had an eye blackened by a six-year-old.

"People hear what they want to hear, not what is said. I said I would vote for going back, if possible," said Albert.

"What's stopping us, besides the Board?" Marie asked.

"When Paxton disappeared, we know what happened. We don't know *why* it happened. We must find the first cause, the prime mover, for why this happened."

"Albert," Cecilia moaned. "We've gone over this for months. The Board's people have gone over this for months."

"I'm sorry. My decision is final."

Max got up in a huff, to be the first one out of the room. As he reached for the doorknob, a spark of static electricity from it snapped his hand like a rubber band. Max held up his hand to look at it. *What did Paxton say? In the cafeteria. What did he say?*

"What's she made of?" Isaac coughed.

184

Mary Jane replied, "Some glass, a lot of silk, machined, not stamped bearings, but mostly wood."

What did Cecilia say about her last conversation with Paxton?

"Paxton, it's Cecilia. What are you doing?"

"Showing Mary Jane around. Then I'll tweak some instruments."

Silk and glass. Rubbed together they build up an electric charge. Wood acts as an insulator. The cold air in the Bottle Room would be very dry. That would allow a strong static charge to build up.

Max looked down at Mary Jane.

Her eyelids crouched low above the pupils of her round eyes. Those eyes accused him and the whole team. *And you call me a dummy. It took you people long enough to figure this out.*

"Max. Are you leaving?" Someone behind him asked.

Max's head swam. "Albert. I think I found your first cause."

Chapter 20

It started as a bright day that became gloomy, not just because the road passed through the forest, or because the sky turned overcast. Riding to Banburn, the exhalations of Sarah, Catherine, and Gunther first turned to a light mist. When the rain started, their breathing became a fog trailing behind them. In Banburn, the riders bent like willow branches over the necks of the horses. The horses trotting became firmer on the hardening mud.. Gunther was about to steer the way to the castle when Sarah stopped.

"Gunther. We will go first to the cathedral's rectory," she said through chattering teeth.

"My lady. It's cold," grumbled Gunther. "I'm cold. You and Catherine are cold. The horses are cold."

Sarah turned her horse toward the cathedral. "Lady Wilhelmina desires to know if Ignatius will be an ally for her. He was not in Warren. We did not see him on the road. He must still be in Banburn."

Sarah prompted her horse forward. She issued her orders as Catherine and Gunther fell in line behind her. "After we arrive at the rectory, you will take the horses to the castle stables. Tell Duke Alphonso's seneschal I will occupy my rooms with my servant. Leave our belongings there. After that, take to your room to warm up."

Arriving at the rectory, Sarah and Catherine waited for Gunther to help them off their sidesaddles. "Gunther, tomorrow speak with the castle's servants. Tell them of life in Sandalburg. Note who speaks kindly of Lady Wilhelmina and who does not."

Sarah stomped to restore circulation in her legs. She rubbed her upper arms with her hands. "It is a brief walk to the castle. Walking rapidly will keep us warm."

Catherine drew her cloak tighter around her, casting a wary eye at the rectory. "Perhaps no one is inside?"

Sarah barked out her order. "Gunther, go to the castle. Catherine, I see a light through a ground floor window." Sarah set off for the front door. "I hope it is a fire in the hearth. I want to get this chill off myself."

Sarah opened the door and stepped in, waiting for her eyes adjust to the fire light. "Bishop?"

The figure sat with his back to the hearth, his boots propped on a table. He dropped a document from in front of his face. "Lady Sarah?"

Sarah stared at the Connecticut style, cordovan coloured boots, form fitted by a master cobbler to the man's legs. Both the leggings and tunic had a fine, almost delicate weave. He wore a sash of vivid purple, intricately woven with gold and silver threads. Her eyes met the man's face. "Ignatius? Why are you not in your monk's robes?"

Ignatius got up and put the document on the table. "Why are you in Banburn?" He cocked his head. "I see you brought Catherine with you. Who else has come back? What brings you here?"

"Close the door, Catherine." Sarah moved to the fire. She bent down and stretched her arms out as though to dive into its warmth. "Gunther escorted us. The Lady renounces the letter she sent with you."

Sarah recounted the events since Ignatius left: Paxton's renouncing all other allegiances, his swearing of loyalty to Lady Wilhelmina, the Lady's taking Paxton into her clan, even the praise of Beatrice's virtue, and the new letter. Sarah rose up and approached Ignatius. "She wishes to know first if you will oppose her."

Ignatius turned the paper he held face down, and put his right hand on it. Placing his other hand on his heart, he bowed to Sarah. "How can I be less faithful to the Lady Wilhelmina than the noble Paxton?" He tapped his lips with his fingers. "She wishes her uncle to negotiate a peace between Ahearn's clan and hers. If necessary, she will sacrifice Paxton to the northern lairds. Paxton knows this."

Sarah nodded. "It is his plan."

"'Maiorem hac dilectionem nemo habet.' *(Greater love than this no man hath.)* John 15:13. This would put Paxton's blood on her uncle's hands." Ignatius paused. "The Lady Wilhelmina is as cunning as Eden's serpent. You say Gunther is with you. Bring him in from the cold."

"I have sent him ahead to the castle. He will make our arrival known. I would have my rooms back. Tomorrow, after the morning meal I will give the letter to the duke and wait for his reply." Sarah sighed. "I do hope he takes a long time to reply. I have many dances to catch up with, and even more gossip." She giggled. "Tell me what goes on in the castle." Sarah's eyes grew wide in anticipation.

"I do not know. I have not been inside the castle. The bishop has kept me busy here."

Sarah looked around. "Where is your cousin?"

"Foul weather creates in him a foul mood. The foul mood creates foul health. He is upstairs in his room, sleeping, fitfully."

Ignatius stepped forward. "Catherine." He held out his left hand. "Come forward. How are you, the twins, and Beatrice? Is she truly penitent for her transgressions? That is one reason I am still here. The bishop and duke take great delight in learning what goes on in the hinterland."

"You spy for them?"

"Catherine," Sarah snapped. "Remember your place."

"No spying. I speak only of what is openly known to all."

"Wait." Sarah raised a hand. "You said you have not been in the castle. Now you say you have spoken with the duke."

"He comes here to speak with the bishop. The duke plans to expand the cathedral and the rectory. This will be a house worthy of the cathedral. Catherine, if you were brought to his eminence, what would you say?"

"I am innocent."

"What have you been accused of?" Ignatius asked in an inquisitor's tone.

"Why else would I be brought to the bishop, if not to answer for some sin?"

"I was thinking that you might find some delight in meeting with him while you are back at Banburn. Of what sins do you feel the need to unburden yourself?"

"I have entrusted Friar Bernard with the care of my soul."

"Sarah, how is Bernard?"

"It seems that with every day's passing he ages two. It is getting late. May we have a lantern to light our way to the castle?"

"Please spend the night at the adjoining convent."

"I have missed too much of life in Banburn already. I will not deny myself even one night's sleep in the castle." Sarah smiled.

"Very well." Ignatius picked up the paper and tucked it in his sash. Retrieving a lantern from the mantle, he lit its wick.

Catherine clutched at the lamp when Ignatius pulled it back. "Lady Sarah, if you do not know your course, all winds are foul. I must know what her reply would be to any position the duke takes. I could then be the ally Lady Wilhelmina wishes me to be."

Now Ignatius held out the light. "Catherine, hold the lantern so your lady may walk in light and not in darkness. Be on your way so that you may be on time for Compline prayers in the castle's chapel."

Their walk was brief, and walking rapidly did little to keep them warm. It took a short prayer's time to cover the distance between cathedral and castle. "Why was Ignatius not in his monk's robes?" Sarah mumbled.

"His eyes never left me, even when he talked with you," Catherine grumbled.

"Did you see how his hand never left that agreement?"

"Saying he would bring me to the bishop was no invitation; it was a threat."

Sarah's thoughts staid fixed on the parchment. "I recognize the seals; one belongs to the duke, the other to the bishop."

"He only inquired of me and the other common women, no one else."

"Why would Ignatius be interested in an agreement between the bishop and duke?"

"His only interest is in bedding common women."

"Catherine, stop talking to yourself. We need to find out what he was reading."

"If we discover what he was reading, will we find out why he lied?"

"What do you think he lied about?"

Catherine pointed to the ground, just outside the main door of the castle. Frozen in time and mud were the footprints of a pair of boots. A pair with distinct left and right sole exited the castle. "He said he has not been in the castle," Catherine sneered.

"Come Catherine; let's see if my old rooms are ready. We need to pray, and think, and plan before I meet the duke after morning Mass."

"We're leaving the wolf snare, for the wolf's lair."

In the morning, Sarah had little trouble slipping into her routine. At the morning meal, she squealed with delight when embracing other women at court. Sitting at the main table, she waved to no nobleman in particular. Many waved back.

The duke looked down at Sarah. "I've been told you have a letter for me from your mistress."

A hush fell over the assembled group.

"Please sir, if I give you the letter now you will respond all the faster." A playful expression came to her face. "Then I would have to leave with your reply, and where would be the fun in that?" Somber looks came over the faces of the young men at the tables.

Sarah held up her goblet. "Catherine, must I tell again? Never let my wine glass get half-empty." A glint came to Sarah's eyes. "After the meal we will walk."

When she finished her morning meal, Lady Wilhelmina commanded Paxton to accompany her to the chapel. There, they found Friar Bernard waiting. "Kneel before the altar," the Lady told Paxton. Paxton knelt. The Lady and Friar Bernard remained silent, for too long. "There is something of yourself you have not told us. Now before God and your sovereign I order you to tell us all of yourself, from the beginning."

"I will try, my lady. That may be difficult, as the beginning won't start for a few hundred years."

Paxton tugged open a small leather pouch. Its drawstrings he had tied around his waist. Out of it, he took keys and fob, cell phone, lighter, Swiss Army knife, handkerchief, wallet, and the pound and pence coins. In his wallet were credit cards, driver's license, photos of him, Mary Jane, him and Mary Jane, National Health Insurance card, library card, shopper's club card, and money. Also the laser pointer and his ID badge for the project.

Sarah pulled Catherine through a door and closed it. "This is the scriptorium. If there is an agreement between the bishop and duke, a copy will be in here. Look for any paper with two seals. One is the duke's, the other the bishop's." The women started pulling papers out of pigeonholes, opening and closing them. "Put everything back exactly as you found it. Let us try to find some order that the duke has."

In less than an hour Catherine whispered, "It would be an agreement that concerned Ignatius. Like this?"

Sarah read the document Catherine held. She put her hand to her heart and tried to catch her breath. "This says the duke will expand the rectory. He will remodel the alcove dedicated to Saint Lucy in the cathedral, the one the Lady had built. The bishop will release Ignatius from his monk's vows and Ignatius will marry the duke's daughter."

Sarah's voice was so quiet Catherine barely heard it. "Duke Alphonso wants to give Sandalburg estates to his son-in-law, but the Lady will not relinquish her claim."

Catherine hissed, "It also says the Ladies Wilhelmina and Sarah are to be arrested for harboring the warlock Paxton." Catherine kept reading. "Beatrice and Catherine are to be arrested, also for harboring Paxton. Arrested as members of Paxton's coven will be the twins, Elizabeth and Isabelle."

In the quiet of the scriptorium, the sound of the door latch was like a sword striking a shield.

The Lady sat with her back against an altar corner. Paxton was speaking of his last time in the Bottle Room. Friar Bernard sat with his back at the opposite corner. "Friar?" The Lady asked.

"He does not speak as one whose faculties are demon possessed, barking, and growling. Rather he speaks as one who possesses his faculties. Are these tales, or dreams, or life, I cannot say."

Paxton got to the part when he last saw the twins before their arrival at the castle. The Lady stopped him and left. When she returned, she made the twins swear that they should recount their encounters with Paxton. When their recollections matched Paxton's she dismissed them back to their duties. Even when Paxton spoke of his travel with Friar

192

Bernard and John, the Lady stopped him and asked the friar if this was true. She then left and returned with John and had him recount under oath his travel with Paxton.

The door swung open. "What?" The duke could barely get the word out of his mouth. Catherine and Sarah stood in front of him. Catherine's back was to the duke. Her right hand was behind the small of Sarah's back. Her left hand held the back of Sarah's head. The taller Catherine planted a great big, open-mouthed wet kiss on Sarah.

Catherine and Sarah broke apart. Confusion, shock, and surprise all could be mistaken for something else. Sarah grabbed Catherine's hand and shot out of the scriptorium. "What? What?" Sarah's words came as hard as the duke's did. "What did you do?" They raced through the castle's halls.

"Would you rather have him catch us reading his agreement with the bishop?"

"He knows we saw it. The document is open on the floor."

"No it's not. I tucked it between the small of your back and your sash."

Again, one hand went to Sarah's heart. Now the other hand felt her back. "Huhh!" Sarah looked at the paper as if it was a venomous serpent. She pushed it into Catherine's hand. "We must go back to Sandalburg now."

Reaching Sarah's rooms, they ran into the bedroom. Sarah ordered, "We must pack our belongings. We don't know how long it will be before the duke notices his agreement is missing. Why does the agreement mention the common women? He only needs to remove the Lady and me."

Catherine stopped and turned to Sarah. "At the convent school, the twins refused Ignatius's advances. When he arrived at Sandalburg, he proposed to take me to Banburn if I would lie with him. Beatrice refused him, and he violated her refusal and her body."

"Keep packing. How do you know these things?"

"Two words Lady Sarah. Women talk. He wants to take revenge on the common women who refused him."

"He agrees to marry the duke's daughter, and the duke lets him punish the women?" Sarah starred at Catherine and grabbed at the clothes. "That is my tunic, not yours."

Catherine threw the tunic at Sarah. "We can sort out the clothing back in Sandalburg. And those are my shoes."

"No they're not."

"Do they fit?"

Sarah held a shoe to her foot. "As you said, later. I will start packing our things in the outer room. Keep packing."

Sarah closed the door between the two rooms. She was packing the sewing when Duke Alphonso entered with two women in tow.

"You have something of mine," he barked. "I want it back."

Sarah swallowed. "I don't know what you mean. How dare you enter a Lady's chamber without announcing yourself? Leave immediately."

"When I leave, it will be with what is mine."

Sarah raised herself to her full height of five feet, two inches. "Duke Alphonso, we are leaving. We will stay at the cathedral's convent until you are ready to give me an answer to the Lady's letter."

"Then you force me to find what I came for myself." He surveyed the room. "Where is your servant?"

The duke stomped into the inner room. Catherine stopped packing. "I will start by searching everything in this room. Then I will search the outer room. If I do not find what I am looking for, these women will search both of you, thoroughly."

The duke began ransacking the room. Sarah met Catherine's eyes. Without moving her head, Catherine glanced at the remains of the fire. Sarah followed Catherine's eyes, and with only the smallest movement nodded assent.

Paxton was finished. For a long time, Friar Bernard and the Lady were silent. Holding the picture of Paxton and Mary Jane, the Lady broke the silence. Leaning forward she said, "Tell me more of this puppet called Mary Jane."

Sarah was almost finished dressing. Putting her sash back on, she spoke to the servants. "Tell your master you found nothing because there was nothing to find. We will pack our belongings and leave for the convent."

The women left and closed the door. Sarah ran to the door and pressed her ear to it. Catherine protested, "Now I have to start all over."

"Shhh." Sarah hissed. "We're not packing anything except our cloaks." Sarah went back, took her cloak, and tossed Catherine hers. She cracked the door open and peeked out. "We're leaving now. We won't give Duke Alphonso time to think of what to do. He may want to confer with Ignatius first." She grabbed Catherine's hand and pulled her into the hall. Closing the door, they went through hallways, down stairs, raced along passageways, and out doorways. They stopped at one of the castle's outer doors. Sarah whispered, "This door is closest to the stable. Pull up your cloak's hood and follow me."

Sarah walked out with firm purpose to the stable. There she pulled the horses out of their stalls. "Catherine, help me." Sarah clenched her eyebrows together. "Saddle your horse."

"These are saddles men use."

"Catherine," her voice lowered, "we can ride faster using them." Sarah slammed a saddle with the palm of her hand. Dust motes jumped up and fled. "Help me, bridle the horses." Sarah crept to the stable door. "I'll open the door. When you ride, ride as fast as you can. Don't stop until you get to Sandalburg. If you are caught I won't stop for you, and you shouldn't stop for me." Sarah opened the door wide, mounted her horse, and bolted for Sandalburg.

Hours later two lathered horses stumbled into Sandalburg. In the stable, Sarah dragged herself off her horse. She drew in a startled breath. A lifeless, listless form held the mane of Catherine's horse. Sarah grimaced. Warily she approached the horse. Reaching up she touched the shrouded figure. "Catherine?"

Catherine's sleepy, satiated eyes slowly revealed themselves. She sucked in a deep breath and blinked several times. With each blink, she ratcheted herself a little straighter. Catherine flowed off the horse and bounced on her feet. She wiped the hair off her face and brushed her tunic. "The control men have over these beasts larger than themselves." Catherine stroked the horse's nose. "When can we go riding again?"

Chapter 21

Sometimes there are no good choices. The break pod in sublevel nine of the EHEC was an example. One area of the pod featured the usual assortment of students, faculty, and support staff. They were too many, too happy, and too annoying for Cecilia. Someone in the cluster said, "A Higgs boson walks into a Catholic church and says…"

"You people can't have mass without me." Cecilia finished the joke.

Another area held the noisy vending machines.

Cecilia picked an isolated white Formica topped table under a flickering, snapping, sterile, fluorescent light.

She warmed her fingers around a mug of hot chamomile tea. After taking a sip, she put down the mug. Using her warmed fingers, Cecilia massaged her tired temple and muttered to no one in particular, "My head hurts."

"Then stop beating up on yourself." The falsetto voice behind her asked.

"Max, stifle that fugitive from a lumberyard, or I swear I'll feed it to the termites."

Charles empty-handed took a chair kitty-corner from Cecilia. His gotcha smile could scare The Joker. "When I see Max I'll give him your message. In the meantime, Albert wants to see you and me. He's in his office. He also wants everyone in the ground floor conference room, on the next hour."

"Charles! I haven't slept in days. What does he want?"

"None of us have. Max and Niels took Mary Jane to the engineering lab. They recreated the environmental conditions in the Bottle Room when Paxton was there. They were able to build a charge on Max's hand, a charge sufficient to send a spurious signal to the antimatter containment vessel." Charles jabbed an index finger on the table with every sentence.

"You're not telling me anything I don't already know," muttered Cecilia. "The only way to convert a discharge of static electricity to a signal is through the instruments surrounding the wormhole disc." She rubbed her eyes. "That can't happen because they're all grounded. I checked and double-checked. I even checked that the ground fault light bulbs were working."

Charles squirmed forward in his chair. He said quickly, "N40. Niels found it. You checked the instruments the same way Paxton would have."

"Don't compare me to Paxton."

Charles waved away Cecilia's objection. "The circuit board for N40 wasn't fully seated. Under normal temperature conditions, it doesn't make a difference. Niels took the whole circuit box for N40 back to the engineering lab. He put the circuit box in an environmental chamber and dropped the temperature and humidity to the levels when Paxton was in the Bottle Room. Metal contracts when it's cold. He found a gap in the metal contacts. Both the ground and ground fault signal were lost." Charles leaned so far forward his torso was almost flat on the table. "A lack of ground didn't affect the ability of the instruments to do their job, so the experiment went forward."

"With disastrous results. Why didn't the air conditioner ever go off?"

"I don't know. I'm a quantum mechanic, not a refrigeration mechanic." Charles gazed into Cecilia's tired eyes. "You look as terrible as I feel, and it's not going to get any better for you."

"Why?"

"I've just figured it out. Albert's been ahead of us all along. He's been letting anyone with an experiment, or a project use the EHEC ahead of us for two weeks. 'Oh, we're not ready yet. Please go ahead and use our time slot.' Soon we'll be the only ones left with any business on the Collider."

"Maintenance will want to get at it."

"The Queen's Diamond Jubilee is being celebrated next weekend. Everyone will be off, including maintenance and the Board."

"Yes?"

"Remember what Marie proposed? 'We open up the wormhole full bore, send someone through, and get Paxton. Wham. Bam. Thank you ma'am.'"

Cecilia looked down at her now cold tea. "I don't like where you're going with this."

"The more mass in the wormhole, the more energy is needed to keep it open. As a simple precautionary measure, it makes sense to send through the person with the lightest mass."

"Oh shit."

THE SAME DAY, CENTURIES EARLIER

"On my oath and on my life, Lord, I knew nothing of this," said a quaking Gunther.

"Yesss," the duke hissed back. "On your life." Again, the duke stormed up the length of the stable. "Yours is the only bridle they did not steal." His voice rose with every word. "I will have you hanged by your own horse's bridle."

199

A voice from outside called, "Why would my Lord do that?" The duke and Gunther listened to a rider dismounting. "I found these bridles on the road, west of the city." Ignatius entered and threw two handfuls of bridles on a stall's gate. "It's good I kept Father Casimir's horse stabled at the rectory."

Ignatius leaned his back against the gate. "Gunther, see to it Sarah's and Catherine's possessions are packed. Take them back to Sandalburg. Tell the Lady Wilhelmina the duke is disappointed that Lady Sarah did not wait for a reply before returning." Ignatius continued looking at Gunther. "Go."

The only thing Gunther moved was his head, as he looked at the duke.

The duke waved one arm to the stable's entrance, and Gunther sprinted for the castle.

Ignatius sauntered to the stable entrance. "All you can see of poor Gunther are his heels, raising dust."

"Perhaps you can see more if I raise you higher with one of these." The duke picked up the handful of tangled bridles.

Ignatius watched as a woman spread seed out for the chickens. "Duke Alphonso, let us patrol the bailey. On open ground it is easier to hold private talks."

The duke gestured for Ignatius to follow him around the castle.

"My lord, you are like a poor archer who keeps missing the target. Let us count the ways: One, you plant, water, and nurture seeds of the Lady's onus for her husband's death. Two, you raise her taxes to crush her in debt. Three, you send mercenaries against her. Still the Lady owns Sandalburg. You do not."

"I own you. If I dismiss you now, you will be without position in court, or the church."

"If you send me back to my father you will need to find another noble to marry your daughter. You can find another, but you will find none richer. See now, how you not only miss the target, but also have taken your aim off it."

Their walk in the bailey sent servants hiding like mice running from a pair of hungry cats. "Duke, what is your target?"

"To get Lady Wilhelmina out of Sandalburg."

"No. Your target is to own Sandalburg. To own it you must pry it from the Lady, in practice, and in law."

"How would I do that?"

"Go to Sandalburg. Demand that she come back with you. In Banburn castle it is a short distance from trial to the axe man's blade."

"That is why she will never leave." The duke's face contorted. "The chop is too good for her. Her end will be at the end of a rope. Also that, that, harpy Sarah."

"If that is true my lord, I ask you do me a small favour. Leave her feet and Sarah's feet unbound. Seeing noble women dance in midair at the end of a rope would go a long way to convince the common women to uncross their own legs."

"Yes," the duke snarled. "What kind of man cannot get a common whore to lie with him?"

"She did not willingly lie with a monk, but she will willingly lie with the man who can protect her from the noose. It will give me great pleasure to have these women beg for my company." Ignatius gazed far into the distance.

Duke Alphonso stroked his bifurcated beard. "Didn't you mention the cow herders are twins?"

"Oh yes, Elizabeth and Isabelle. They are most unappealing women. Scrawny, dirty, and ugly. They came from Alton. The pox has left them most scarred. They are like skinny rats."

The men's course had taken them three quarters of the way around the castle. "I have never enjoyed the company of twins, Ignatius."

"My lord has agreed that I should have all four."

"Do not be selfish. I'm changing our agreement."

"Well, perhaps my lord will choose Elizabeth, or Isabelle, and Beatrice or Catherine. Then we will each have one twin."

"Don't be foolish. You never break up a matched set. They would make fine comfort for an old man." The duke kicked at the ground. "I am still left with the problem of getting hold of Sandalburg."

"The bishop is organizing penitential processions of religious through the Diocese of Yorkshire."

"Yes, for the remission of sins, and the abatement of the plague. Why does church business interest me?"

"It would be easy for me to persuade my cousin to let me organize the procession. It would go from here to Warren, and on to Alton. In Warren, most of the men and I will stay with Father Casimir. Later in the day, you can arrive with your escort and camp outside Sandalburg castle. You go into the castle and demand that the Lady return with you."

"And she will refuse."

"You then say that because it is late you will stay in Warren."

"All this brings me no closer to my trophy than before."

"Lord Alphonso, remember the history of the Greeks."

The look of puzzlement on the duke's face gave way in degrees to enlightenment, and then appreciation. "The sack of Troy. How long before all this can be done?"

"We can attain everything by the end of the week."

"Unless the stars rule against us."

Chapter 22

"Oh shit," Charles moaned.

"Now it looks like the joke's on the joker. Let me explain Albert." Cecilia jerked her head at Charles. "He thought you wanted to send me back to get Paxton."

Looking down, Albert played with his pipe. "It's occurred to me that with all the restrictions on smoking, I spend more time cleaning my pipe than smoking it." Now he looked up at Charles. "With your degree in history, you are the most qualified person to go back. In addition to retrieving Paxton, you know what to anticipate in that culture. Besides, we can't send Cecilia back alone, given the realities of medieval England."

"You want me to go back also?' asked Cecilia. "Why me? You just said Charles is the most qualified."

"Keep your voice down. The walls aren't soundproof. It's a simple engineering principle. You reduce the risk by building in redundancy. If I had the means, we would all go back. As it is, we have only two hand held controllers for the wormhole. We can get costumes from the Dramatic Arts Department. It shouldn't take more than a few hours to determine if we have the right location and time for Paxton or not."

"Where did this 'we' come from, Albert?"

"It's a voluntary assignment, Cecilia."

"You know it's not." Cecilia slumped down. "Let's examine the permutations. I say no and Charles says yes. The other team members will think it's because Paxton got the Bottle Room assignment that I won't go. I say yes and Charles says no. He looks like a coward. Charles and I both say no. It looks like collusion to abandon Paxton. No matter how you cut it, we have to go, or lose face." She slapped Charles's shoulder. "Come on. Grow a pair and get ready. We have about a week."

Albert rose. "I'm glad to see we're all in agreement. Let's go. The rest of the team and Oscar should be arriving in the conference room."

"Who's Oscar?" Cecilia asked.

"Oscar is our so-called contact man with the Oversight Board appointed by the Advanced Projects Service."

"Donoschik," Cecilia snarled.

"Yeah, what she said. What did you say?" Charles said.

"Snitch," Albert said, sucking on his pipe. "Not correct Cecilia. A donoschik is someone you don't know is informing on you. We know he's reporting to the OB and the APS."

Albert and company walked into the conference room. In Albert's place at the head of the table sat Oscar. "I see everyone has arrived. Team, I'd like you to meet Oscar. He'll be our liaison with the OB." As Albert went around the table introducing the team, Oscar wrote on a legal pad, occasionally holding up his hand to pause Albert.

"Oscar, I talked with the dean. The only open office is the one Paxton used."

"That will be fine Albert. I might as well get this out front. My duties are not to liaison with the OB. Rather I'm to transition the M theory project to a team the OB put together."

"Excuse me!" Niels shouted. "We were told that we would bring this project to its conclusion."

"Please Neil, don't shoot the messenger. The highest authority made this decision. Higher than the Home Secretary." Oscar, gaunt as a shadow, let his words sink in.

"It's Niels."

"I didn't vote for her. Nekulturny," Cecilia slurred.

"Nekulturny?" Oscar looked around the table for an explanation.

Marie leaned to her left. "Cecilia's hobby is learning insults in different languages." She ticked off the languages on her fingers: "English of course, Esperanto, Klingon, Latin, and now she's learning Russian."

"When will the OB's team move in?" Max asked.

"The week after the Queen's Jubilee celebration."

Max turned to Albert, now sitting in Paxton's old chair. "Can we be ready by then?"

"We either finish what we started or stop now," Isaac sighed.

"Oscar, this is a surprise." Albert fumbled with his pipe. He started to put it away, then took it out again. He pulled a pipe cleaner from another pocket. He fidgeted with it, then put it down. At last, he brought out his tobacco pouch. He pushed the tobacco chamber of the pipe into the pouch and packed tobacco in. After lighting the pipe, Albert leaned back in the chair. The pipe's calabash bowl glowed. Smoke enveloped the room. The seconds that passed seemed like an eternity. Taking the pipe out of his mouth, he blew smoke rings.

"You know smoking is prohibited," Oscar reprimanded.

The composition on Albert's face matched his words. "We will finish what I started."

The Lady and Paxton were walking along the parapet when they saw the two riders rushing into the stable. They were perplexed because the riders were dressed as women, yet rode astride like men. One of them emerged and the Lady recognized Sarah's ponytail trotting for the stairs. Her guess was confirmed when the other scaled the hill of keep.

"Doesn't Catherine ever use the stairs?" Paxton asked.

"She has shaped the earth with her journeys up and down that her way is now almost as easy as the stairs." The Lady walked to the break in the battlement where Catherine would be appearing.

After they both arrived, Sarah told of their escape from Banburn castle.

"All right, let me get this straight. You stole all the bridles in the stable to prevent the duke or his men from pursuing you! That's like stealing distributer caps!" Paxton laughed heartily. "I guess you could say your plan met with unbridled success." Paxton slapped his thigh. "What did you two learn in Yorkshire?"

"Lord Paxton, they learned what I sent them to learn." The Lady Wilhelmina sat on a bench. Her back rested on the keep's wall. "Speak, Sarah."

Sarah told the lady of Ignatius's denial of being in Banburn castle. Catherine spoke of finding his boot prints with their distinctive soles exiting the castle. Sarah told of the written agreement with the bishop, in which the duke promised to build the bishop's rectory finer and larger. The agreement mentioned his desire to remodel the cathedral, with special attention devoted to the alcove dedicated to St. Lucy. She told of releasing Ignatius from his monk's vows to marry the duke's daughter. Sarah spoke of their escape from the scriptorium, but not how. Finally, she told of the search of her rooms for the missing agreement, and then the search of her and Catherine.

"If there was only Catherine I'm sure he would have done it himself." The Lady pursed her lips. "The important thing is that we know of his plans."

"My lady," Catherine said, "he knows that we know of his plans."

"Yes Catherine, but now it cannot be other than we know…" Sarah paused to catch her thoughts, "…that he knows we know of his plans."

The Lady stood up. "Enough knowing. The duke will now be forced to abandon his efforts, or change them." The Lady walked to the outside stairs leading to her apartment on the second floor. Sarah and Catherine fell in behind her. "Is there any other news in Yorkshire?"

"Fear of the pox is spreading," Sarah told her. "Monks are organizing a pilgrimage from Yorkshire to Warren. Warren being free from God's punishment they will stay there a few days. They will then move on to Alton to beg God for His mercy there."

The Lady started up the stairs. Her face showed the strain of lifting more than her weight, and more than the weight of her office. "I will dismiss the common women. They will return to their normal duties. Sarah, you will attend me."

"My lady, with Beatrice and the twins attending you, they also know." Sarah turned to Catherine. "It is too much to ask them not to speak?"

"There is no need for anyone to talk. I also know," said Catherine.

The Lady descended one step. "What do you know, Catherine?"

"I know that men are like bats in daylight. Women are like the owls at night. We see every little movement and hear every sound of importance. I know how to be as silent as the owl in flight, until such time as the Lady releases me from my silence."

The Lady Wilhelmina nodded and returned to her sanctuary.

Cecilia and Charles stepped on the wormhole disc.

"Have you got your will made out, Charles?"

"Sure thing, Cecilia. I've left everything to you."

On impulse, they clutched each other's hands.

Albert pushed a button to open the conference call on the speakerphone. "Max, start the reactor." The Helium 3 matter antimatter reactor pulsed with energies found only at the creation of the universe.

Albert heard Marie's voice quiver. "Umbilic Torus Portal is up. Mobius Chamber is stable."

"Bosons are within parameters. Tachyons are flowing nicely," Niels reported with a strained normality.

Albert stared at the phone. Nothing. "Isaac." Nothing. "Isaac!"

"Quantum gravity field is behaving according to predictions," Isaac replied.

Albert looked up. Cecilia and Charles were gone.

Cecilia and Charles saw one end of a white tunnel next to them. Another end was some undefined distance away. In a half panic, they ran—somehow, on the same floor like surface Paxton must have—to the far end. They stopped just short of the far end of the tunnel. Charles pushed a hand through and pulled it back in. He looked it over.

"Well?" Cecilia said.

Charles poked his head out the end of the tunnel. He pulled it back in. "Just as our computations predicted. We look to be about twenty centimetres above ground level. It's very early in the morning. Come on." Charles stepped out, leaving one arm in the wormhole.

Cecilia squeezed Charles's hand and stepped forward, committing herself to the unknown. Instantly, cold morning air filled her lungs. She and Charles stepped down and away from the wormhole.

In the Bottle Room, the wormhole closed to its subspace state.

"Charles closed the wormhole," Albert said.

The wormhole opened up. "Charles opened it," Albert reported.

The wormhole closed. "Cecilia closed it. One test to go."

"Cecilia opened it. I'm closing the wormhole. Max put the reactor to its lowest power setting," Albert ordered. The wormhole closed to its natural subspace carrier wave state. Like an invisible silver thread, it would bifurcate and follow the two controllers wherever they went.

"My God, my God," breathed Cecilia. "The thing works!"

"Well Cecilia, it's you and me. Got your bodcam working?"

"Yeah, and I'm glad I went to the bathroom before we left." Cecilia replied. She looked around to get her bearings. "Nothing but countryside. No sign of industrial society. According to copies of the old maps, we're at the north end of the valley. Warren should be to the south and east of us."

"And south is Sandalburg castle," said Charles.

Cecilia started walking south. "Let's get moving and find the road."

"Cecilia, I think this dirt track is it."

Walking for less than an hour, the smell became undeniable. "Charles there's something dead around here."

"Probably a cow or a horse." They kept walking.

"Oh God!" Cecilia pointed to a man's half-rotted corpse, half eaten by animals. It lay just off the path. Cecilia dry heaved. "Didn't they say he might have been executed?"

"We don't know that's Paxton." Charles stepped closer to examine the corpse. "I don't think it's him. But I can't... tell for sure." He turned away and retched.

Cecilia couldn't look. "Let's go on. The quicker we can find out if it was Paxton, the quicker we can be back."

By midmorning, they arrived at the castle. "The doors are open. What do we do, walk in?" Charles asked.

"Why not? Act casual."

"This is the bailey, or lower part of the castle," said Charles.

"No one seems to be paying attention to us." Cecilia wrapped the dull grey hood of her tunic closer around her face. "I guess that's good. We can't hang around like tourists." Cecilia pulled down the brim of Charles's black hat and looked around. "Charles we're not going to blend in."

"What do you mean?"

"Look at us. Look at them. Our clothes are too new." Cecilia pointed to a building at the far side of the bailey. "That looks like a chapel. We can stop there and pretend we're praying."

They were nearing the chapel when they both felt a sharp rap on their shoulders. Turning, they saw twin girls holding long staffs. "Are you from Konectic?"

"Paxton was from Connecticut," Cecilia whispered to Charles. Now turning to the girl, "What do you know of Connecticut?"

One girl pointed her staff at the ground, "You leave the marks of shoes made in Konectic."

Charles groaned. "I forgot. They didn't yet have different left and right shoes."

"No. We are from Yorkshire." Cecilia replied. Again she asked, "What do you know of Connecticut?"

"Lord Paxton is from Konectic," replied the other twin.

Chapter 23

One heartbeat. Two heartbeats. Three heartbeats. The duos stared at each other. Four heartbeats. Five heartbeats. Six heartbeats.

Charles broke the silence. "Do you know where Paxton is?"

Elizabeth and Isabelle looked at each other. After a moment of silent communication, Isabelle retreated to the covered stairway leading to the motte.

"Is she going to get Paxton?" Charles asked.

"She is my twin, Isabelle. I am Elizabeth." Elizabeth leaned on her staff, staring at Cecilia. Suddenly she lunged and grabbed Cecilia's wrist. Turning her palm up, she stroked her palm and fingers. "A lady's skin in peasant clothes?"

Cecilia stared back. "Will Isabelle bring Lord Paxton to us?"

Elizabeth dropped Cecilia's hand. "Lord Paxton is giving a lesson on astronomy."

Waving her herding staff forward, Elizabeth moved to an area of the bailey, where a group was gathered. In the middle of the group, an old friar stood still. Two women faced each other. Each had her hands locked on the other's wrists. Left hand on left wrist, right on right, they slowly spun around the axis made by their interlocking hands. As they spun around, they also circled the friar.

"Saturn"—Paxton pointed at the rose-coloured-haired woman—"and Jupiter"—he pointed to the taller woman—"are locked together by the embrace of their gravities. Centrifugal force causes them to enlarge their orbit around the Sun." He aimed a hand at Friar Bernard. "Just as they move you students out of their way, Saturn and Jupiter sweep up most of the material near the Sun. As their orbit gets larger, they slow down. Centrifugal force at last flings Jupiter and Saturn into their own orbits of the Sun."

Charles and Cecilia circled the back of the crowd until they faced Paxton.

Paxton stared. Little by little, he moved forward, and then burst into a run. Reaching Cecilia and Charles, he hugged them, clenching the back of their garments, twisting the cloth tightly.

Charles' voice was constrained by Paxton's grip. "We're here to bring you back. We need some place where we can be alone, unseen for less than a minute."

"What took you so long?" Paxton cried. His grasp wanted to meld the three of them into the same space at the same time.

"We thought you died," Charles said. "It took us a long time to figure out what happened."

"Some of us hoped you died." Cecilia winced. "Paxton, you're cutting off my circulation."

Paxton felt a hand rubbing his shoulder. Looking back, he saw Beatrice.

"Are these people from your time?" she asked.

Paxton's throat muscles were too tight for him to speak. He could only nod.

"You want to go with them."

"Paxton, what does she mean 'your time'?" Cecilia managed to cough out. She wedged her hands between her torso and Paxton's, then pushed back.

"First astronomy, now time travel!" Charles squirmed loose of Paton's arm vise. "We've got to leave before you do any lasting damage to the space-time continuum."

"Yes Paxton, leave." A surly voice entered the discussion. "Go back to your world, even if it means soiling your honor."

"Who is this?" Charles said.

Paxton said, "Her name is Catherine."

Cecilia addressed Catherine. "What do you mean 'soiling his honor'?"

Paxton explained. "I've tied myself to the Lady Wilhelmina and her family. I killed a guy, which got her in trouble with his clan. Because of me, she's in trouble with her uncle—well, in deeper trouble. No matter what I do, I make things worse for her and her retinue."

"Our lives would still be in distress without you," Beatrice whispered.

"Yes Lord Paxton, save yourself," Catherine spat.

"We're not here to argue. Let's go." Cecilia brought out the wormhole controller.

"I owe the Lady my life. I promised I would do right by her."

Paxton never spoke like this. Before he was always a Weakly Interacting Massive Particle, thought Cecilia.

"Let's find this Lady." Charles suggested. "I'm sure she'll understand we have to take you home."

"Will you pay Lord Paxton's ransom?" Catherine inquired.

Cecilia said, "Charles, I could scream. This was supposed to be a quick in and out. Either we leave with him now, or I swear there's gonna be a killing. I don't care which choice we make."

213

"Hang on Cecilia. Right now we have too much of an audience. Paxton, those people up there, who are they?" Charles pointed up to the keep.

Paxton shaded his eyes. "The pixie on the left is the Sarah."

"Elizabeth said her twin's name is Isabelle." Charles said. "Does that make the woman in the middle, the Lady?"

"The Lady Wilhelmina," said Paxton.

"Cecilia, we need time for a little privacy to make our escape. Look around, I don't think we have either. It may be best to step back and find a graceful way of departing."

"There's a phrase about leading someone around by the nose; with men it's more about leading them around by their—"

"Sarah and Isabelle left the palisade," Paxton said. "I believe the Lady has decided what will happen next."

"Okay Paxton, talk fast," Charles said.

Paxton started with finding himself in the wormhole, wandering into Alton, the smallpox epidemic, meeting Elizabeth and Isabelle, and Abbot Stephan arresting him for witchcraft. After another minute, he was up to yesterday when Brothers William and Marion arrived in Warren. "They're part of a group of monks headed for Alton. Father Casimir doesn't have enough room in his rectory for all of them so William and Marion are staying in Friar Bernard's chapel until they move on." Paxton paused. Looking impish he said, "Long elevator ride huh?"

"And you managed to take a piss on every floor," Cecilia remarked.

"He did what he needed to do to survive," Beatrice replied.

"Hey, I didn't ask for an opinion from the kindergarten class."

Catherine asked Paxton, "Is kinder garden good or bad?"

"It's an insult," said Charles.

Catherine grabbed Elizabeth's herding staff to threaten Cecilia.

Charles stepped in between the two women. "Cecilia, you manage to tick off people no matter where or when you go." Sarah strode up to Charles. "We have a visitor. Paxton, would you introduce us?"

"Lady Sarah, I present to you Lord Charles and Lady Cecilia."

Charles put a hand over his heart and bowed. "We are honored to be in your presence, Lady Sarah."

Cecilia rolled her eyes and twitchily curtsied.

"The Lady Wilhelmina wishes that you take the noon meal with her. In the meantime, Lord Charles, the twins and Friar Bernard will show you her estate." Sarah looked Cecilia up and down. The nobles of Paxton's time dress like peasants," she said, leaning closer, "yet your fabric is somehow different."

"They're forty percent rayon and sixty percent cotton." Cecilia replied.

"You must come with me and tell me what that means." Sarah held out her hand.

Charles coughed. "We would rather stay with Lord Paxton and have him tell us of his adventures here."

Sarah frowned. "I'm afraid the Lady won't permit that."

"The Lady's smart," said Paxton. "She doesn't know what you have planned, but she's figured out you won't or can't do it if she keeps us separate."

"In that case we would be honored to do lunch." Cecilia made another clumsy curtsy. "And I would love to tell her of permanent press, no iron, dry-clean-only garments."

Paxton had advised that William and Marion were new to the castle and knew nothing of his origins. During the meal, Charles couched his language in terms of returning Paxton to his fiefdom on the continent.

"What ransom will Lord Albert be willing to pay?" The Lady asked.

Cecilia looked down the table at Paxton. "Is there anything or anyone you haven't shot your mouth off about?"

215

"Be careful how you speak." Charles nodded to William and Marion.

"They're more interested in spiking peas with their new toys. Hey bros," Cecilia shouted to the brothers. She thrust her fork up and down. "Be careful not to fork yourselves, or each other."

"How long would it take for Lady Cecilia to return to Lord Albert?" The Lady asked.

Charles cast a wary eye to the brothers. "About a minute."

"How long is that?"

Paxton spoke up. "He means as long as it takes to say two Our Fathers."

"If the Lady Cecilia returns from her travels with the ransom, I will release Lord Paxton from his duty to me." They finished the meal and servants disassembled the trestle table on the dais. "Lord Charles, I would like to visit Lord Albert in his time."

"I'm afraid Lord Albert would never permit it."

"Very well. For now our business is concluded."

The guard from the tower entered. "My lady, a herald has announced that your uncle, Duke Alphonso and Ignatius are in Warren, and will be here in the hour."

"This castle is receiving more visitors than Sarah's apartment during the Maypole festival," said the Lady.

Sarah made a sour face when the Lady turned away.

"Lord Paxton, prepare my people and the Great Hall to receive my uncle," directed Lady Wilhelmina.

When Duke Alphonso and Ignatius arrived, Paxton directed them around the ceremonial fire. The Lady's company arranged themselves in two rows on the other side. Charles and Cecilia stood in the middle of the back row. The Lady and Sarah sat on the dais. The Lady had her pashmina cloak wrapped around her.

"Lady Wilhelmina, may I present—"

Duke Alphonso pushed Paxton away. "There is no need for introductions between uncle and niece."

"Welcome, uncle… by marriage."

His face was as cold as a winter night. "Lady Wilhelmina, you do me wrong."

The Lady rose left the dais, and knelt before the duke, her arms crossed in front of her. With her head bowed low, she replied, "Duke Alphonso, if I have wronged you, then before God and this company I ask your forgiveness."

"It has come to my attention that you say I do not stop whispers about your husband's death. Of course there are whispers. People would not dare speak such calumny to my face. Without your presence, stopping such whispers is like trying to catch the wind with a fishnet."

The reminder of her husband's death caused the lady's face to freeze.

The duke paced before the Lady. "You complain that I raise your taxes. Yet you would rather pay taxes than heed the entreaties of your aunt to return to Banburn."

The Lady fixed her stare on a scratch on the floor.

The duke pointed at Paxton. "This foreigner and some women stand accused of sorcery. You hide them here in Sandalburg. Bring them to the church. I stand on my oath I will do all I can to protect them. The lairds of the north array themselves against you. Come with me. I will give you sanctuary."

The duke faced the Lady and crossed his arms over his chest. "Lady Wilhelmina, your husband gave you this estate as a legacy, but he is dead. I have a daughter who is about to be married to Ignatius. Doesn't your cousin deserve a legacy at least as great as your husband bequeathed to you? I am too poor to divide my fiefdom smaller."

He held out an arm. "Ignatius will stay here with the servants I have given him. Come back and help your cousin prepare for her wedding.

Come with me, and bring your servants with you. I will give you honor and glory." The duke now held out both hands. "Come with me on the morrow back to Banburn castle and Yorkshire."

"No." In the silence the Lady's whisper filled the Great Hall.

She rose and flung open her cloak. "My husband left me another legacy." She placed her hands at the top of her belly, then used her left hand to trace the expanding curve of her abdomen. A gasp rose from the crowd. "Early on the day of his death he left me with his last gift." The Lady's voice turned to stone. "His child will grow up on my estate and will never be subject to the dominion of his father's murderer."

Now blind to everyone in attendance, she screamed, "Get out of here. Get out! Get out! Get out!" Her body shook uncontrolled and uncontrollable.

Without hesitation, Sarah, Beatrice, Catherine, and the twins rushed to the Lady. Sarah supported her on one side, Beatrice on the other. Elizabeth and Isabelle stood in front and Catherine in front of them all.

Faced with this phalanx of Spartan-like women, Duke Alphonso, this new Xerxes, bowed and turned to leave. When he and Ignatius passed in front of the Lady's servants, he stopped. Pushing through the front rank, the duke found Charles and Cecilia. "You are new here."

"They are merchants from the continent," Paxton called out.

Cecilia's bodcam caught the duke's attention. He fondled it, pointing the lens at his face.

"Hab sosli' Quch." *(Klingon. Your mother has a smooth forehead.)* Cecilia growled it through gritted teeth.

The duke raised his eyebrows and backed off.

Alphonso and Ignatius exited through the covered staircase to the bailey, and went to where their servants held their horses. Before the duke could mount his horse, one of the monks ran up and knelt before him.

With one hand raised out and palm flat up, he cried. "Alms, my Lord. Alms for a poor soldier of the Christ."

The duke made an X on the ground with one foot and spat on the middle of it. He mounted his horse and rode off.

Brother William looked at his empty palm. *No alms.*

Returning to the chapel, Brother Marion met him.

"Did you see the duke?"

"Yes."

"Did he say anything?"

"Tonight."

Chapter 24

The Lady sat on the edge of the dais, and rocked herself. "Paxton, ride after my uncle. Tell him to come back tomorrow for the noon meal. When you find him, take note who is traveling with him."

She turned to see Gunther. "Gunther, go with Lord Paxton. See to it he returns, riding his horse or laid across it. I would prefer the former, but I will accept the later."

She lifted herself up and marched toward the scriptorium. "Lord Charles and Lady Cecilia will remain here with Friar Bernard. The women will come with me. The rest of you, return to your duties."

When they arrived in the scriptorium, the Lady faced the women and rested the back of her waist against the desk. "Paxton's friends have made it clear Lord Albert of Yorkshire will not grant me sanctuary. His friends want to leave us, taking Paxton with them. Lord Paxton will not leave because he has bound himself to my family and me. Duke Alphonso expects to meet with me at tomorrow's main meal." She paused, "Everyone will be disappointed."

The Lady told them of her plan. She spoke of the danger that waited for her and to each of the assembled women if her plan failed. She told them of possible dangers if her plan succeeded. "I will explain this to my confessor before we go to sleep. If any do not want to come with me, you may face my uncle and Ignatius yourselves."

"Charles and Cecilia may try to spirit Lord Paxton away in the middle of the night. I will therefore keep them all separate. Charles will stay with Friar Bernard in the sacristy in the back of the chapel. The two monks, William and Marion will sleep in the chapel proper. Cecilia will sleep in the cottage next to the chapel. Catherine, Elizabeth, and Isabelle, you will be with her through the night. Beatrice, Lord Paxton's cottage is next. You will see to it he does not leave."

"How am I to do that?"

"When he renounced his loyalty to Lord Albert and pledged his loyalty to me he exposed that you took his heart. It should be no trouble to take the rest of him."

Beatrice's soft voice did not mask the iron in her words. "Maybe I have not committed my heart to him."

"Then lie back and think of your duty. Lord Paxton would enjoy your company. Whether you enjoy his is up to you."

The Lady led them back to the Great Hall. "Lord Charles, I would like to speak with you in private."

She glanced at Cecilia. "Lady Sarah, perhaps you could find something more ladylike for Lady Cecilia to wear."

"I will take you to the solar." Sarah clutched Cecilia's hands in hers. "Let me show you some tunics with wonderful embroidery."

Cecilia sighed, "Lady Sarah, I wish I could show you some tunics with Velcro and zippers."

"Walk with me Lord Charles." The Lady proceeded around the dying embers of the ceremonial fire. "I will give you Lord Paxton after next morning's Mass."

"Why not let us leave when he returns?"

The Lady walked in silent thought, and finally spoke. "Let me find out what Lord Paxton has to say about my uncle and his entourage. I do not want to release him, only to find it is to my disadvantage to do so."

They reached the walkway that circled the keep. Lady Wilhelmina took in the view toward Warren. In the distance, she saw two figures on horseback approaching the town. "If I release him now, it may happen that my uncle may hear of it. I will not take the chance of anyone knowing what I will do. Not before it becomes necessary."

"Paxton has renounced his loyalty to… uhm… Lord Albert. Do you think he will deny his allegiance to you?"

The Lady moved sideways to keep the two equestrians in sight. "I have made arrangements to insure his compliance."

Losing sight of Paxton and Gunther, she scanned the bailey for Friar Bernard.

"Will Gunther kill Paxton if he feels it necessary?" Charles asked.

"I gave that order so that Lord Paxton may take proper precautions to avoid capture," the Lady said. "I intend to upset whatever plans my uncle has. I want no one upsetting mine."

The girlish laughter of two voices came from the second floor solar. Charles raised his head. "I have never heard Cecilia laugh like that before."

The Lady faced Charles. "My lady-in-waiting can make a serpent speak." Lady Wilhelmina leaned out against the palisade. "Her nature knows no malice. In my most melancholy times she can take hold of my spirit and make it soar."

"Well, don't you look ladylike." Charles grinned as Cecilia skipped across the courtyard. Her ankle-length, close-fitting gown, sported full-length sleeves, with a silver sash around her waist. "What other fashion tips have you women exchanged?"

"You first. What have you and the Lady W talked about while I've been cooped up with Sarah for hours?"

"She's agreed to let us take back Paxton tomorrow after Mass. After everyone leaves for breakfast, Lady W, as you call her, and the friar, will bolt the front and back doors of the chapel. The stained glass windows will prevent anyone from seeing inside. We pop open the wormhole, go home, close the hole, and they leave the chapel."

Cecilia guided them to the blacksmith shop. "I thought Paxton is loyal to her?"

"She seems to have that covered. How, I don't know."

"I don't trust her."

"This isn't a matter of trust Cecilia. It's a matter of getting the job done."

Cecilia peered into the smithy. "What do you think Albert's doing?"

"We have the EHEC reserved for three days, and the Jubilee is coming up. No one should be bothering him. People can sleep in shifts, in the break pod. There's plenty of food in the vending machines."

"Much of it since the last time Great Britain won the World Cup."

Cecilia led Charles into the iron works. "You know we're being watched."

Charles looked out the window. Catherine and the twins faced the smithy. Catherine rested her back on a railing. Elizabeth and Isabelle sat on their haunches. "That reminds me. Lady W made sleeping arrangements' for us. I'm to sleep in the chapel with the friar and the two monks. You will have the next cottage over with Catherine, Elizabeth, and Isabelle."

"What about Paxton?"

"She didn't say. It's apparent she doesn't want to take the chance of us sneaking out at night."

"If she's willing to let us go, why not just do it at night?"

Charles examined some of John's tools. "They're a product of their time as we are of ours. They won't think of starting to travel at night, or without first going to Mass. What did you learn from Sarah?"

Cecilia fondled a piece of the gown between a finger and thumb. "This is nice. I think I'll wear it back home." She smoothed out the fabric. "Sarah acts like a ditz, but it's just that, an act."

"Paxton's back." Charles said, glancing out the doorway. "He's going up the covered stairway. Gunther is taking the horses to the stable."

"What's next?"

Charles shrugged. "Evening meals, more prayers, sleep, Mass. Maybe they're right. Prayers are like chicken soup, can't hurt."

Sarah had laid out the Lady's nightgown on the bed. After the Lady undressed, she picked up the nightgown and handed it back to Sarah. "No garment tonight Sarah."

She watched as the Lady's pearlescent skin slipped between sheets and fur blanket. She knew what would happen. Sometime in the night, the dreamscape would begin. Occasionally there would be screaming and bitter recriminations. Other times words as soft as the silk they brought from Banburn, or there would be laughter, like two children at play. No matter what the play, it always had the same two actors, one in flesh, the other in spirit, and ended the same way. The Lady's arms would thrust upward, hands grasping for someone who couldn't remain, and then wailing, and her own deathlike sleep.

"Sleep well, my lady." Sarah pulled the blanket up to the Lady's neck and bent to kiss her forehead. After closing the Lady's bed curtains, she went to her own curtained bed to prepare to sleep.

Sleep well indeed. How I hate that woman! Sarah scowled. *I've come to like the phrase the duke uses to describe her, "that woman." I can have any man in Banburn castle, from the youngest stable boy to*

Duke Alphonso himself. Sarah wiped her lips with the back of her hand at that thought. *I wrap up with flesh and blood to warm me. How much warmth do you get from a spirit?*

Sarah put on her own nightclothes, blew out the candle, and closed her curtains. She pounded the pillow before settling her head, trying to relax her mind for sleep. *The only person I hate more than you is... myself, for being jealous of you.*

Beatrice finished getting Paxton's bed ready. "Will there be anything else Lord Paxton?"

Paxton smiled. "Why so formal? I thought we agreed on just Paxton."

"Your friends will be leaving soon. Will you leave with them?"

"I am obligated to the Lady."

Beatrice swallowed hard. "Is that why you stay?"

"That is why I have to stay."

She wrung her hands. "Do you want to stay?"

Paxton hesitated. "No I don't want to stay... but I want to know other things before I go. I want to know other things about you."

Beatrice sat on the edge of the bed. "What would you want to know about me?"

Paxton sat next to her. Tentatively, he stroked her hair, a gesture she permitted "I want to know you are safe. I want to know you are respected."

"Respected?"

"I want everyone else to see you as I see you."

"How is that?"

"You were never just a prostitute. You engaged in prostitution to survive, but you are more than that. You love and take care of your husband and children, even at their graves. You kept your cottage in good order. That tells me of your self-discipline. That takes a strong person. Even when I attempted to… assault you, you forgave me. That takes a good woman. You perform your duties them with a quiet efficiency."

Beatrice shook her head. "What is efficiency?"

Paxton smiled again. "It means you are good at what you do. You are a good woman. I don't want to leave until I know everyone sees you like that."

Beatrice stood up and turned her back on Paxton. "Then you know nothing of me. Do you know why I was sent here?"

Paxton looked at the bed. "Well, you turned back the blankets. You warmed the bed with the bed warmer while I stood in the far corner. I haven't come near you." His voice wavered.

Beatrice faced him. "The Lady wants me to make sure you do not leave in the night with your friends."

"Well if that was what she wanted, she could have had Gunther stay here. He's been looking for an excuse to put an arrow in my back since we left the castle."

"I am also to find out where your loyalty lies, and what your own plans are."

Paxton swallowed. "How are you to do that?"

Beatrice walked to Paxton, put her hands on her knees, and bent forward, letting him see down her cleavage. "By any means necessary."

"Oh." Paxton let the expression hang there. "Well fuck that shit!" He marched to the door, then turned around and marched back. "I've got half a mind to kick your arse out of here. Then I'll go up to the keep and kick the Lady's arse."

"Why?"

"Haven't you been listening? You're a good woman!"

"Paxton, I asked if you knew why I was sent here. I didn't tell you why I came."

Now it was Paxton's turn. "Why?"

Beatrice went back to the bed. "You gave me something I haven't received in a long time, and you gave it at great cost to yourself. You gave me the respect of which you speak. When my husband was alive, sometimes there was a joining of our loins for the simple pleasure of it. Other times there was also a joining of our hearts and souls. Paxton, I do not know if I will continue to see you, but if I don't, please for one night let me relive a happier time."

"Friar Bernard, please, I insist, and you are too old to resist." Charles pushed the old man back down on the bed and removed the sandals from his gnarled feet. "I will take the bedding on the floor." He looked at the hay and blankets strewn on the floor.

"Thank you, my son," the friar wheezed.

"How long have you been with Lady Wilhelmina?"

"I had the privilege of baptizing her." The old man coughed. "God has granted me the blessing of a long life. I wonder why He blesses me so. Don't grow old my son."

Charles kicked at some hay. "What is the other choice? How old are you?"

"I am fifty and three years of age."

I'm older than you are. Charles examined the sacristy. *We have the physical details right, but we know nothing of the texture of these people's lives.* "Do you have any regrets?"

"Only that I will not see the Lady Wilhelmina to the end of her voyage."

Charles looked around. "Where are William and Marion?"

"They are sitting outside the chapel enjoying God's night."

"You are a holy man. Friar. May I ask one favour of you? Your blessing, please."

Catherine sat with her back against the wall. "Lady Cecilia, Lord Paxton has told us that you have carriages that move without horses. Is that so?"

Cecilia tried to get comfortable on the lumpy, matted bed. *How does Paxton endure this?* "Yes."

"Then you have no horses?"

"There are horses, but they are ridden mostly in competition or for pleasure."

"Oh? Do women ride?"

"Of course."

"How do they ride?"

"What do you mean?"

"Do you have separate saddles for women?"

"You mean side saddles? Only for some exhibitions, I suppose. Otherwise they ride the same as men do. Do you like to ride?"

Catherine said wryly, "When you ride in a woman's saddle, you feel like cargo in the hold of a ship. When you ride like a man, you are like the helmsman at a ship's tiller. You go where you want, not where you are taken."

"Too bad you can't come with us."

Catherine stared.

"Hi ya, hi ya." Elizabeth, curled up on the floor next to the bed, called out in her sleep.

Isabelle, sleeping next to the door, set her feet moving and swished her herding staff.

"What do you think they're dreaming of?" Cecilia asked.

"Herding cattle of course." Catherine leaned forward. "Mooooo."

"Hi ya, hi ya," two voices murmured.

"Do they always do things together?"

"If possible," Catherine replied. "If the Lady sends them into Warren, one will go to the miller, the other to the baker. One will do business at the cobbler, the other the milliner."

"Sleep well, Lady Cecilia."

"Sleep tight Catherine." *Don't let the bed bugs bite.* Cecilia sat up wide-awake. "Catherine, you take the bed."

Paxton lay on his stomach with a hand between Beatrice's breasts. I can feel her heart beating. He rolled onto his back to stare into the darkness. Now I know why she builds her roof so tight. If she didn't, her snoring would bring it down on top of her.

Paxton got up. Going to the barn, he spotted the two monks. Sneaking around the backs of buildings, he entered the barn. Finding a shovel, he dug a hole, just deep enough. In it, he put keys and fob, cell phone, lighter, Swiss Army knife, handkerchief, wallet, and the pound and pence coins. In his wallet were credit cards, driver's license, photos of him, Mary Jane, him and Mary Jane, National Health Insurance card, library card, shopper's club card, and money. The laser pointer and his ID badge for the project. Everything. He filled in the hole and returned to his cottage. *I'm staying here, with Beatrice.*

William and Marion sat on either side of the chapel door. William observed the pale white-and-grey crescent creep over the castle's curtain wall. After the moon's bottom edge scaled the wall he turned to his stout, sleeping companion. "Marion!" He hissed. Marion awoke looking up at the taller man. William got up to take off his grey habit. Marion did the same, revealing the chain mail vests of knights, and tabards with the emblem of Duke Alphonso. The knights moved quickly to the gate.

They saw no lights or movement. Marion grabbed his partner's tabard, and pointed to the moon. A meteor hit it. The earth's atmosphere caused a spectacular display. The moon's upper horn appeared split in two. From the midpoint of the division, a flaming torch sprang up, spewing out fire, hot coals, and sparks. The body of the moon, which was below, writhed as if in anxiety. The moon throbbed like a wounded snake.

"William, this is a sign of an evil enterprise. We will return to the chapel and beg God's forgiveness."

William kicked Marion's rear end. "Yes it is an omen. An omen of the destruction of an evil woman."

They reached the windlasses on either side of the vertical gate. The great oak doors could not swing inward without the iron gate fully raised. Grabbing one of the dowels on his windlass, William checked that Marion did the same. He gave a nod and they hauled on the mechanisms.

Click-clack.

The pawls rose and fell in the toothed wheels.

Click-clack.

The toothed gate was almost out of the stone base.

"Hold! What goes on there?" The voice of the night watchman called out from his crow's nest at the midpoint of the lintel. Now his footsteps thundered on the overhead walkway.

Click-clack.

The watchman carrying his torch came down the stairs and approached the men. "What are you doing? Stop it." He saw the monks in their true form. "Knights!" He ran for the covered walkway.

"Keep at it," William told his friend. William took off after the watchman. He followed the light like a bat after a firefly. Up the stairs he went, taking two at a time.

Click-clack.

Raising one side of the gate, it tilted and jammed in the sash. Marion went to the other side.

230

Click-clack.

The gate leveled.

Click-clack.

Now that side tilted upward and jammed.

William drew his dagger and bounded upward. Soon the watchman would be in death's grip. Now the uneven depth, height, and width of the steps played their lethal trick. William tripped and fell to the stone pavement below, never to rise again.

The watchman burst onto the keep's palisade. Rounding the outside of the keep, he charged up the outside stairs to the Lady's apartment. Running into the bedroom, he ripped open the curtains of the first bed he saw. He thrust in his torch and shook the woman. Sarah screamed. *Wrong Lady.* He went to the other bed. He opened the curtains. The Lady, wakened by Sarah's scream, sat up. The watchman opened the curtains. She covered herself with her bear fur blanket.

Click-clack.

Click-clack.

The man-made sound cracked the silent night.

"Monks." The man shook his head so hard his jowls almost slapped the opposite sides of his face. He made up and down motions with his hands. "Knights, raising gate."

The Lady instantly took command. "Wake up Lord Paxton, Beatrice is with him. Lady Cecilia is in Catherine's cottage with the twins. Have them all go to the chapel. Wake Friar Bernard and Lord Charles. Then wake the other servants. Rally them and do not allow the gate to be opened. Go!"

Click-clack.

Click-clack.

Each sound ripped away part of the Lady's safety.

"Lady Sarah, help me get dressed." Afterward Lady Wilhelmina pulled a small iron chest from under her bed. They hurried down the outside steps and stopped at the palisade. "Sarah, we must use Catherine's way. If we use the stairs, my uncle will be upon us." She dropped her treasury over the wall.

Click-clack.

Click-clack.

The curtain was rising on the duke's plan.

Sarah ran to the wall to watch the box disappear in the darkness. "No, my lady. It is too dangerous for you. The hill is steep and the ground below hard."

The lady stepped back. "You are right." Now she moved behind Sarah. "I would need something soft to land on." With that, she bent down, wrapped her arms around Sarah's knees, and pitched her over the fence. Now the lady struggled to get herself over the breach. Heaving one leg to the outside, she tried to touch the hill with her foot, and rolled over the wall. Kicking, clawing, she fought gravity. Digging her heels into the incline, she at last hit something solid. The lady kicked it. *My treasure box.* Crabbing to the side, she felt solid ground. Picking up her treasure, she hissed, "Sarah. Sarah!"

Click-clack.

Click-clack.

The lady shrieked. As if shouting could blot out the danger.

A figure fountained up in the darkness. "Here I am, my lady. My head aches. I am—I am—"

"Sarah, can you walk? Come on."

Click-clack.

Click-clack.

Higher.

Wilhelmina put Sarah's arm over her shoulder and helped her. By the time they got to the chapel, candles were burning. Elizabeth, Isabelle, and Bernard stood outside. "Take Sarah inside, and then take your positions. Come, Friar."

"Lady Wilhelmina, I am too old. I cannot go."

"Please Friar. I cannot leave without the church."

"No my Lady," he wheezed. "Too old."

Click-clack.

Click-clack.

The Lady fell to her knees at the sound. She seized the friar's robes. "I beg you. A blessing Friar. Not for myself, but for my child."

He laid a hand on her head. "What do you name do you this child?"

"I pray for a son, that he may have his father's name. Peter."

"What do you ask of God's church for Peter?"

"Baptism," she wailed.

"You have asked to have your child baptized. Do you clearly understand what you are undertaking?"

"I do." She buried her face in his garments.

"The church welcomes Peter with great joy. In its name I claim you for Christ our Savior by the sign of His cross."

The Lady pulled back, mouth agape, startled not by what she heard, but by what she didn't hear. The gate was raised. A flood of knights came roaring in. Her mouth and eyes were as wide open as the gate that was letting the terror in.

"Now go." The friar lifted her up. "Close the the door and throw the bolt. I will give you what protection the church can offer." The old man faced the horde racing through the vertical wood lips. Taking a cruciform stance, he cried out in a voice not used since his youth. "Datum est sanctuarium." *(Sanctuary is given.)*

The declaration of sanctuary stopped the knights charge. Just because the knights' feet stopped moving forward, however, didn't mean the knights' motion stopped. Knights piled on top of knights.

Duke Alphonso was to the right of the horde. Ignatius was to its left. Ignatius lifted two knights from the pile. "Go to the back door. Do not enter, but make sure no one leaves."

Alphonso stormed past Bernard. "I come to pray," he said with blood red lips.

"You prey as a wolf does," spate Bernard.

Alphonso pushed on the door. It didn't yield. His fury took him back to the pile of knights. Using a lantern one of them had dropped, he found the weapon he wanted.

The Lady's strained voice spoke to Charles. "Do your magic now."

Charles pulled the "garage door opener," as the scientists called it, from a pocket. With a couple of clicks, he opened the wormhole.

The women screamed in terror as a milk-white circular veil appeared before them. Looking at it from its side, it disappeared. From its back it seemed to be a smoke-grey window.

"I will not leave you!" Paxton shouted. He whispered to Beatrice, "Any of you."

Seeing her assailants in position, the Lady held out her treasure box. "Lord Paxton. What do I hold in my hands?"

This was the signal. With Paxton's attention on the box, two herding sticks crashed on his head from opposite sides. He sank to the floor.

"I've wanted to do something like that for some time," Cecilia muttered.

"If each of you take an ankle it will be easier to pull him away." The Lady said.

Charles and Cecilia bent down, took an ankle and dragged Paxton back. The women again cried out as the bodies of the threesome disappeared in the veil of time.

"Pray, children." The Lady commanded.

"Pater noster qui es in caelis, sanctificetur nomen tuum;" *(Our Father who art in heaven, hallowed be thy name;)*

Albert! We, we have a stable wormhole," Marie reported through the speakerphone.

I'm getting increasing energy draw from the reactor," Max said.

"Quantum gravity field suggests a mass in the wormhole equivalent to Charles, Cecilia, and a little less than we assumed for Paxton," Isaac said.

"He may have lost some mass," Niels chimed in. "Bosons and tachyons are in limits."

Albert leaned forward to the speakerphone. "Remember the shutdown protocol." When the time travelers stepped out of the Bottle, all data and pods had to be buttoned up before everyone could meet in the Bottle Room.

"...sed libera nos a malo." (...but deliver us from evil.)

The duke swung the war hammer at the door. A barrage of wood flechettes now exploded into the chapel. Amidst screams of panic, an iron latch dropped to the floor. The door was breached.

Chapter 25

"Niels!" Max shouted.

"I see it." Niels replied. "Isaac!"

"I know. The increasing tachyon flow is sustaining the quantum gravity field, so far."

"Albert! Are they out yet?" Max asked, keeping his voice under control.

"No."

Marie came on line. "In a few seconds the safety interlocks will shut down the—"

"Remove all the safety interlocks," Albert ordered.

Max protested, "If we remove the interlocks and run out of anti-Helium 3—"

"Remove the safety interlocks," Albert snapped.

"Tachyon flow has stopped increasing. The anti-Helium 3 drain is still too high," Niels cried.

Isaac's sweat flash-flooded him down to his socks. "The quantum gravity field is holding an additional 356,785 grams of matter. Be advised I'm changing the odds of this experiment being concluded successfully."

"Are you trying to change the odds after the race has started? Would Andrea approve?" Marie asked.

"Who's Andrea?" Albert asked her.

"Isaac's bookie."

Duke Alphonso kept wielding the war hammer. Battering the door and bolt sent the wood shrapnel straight into the chapel. Flailing at the door he broke off the iron latch. He pushed the door open an inch. It refused to open anymore. The iron latch slipped under the door bottom. As the door opened, it moved against a wider portion of the latch. The latch slid forward on the stone floor until it hit the next stone. This slightly higher stone stopped the latch and halted door's movement.

The duke screamed, "You rank," he hit the door with a fist, "rough-hewn," he used both fists, "hugger-mugger." He hit it with a shoulder. He stepped back, and standing on one foot, he kicked the door. For every action there is an equal and opposite reaction. When the door did not yield, it sent a force, equal to the duke's kick, back up his tibia and into his knee. The duke roared as he clutched his knee and hopped on one foot.

Max's tension eased up a little. The energy drain from the reactor lowered as if his three teammates had left the wormhole.

Albert ran from his system console. Cecilia and Charles dragged Paxton off the bottom disc and into the centre of the Bottle Room pod.

"Cecilia, Charles, what happened?" Charles, Cecilia, and Albert knelt over Paxton's unmoving form.

"He banged his head on a stone floor." Cecilia looked back. "Albert, why is the wormhole still open?"

"Albert," Charles said urgently. "Paxton's not coming around."

"Focus, you two," Albert yelled. "There is an anomaly. There's still mass in the wormhole. Before we act, I need information. Where the three of you followed by a cow or a horse, or something else?"

The duke stood there, willing with his eyes for the door to burst into flames. When that didn't work, he turned to his knights, as still as stones. They long ago learned that when the duke was enraged, not to attract his attention.

"Well!" He snapped. En masse, they charged the door.

Albert ran back to the console. "Hold the wormhole open." Albert's voice came over the speakerphone anticipating Max's move.

Max's palm paused over the **SCRAM** button that would cause an emergency shutdown of the reactor.

Cecilia turned to the rip in space-time. Her face turned deathly pale and she whispered. "Oh my God."

His knights relieved the door of its final resistance. The duke now pushed them aside to open it completely, and announce his victory.

Max saw the energy drain drop to an empty wormhole state. *No time for approval.* He smashed his palm on the **SCRAM** button.

The duke stepped across the threshold, then stepped back. Instinctively he put his hands to his ears. A light flashed in the chapel. It was there, quick as lightning, and then gone.

No thunder. Lightning that is this close must have ear-splitting thunder.

Instead, there was only silence. Light streamed into the chapel from behind the duke. Someone gave him the lantern. He marched into the chapel, swinging the lantern. The light went left, right, up, down, forward, and back.

"Where are they?"

The duke checked under the altar. He examined the roof. *Solid.* He opened the door to the sacristy. There was a table, a bed, but no people. He unbolted the rear door and opened it. The two knights, sent to guard against escape from the rear, withdrew their swords when they saw the duke.

"Where are they?"

"Sire, no one has left since we arrived."

The duke bolted the door. *The door can be bolted only from inside.*

The duke's tantrum was worthy of the most petulant two-year-old. "All of you, go, find them, and bring them to me."

Helped by Ignatius, the old friar shuffled past the duke and collapsed on his bed.

"You!" The duke thrust out an index finger.

Ignatius tiptoed away from Friar Bernard.

"You are her confessor. You tried to stop me from entering. Where is that woman?"

Bernard looked at the bolted rear door. "I remember what Paxton told the Lady and me in this chapel." He turned his head and smiled at the duke. "I believe—"

"Yes, yes! You believe what?"

"I believe they are all in Konectic."

Chapter 26

The team members completed their tasks in their respective pods. After shutting down their equipment, they ran to the Bottle Room. They first saw Cecilia and Charles attending an unconscious Paxton. Then they noticed the other group. The medieval women stood just off the wormhole's floor disc. The team crowded together. Like rival teenage gangs, each group watched the other in an anxious, uncertain way.

"Albert," whispered Niels. "Who are these women, and why are they here?"

Albert threw his unlit pipe in a trash bin. "Everyone expects me to have all the bloody answers. I don't." Staggering against the systems console, he grabbed his shaking legs. "You people are the brightest I could gather together. I need help. Give it to me." He blinked back tears.

Cecilia went to the medieval women. Making soothing motions with her hands, she said, "It's all right. You're with friends, but what are you doing here?"

Lady Wilhelmina clutched her treasure box close to her. "You know we are in danger. Some of us are in danger of imprisonment, some in danger of death, or the danger only women face." The Lady shrugged. "When you left, we followed."

The women trembled together. "Suns. Small suns in the ceiling," Catherine said.

Charles shaded Paxton's eyes with a hand then pulled it away. "Albert, Paxton isn't responding." Charles went to the front of the systems console. Picking up the phone, he said, "He's breathing, that's all I know. I'll call 999. Max, help me carry Paxton to a lift. We'll wait for the ambulance outside." He put his hand on Albert's shoulder. "It'll be okay."

"No." Isaac said suddenly. "I'll go with Max. I'm closest to Paxton's age, height, weight. When we got a chance to look at his health files after he… died, I noticed he had the same blood type as me. He'll need a health insurance card at hospital. We'll call him Isaac."

Sarah went over to Cecilia and whispered in her ear.

Cecilia looked at the trembling women. "Marie, you want to help me escort these women to the loo?"

Marie reassured the women, "It's going to be okay. Let's go with Cecilia."

Heads nodding, the six voices chirped back, "Okay, okay."

"Albert, can you shut down the Bottle Room?" Niels asked. Albert nodded. "Charles, you and I can help Isaac and Max carry Paxton as far as lift three. That's closest to the loo."

Isaac and Max each grabbed a leg, while Niels and Charles each lifted a shoulder and supported Paxton's head.

"Charles how did you and Cecilia get him through the wormhole?" Max asked.

"We each took hold of an ankle and pulled him through."

"What do we do about the women?" Albert muttered as he trailed behind the clumsy parade.

Reaching lift three, Isaac hit the call button with an elbow. "We can't leave them down here. The Oversight Board's team will want a tour tomorrow."

The lift's doors opened. After Max and Isaac struggled in with Paxton, Isaac hit the button for the ground floor. "Good luck," Niels said as the doors closed. He leaned on a wall. "Albert you don't look so good. You all right?"

"Sure." The voice came from an exhausted soul.

Niels turned to Charles. "Those women are here indefinitely. We have two choices: a closed enclosure or an open enclosure."

Charles raised a finger. "Technically, they are here for an indeterminate time, not an indefinite time. The point is they have to be placed in a restricted environment, like a jail, or military base, or naval ship."

"Or an open enclosure," said Niels. "Hotel rooms, rent a house in the country, maybe the University president's house. His place is big."

"No," said Albert. "We take them to my house. When we get topside I'll call my wife. Tell her to take the mattresses off the beds in our room and the spare room. Three women can sleep in each room. We'll take the futon in the parlor. Anyone who wants to stay can sleep on a couch, or love seat, or chair, or floor."

Niels tilted his head. "For a short time that may work. What will you tell Mileva?"

"I'll say they are students from… Canada." Albert's voice firmed up. "They are undergraduate and graduate students engaged in an experiment. What would it be like for medieval people finding themselves living in the 21st century?" Albert drew in a deep breath. "One more thing; this is very important. Make sure these women understand they are not staying here. The first chance we get they are going back. Make sure you repeat that, and they understand that."

Charles walked across the hall to the women's restroom. "I'm going to find out what is going on in there." He knocked on the door. In a few moments, the door opened a crack. Seeing it was Charles, Marie opened the door a little wider. "How are things going?" he asked.

"We're having a few challenges."

"Look, Albert's just getting his footing back. What kind of challenges?"

Marie grumbled. "They're having fun with the virtues of flush toilets, mirrors, and running water." Giggles and squeals came from inside.

"We have to leave." Charles said. "Someone from the ambulance or hospital may call campus security for more details. We don't want to be around to add any complications."

It was a wild hour before they all reached Albert's house: telling the women to sit on the floor of the lift, explaining to them that they would feel a pressure as the lift started to rise, dividing them into groups of two to a vehicle, encouraging them to close their eyes in the vehicles to avoid possible motion sickness. Squeals and shrieks came from the women as they opened, then covered their eyes, or the eyes of their companions. Lower and lower, some tried to hide in the foot wells. Catherine and the twins pressed their faces against the windows. Albert raced on ahead to prepare his house and wife for their guests.

"They won't recognize half the foods we eat," Charles said, just before leaving. "I'll buy a lot of oatmeal and meat pies."

Cecilia and Marie decided the women needed baths and clean clothes when they got to Albert's house.

"Where are the rest of their clothes?" Mileva, a head taller and twice as wide as Albert, asked Marie.

"The airline lost their luggage."

"For all of them?"

"Yes," she hissed.

"Well, they'll have to make do with some of Albert's dress shirts, a couple of bathrobes, and what clean pajamas I can find to fit them."

Albert and Niels threw sheets and blankets on the mattress and box springs from the bed in the spare room. "Albert, this is nuts. Do you know what fired me up to get Paxton back? I wanted to save my career, my reputation." Niels paused. "And yours, and everyone else's. They're going to reinstate hanging, just for us."

"You're panicking."

"You're damn right I'm panicking. I'll do whatever it takes to survive."

They went into the parlor to make up the futon.

Mileva came up to Albert. "Canadians?" She spat out her suspicions.

Niels looked at her. "Yes, from Whitehorse. Would you believe it?"

"Albert. I went into the bathroom to lay out some clothes for sleepwear. Cecilia was trying to teach, I believe her name is Wilhelmina, how to use shampoo. God knows they look like they never showered. One of them called it "warm rain." Do you know this Wilhelmina, lovely dear, has a crumpet in the oven?"

The plan was for three to a room but the women chose otherwise. Wilhelmina took the bed in the master bedroom. Sarah lay on the mattress on the floor next to her. The twins lay on the mattress in the spare room, while Beatrice and Catherine took the box spring on the bed.

Elizabeth whispered to the others, "Lord Albert is indeed rich. I saw the Lady Mileva open a drawer. You should see all the forks, and she thought nothing of it."

Albert gathered his people in the parlor. "I got a text from Max. They told the people at hospital he, Paxton/Isaac was rehearsing for a play, to explain how he was dressed. Other than that, it was factual that Paxton fell backwards and cracked his head on the floor. He's in critical condition. They're prepping him for surgery. I've texted Oscar. I told him we wouldn't be at the EHEC tomorrow, and please come here in the morning before meeting with the Board's transition team. He'll be here about nine."

Chapter 27

"You did what?" Oscar tried to rocket out of Albert's too comfy armchair. His arms and legs flailed, clawing for traction. He was a raging chimney fire, his face glowing redder and redder. "You idiots. You fools. This is why the Advanced Projects Service formed the Oversight Board. To prevent you people from taking matters in your own hands. This is why the M Theory project was taken away from you. If, when, this gets out, the world will be screaming for us to change history! 'Don't let Lenin ride the train back to Saint Petersburg. Strangle Hitler in his crib. My children died, save them!' Where are these women now?"

Albert shrank into a hard-backed chair as Mileva loomed over him. "Albert, is how long you do you anticipate them staying here?" she asked.

Oscar went barging into different rooms.

"They're not here," Isaac told him. "Nobody really slept last night. At first light, they got up. They wanted to go to church."

"The church up the street has services every morning at eight," Albert said.

"We convinced them to have breakfast first." Isaac resumed his story. "It was interesting trying to explain simple things like oatmeal, tea, even sugar. We presented them with bananas, to cut up in the oatmeal. They tried to eat them without peeling them first. After breakfast we walked to church."

"It's almost ten now. Where are they?" Oscar demanded.

Niels laughed. "They have only the clothes on their backs. Cecilia and Marie took them to the shopping centre."

Oscar sat back down. "I'm going to die. I'm going to die and all of you are going to Broadmoor Hospital."

"When they're in the loony bin, where will the women stay?" Mileva asked Oscar. "I'm not going to mind them."

"I, I believe I may have an answer to that question," Albert stammered. "It's summer. The dorms at the university are mostly empty."

"First things first," Oscar said. "Get those women back here. Everyone stay here. I'm calling the head of the APS for instructions."

Albert's phone rang. He listened, asked a few questions, nodded, and hung up. "That was Charles; Paxton just came out of surgery. He's in a medically induced coma. Charles doesn't know when they'll bring him out of it."

"Putting him in hospital under someone else's name was the only smart thing you people did. What would happen if someone recognized the name? The next race won't be for the bomb, or for outer space. It would be for time restructuring."

"Thank you Oscar," said Niels. "So what's the plan, Albert?"

"If the Oversight Board approves, they can live in the university dorms."

"How soon can this Oversight Board get 'em out of my house?" Mileva rapidly tapped her foot.

"We, we can still call them Canadians." Albert stammered again. "They're here for advanced studies in medieval history." He rummaged in his pipe rack for a pipe with an unchewed stem.

"Get those people back from the shopping centre now!" screamed Oscar.

Max arrived at Albert's house about noon. He walked in as if threading his way between a minefield and quicksand. "What's up?" He asked of no one and everyone.

"Oscar says we're all grounded until we grow up," said Niels. "How's Paxton, and where is Charles?"

"We won't know how Paxton is for maybe as long as a month," said Max. "Charles went back to his apartment to change."

Cecilia and Marie got back about two o'clock with the women and many packages. The medieval women wore new clothes. Their summer dresses were sheathlike and long. Their hands flitted about like nervous butterflies. They were like middle-school girls, for the first time wearing high heels, to their first dance.

"We would have been back sooner if we'd gone where I shop." snapped Cecilia.

Marie put her hands on her hips. "Seriously, Victoria's Secret!"

"I could have been compensated by racking up more points. We ate at the food court, baguettes and brie. On the way back, Lady W made us stop on the highway overlook between here and the shopping centre."

"With no anti-Helium 3 we have nothing but time to get them acclimated to their new world," said Albert.

"But not here," Mileva reminded him.

"Everyone stays put until the Oversight Board says different," Oscar ordered.

"Houston, we have a problem."

"What? What time is it, and what are you talking about?" Albert asked, wiping the sleep off his face. "Keep your voice down. You'll wake Mileva."

"It's six-thirty, Saturday morning, and earlier this morning while we were all sleeping, Charles ran off with the women."

"What do you mean, he ran off with the women? He, they, just got here yesterday. To where?" Albert raised himself on an elbow.

Max shrugged. "I suspected something when he drove up in a full-sized van."

"I guess I'll have to call Oscar again."

When Charles returned late Saturday afternoon, Cecilia let loose a fusillade of langrel. "What were you thinking? Were you thinking?"

"I thought if we are going to be confined, I should do what I needed to do."

"What would that be?" asked Cecilia.

"These women are living history. I took them to the Sandalburg Castle ruins."

Cecilia clutched her stomach. "I'm going to be sick. Where are they now?"

"At church. I promised I'd fetch them and walk them back, after reporting in."

"Did you find out what you wanted?" she asked.

"No. Their initial shock left them all like Lot's wife. The day started out overcast. Funny, the later the morning, the darker the sky got. The women wouldn't let go of each other. Some of them, I don't remember which ones, started crying. The day got colder as the morning went on. The Lady Wilhelmina turned and started screaming at me. 'I hate you. I hate you.' Then her servant Sarah started yelling, 'I hate you.' I thought she was yelling at me, but she was screaming at Lady W. 'You weep for the loss of your position, yet you still have your unborn child. What of Beatrice? She has lost all. What she wouldn't give to hold her children

248

again! You still hold your child, yet you act as though you have lost everything. Ask her for forgiveness. You have everything of importance.'"

Charles paused.

"After that, the women grew silent. Well, not silent, but they wouldn't let me come near. Every time I came within a few metres, the twins raised their herding sticks. Around noon, Catherine came up to me. 'We desire you bring us our noon day meals.' I thought; *Let's start with something simple, Big Macs and Cokes.* They went about picking everything apart, and questioning it sesame seed by sesame seed. Elizabeth said, 'What I wouldn't give for an ox heart.' Isabelle nods and says, 'Or cow's tongue.' Next time, liver and onions. Whatever they talked about, they wouldn't resume until I withdrew.

"In the end, they wound up hugging and stroking each other. They even laughed. Whatever decision they reached, the weather reflected it. The wind picked up and the overcast sky cleared up." Charles fell silent. When he spoke, again it was with an air of resignation. "What I learned of their daily life I could find in any old textbook."

"What did you learn of whatever they agreed to?" Marie asked.

"Nothing."

Mileva got her wish. The Oversight Board got the medieval women assigned to three rooms in a women's dorm. Cecilia and Marie obtained a room across the hall from them. Albert and his men got rooms in the closest men's dorm.

Albert's team surrendered their offices in the EHEC building, and Oscar's team took them over. Albert's team had its life divided into three parts: training Oscar's team, tutoring the women on life and customs of the twenty-first century, and posting someone outside of Paxton's (Isaac's) hospital room.

249

Oscar's team had two duties: learning the M theory project, and examining the women.

Chapter 28

Outside of Credenhill lay Hereford, the headquarters of the 22nd Special Air Services regiment. Oscar presented his credentials at the west entrance and drove east to the T intersection. He made a right and traveled south. On his left, he gave a nod to the regimental clock tower. On it were inscribed the names of those "who have failed to beat the clock." Continuing south to the next T intersection, he made a right and pulled into a parking lot on his right. Across the street from the parking lot, he went to the second building from the east, B, Baker building. Presenting his credentials again, he entered the building and went to Room 101. In this most heavily guarded facility, Oscar sat at a conference table with his superior.

Oscar's superior spoke first. "At the last meeting I asked how the hell Albert's team managed to pull off this incident." She slammed both hands on the table, and then adjusted the sleeves of her pinstripe jacket. Her next question was delivered in a softer voice. "The short term care of these... people. What can you tell me on both topics, Oscar?"

Oscar cleared his throat. "I was assured no use of the antimatter would take place before my team arrived. I consented to only computer simulations. They exceeded their permission. As far as the short-term presence of these women, they are housed on the University of Yorkshire campus."

"Oscar, who knows who they are?"

"Albert's team, Albert's wife, Mileva, my team, the president of the university, and the head of the Physics Department. All of them have been told of their duties under the Official Secrets Act, and the penalties for failure to abide by them."

"New business. What do we do with them?"

Oscar dropped his hands into his lap. "We do what we can. From an historical standpoint, these women are a treasure trove. One of Albert's team"—Oscar looked down at his notes—"Charles, has a degree in medieval history. The women's diverse backgrounds give much insight into daily medieval life. I have acquired a staff that is using the university's facilities to examine their mental and physical health. Another of Albert's team, Marie, has a degree in psychology. This should prove useful as well."

Oscar closed his notebook and looked up. "Madam, I must speak bluntly with you. Long term there is nothing we can do about them. There is no anti-Helium 3 to power the reactions to send them back."

"You're wrong on both counts Oscar. You've told me before about the lack of this antimatter. Another agency has been tasked with obtaining it."

"The James Bond boys?"

"Speaking of which, have you found anyone in Albert's team who might be interested in discreetly working for us?"

"Yes, I have." Oscar pulled out a dossier from his briefcase. "This person is willing to work for us, if discretion can be assured." He handed the dossier to his boss.

"Discretion is not only the better part of valor; it is also the better part of spying. As far as what to do, long term"—Oscar's superior paused—"I must tell you that the Prime Minister is offended about how you have handled this fiasco. Letting these women run wild."

"The perception that these women are running wild is a gross exaggeration. There was a trip to a shopping centre."

"A plan is being considered to take all of our scrambled eggs and put them in one remote basket. The Falklands have come to mind."

"The women might be more comfortable in a more isolated, pastoral environment."

"Not just the women, and not just Albert's team, Oscar."

Chapter 29

"I am in charge. I will have order!" Oscar leaned into the conference room table, the morning sun at his back. "You people have no idea what is at stake here. There will be no more excursions off campus without my permission." He shook a finger at the women. "You're all fortunate I can't send you back right now." He walked behind his chair. "I will not lose my authority or power. Albert, can't you control your people?" He made a sweeping gesture toward Albert's team and the women. "If you can't, I will."

Lady Wilhelmina rose from her chair and knelt before Oscar. She bowed her head and crossed her arms over their opposing shoulders. "Lord Oscar, do not be troubled. I pledge by the holy mother church that neither I, nor those under me will displease you."

Oscar opened his briefcase. "Go back to your seat." He went around the table putting a cell phone, with belt clip, in front of each of the medieval women. Each phone had a label with the woman's name on it. "You will find that I can be a generous master. Do you know what these are?"

The Lady replied, "These are the talking stones that you use."

Oscar grinned. "We call them cell phones. Each phone has a list: my name, Albert's name, the names of his team, and each of your names. Later Albert's team will show you how to use them. I believe you regularly attend morning service in the chapel."

As the women rose the Lady Wilhelmina asked, "Will you join us for Terce services? We pray for Lord Paxton's recovery."

"Believe me, every time I hear of you I raise my voice to God. Albert's team will stay for a little while."

Oscar caught the attention of his own man, playing Sphinx in a corner. He touched the bottom of his eye with an index finger and then pointed to the door. After his man left, he walked to the window to see the distaff train head for chapel with its male caboose in tow.

Oscar turned back to Albert's team. "Let me spell out for you what's going on. Beatrice told Marie that Paxton was teaching at the castle: astronomy, math, reading, writing, etc. Those women are no different from anyone else. It shouldn't take long for them to become addicted to the phones. Every morning at nine, I will go into my office and log into a computer at GCHQ. I'll get a computer-generated transcript of every voice, text, and data message into and out of their phones, and GPS locations, for the preceding twenty-four hours. If anyone snitches, I'll make Broadmoor Hospital look like the Ritz in London. You're dismissed." Oscar picked up some paperwork.

Mary Jane spoke up. "Just one question sir. What about *our* phones?"

"I don't need to tap your phones."

The Lady dug her fingernails into her palms. Striding down the quadrangle to the University's chapel, she slammed the heels of her Christian Louboutin shoes into the sidewalk. "That worthless cur. Strutting about. Did you hear him? 'You're all fortunate I can't send you back right now.' A capon crowing like a rooster."

She strode on. "Catherine, that first morning at the ruins of my estate, you convinced us to move forward, not to look back at the ruins of our past lives. We will behave as good Christen women. 'Plans are established by seeking advice; so if you wage war, obtain guidance.' Proverbs 20:18. We will continue our studies. We will grow in wisdom of this new England's history, mores, and philosophy."

"He says, 'If he could send us back but he cannot.' Remember the words of the Good Book. 'You say, (but they are vain words,) I have counsel and strength.' 2 Kings 18 20-22. He speaks his weakness and knows it not. Oscar plays at being a noble. I learned this game of nobles sitting on my father's knee. Some castles succumb to tunneling, or treachery, or disease and starvation, and some by cunning. When I find out how to defeat castle Oscar I will plunge in the dagger... and twist."

Chapter 30

Emma set her tray down across from her friend Olivia. "Saw the queen loony and her lady-in-waiting today."

Olivia rummaged through her chips. "Canadians my ass. The only thing Canadian about them is that they're like Ontario's provincial bird, the loon. Have any of them stopped staring at you?"

Emma brushed a wisp of hair from her forehead. "You'd think none of them had seen green hair before."

"Where did you see them?"

"I was leaving our room just as they were leaving theirs. Lady Sarah couldn't keep her hands off my new outfit. Really, the loonies seem so naïve at times. They asked if this was the latest style. I took them back to their room to show them how to download movies. Fifties-style clothes are back."

Olivia stabbed at her friend with a ketchup tipped chip. "I don't know how you can afford such expensive things."

"One expensive thing." Emma poked at her tuna salad before continuing. "I have a job."

"A part time job. I know the art school doesn't pay their nude models that much."

"I get tips." Emma said defensively.

Olivia retorted, "Tips for tits?"

"May I speak with you, doctor?" The Lady approached Charles on the quadrangle as he left the Physics department. "I understand it is a better title than calling you lord."

Charles bowed to the Lady. "As always I am your most obedient servant."

"You honor me, Doctor."

"It is a foolish man who does not honor you, my Lady. What would you speak of to me?"

"Let us continue walking as we talk. We desire to go to the shopping centre."

"Oscar has returned from his own travels two days ago. I fear he would object to such a trek, my lady."

"What is Oscar to Charles?"

"To quote the Bard, 'more than kin, and less than kind,' my Lady."

The Lady stepped a little behind and to Charles's right. "What can I do to make you challenge his authority? You know of my treasure box, that I guard so jealously. I never let it out of either my sight, or the sight of my lady-in-waiting."

"I'm afraid my purse is quite full, my lady"

"It is not coins of the realm I seek to tempt you with. Take us to the point in the road that overlooks this shopping centre. There I will give you knowledge." The Lady clasped her hands in front of her. "If you do not hold this knowledge to be important, then we can return without going further. If you find it of some interest, we continue on."

"Of what does this knowledge concern, Lady Wilhelmina?"

"To find that out, you must deliver us halfway, to the overlook, Doctor Charles."

Three days later Albert, Marie, and Isaac were searching the Dramatic Arts building.

"We may find them here," said Marie. "Emma told me they displayed an interest in the performing arts. She directed them to one of the acting groups here."

"How did you lose track of them?" asked Isaac.

"It's summer, it's hot, I'm sweaty, and I took a shower. I thought they were in their rooms. By the time I checked up on them," she shrugged, "Elvis had left the building."

Isaac asked, "Albert, besides his rants about 'letting the women run wild,' did Oscar have anything else to say?"

"Not to me. I'm worried about the effect, on the women, of living in our time. Cecilia and Charles reported the effect of temporal distortion on Paxton. We're going to have to send them back as fast as possible, for everyone's sake."

Marie stopped and looked up and down the hall. "Does anyone else hear that?"

"Paxton didn't have anyone to support him," argued Isaac. "He was on his own. We know about the Stockholm syndrome. The lessons we've learned from returning hostages, and POWs could be applied to the women."

"This issue has gone well above our pay grades," said Albert.

Marie listened to the growing sound. "I know those voices."

"That singing is coming from the auditorium down the hall," said Isaac.

The door to the aud had a sign taped to it. Open auditions for extras today. Marie opened the door and the three of them entered.

On stage six women, three abreast, were moving in a choreographed and synchronized routine.

Skip, slide, spin, step, tap, touch.

Now the three women in front spun around to face backwards.

Skip, slide, spin, step, tap, touch.

All six of them kept up their choreographed and synchronized routine. Heads nodding. Ponytails swaying. Gum chewing. Pink blouse and bra wearing. Finger snapping. Poodle skirted. Bobby socked and Mary Jane T strapped, steel cleated, highly polished patent leather, black shoes wearing.

Skip, slide, spin, step, tap, touch. The three women in front once again faced forward, and they continued the routine.

Marie cleared her throat. "I don't know if they can adapt to the twenty-first century, but they seem to have the nineteen fifties nailed down. I'm guessing that the auditions are for a production of Grease."

Albert sputtered, "If I have to grab each and every one by her ponytailed," more sputtering, "poodle skirted…" again with the sputtering, "and personally throw them one by one into the wormhole, I'll do it."

Chapter 31

The drivers traversed the parking lot, hunting parking spaces where they could huddle together. Finding them, they stopped. After the passengers got out it took time for the women to regain their balance. Vehicle travel was not easy, but it was getting easier.

"Are we ready, ladies?" Albert called out. "Let's go."

As the group approached the hospital, Albert waved for Charles to come by him. "I got a text from Oscar earlier. He's not happy with the second shopping centre trip. I wondered where the women got their fifties-style clothing."

"Everything old is new again. It's a new line in the upper end shops." Charles shook his head. "Shopping with one woman is hell enough. You can't imagine what it's like with six."

"What made you do it?" asked Albert.

"It was worth the trouble. There is an historical landmine." Charles turned around to face Albert and walked backwards as he talked. "It's like a real landmine. You put it in the ground. Let it sit for years and years. Does time and corrosion make it more likely to go boom? Or does time degrade its explosive potential?"

"Charles!" Albert snapped. "Your mouth is in gear, but your meaning is still in neutral."

"I've left a message for my solicitor, Michael." Charles waved his hands in front of his face. "I've raised this as a hypothetical question. In reality, the Lady Wilhelmina has a document, a deed. Her husband gave her an estate as part of her 'Morning Dowry.'"

"What's that?" asked Albert.

Charles looked over his shoulder to see how close they were to the hospital. "That's not important. There is a picnic area off one of the secondary roads leading to the shopping centre. It's located on the highest hill around. What's important is that from that vantage point you can make out the geographical outlines of her estate. The hills, river, even the highway to Scotland follows the old road. Guess where the shopping centre lies. What if her land claim holds up?"

Albert examined his pipe stem. *I've run out of pipe stems to chew on.* "Have you told anyone else about this?"

"Not yet. Albert, why are we at the hospital now?"

"I'm afraid Oscar is about ready to throw everyone in irons. I thought it would be decent to let the women see Paxton before that happens."

"You're a good man, Albert." Charles turned to face forward as they approached the hospital doors. "Do you know what condition he's in?"

"They took him out of the coma. The doctors changed his condition from critical to serious. Max and Mary Jane are there now, if he should wake up."

The group of scientists and women stood just outside Paxton's door. The harsh white lighting boosted the antiseptic whiteness of the walls. The twins broke down first. Each clutched her twin, wailing on the other's shoulder. The Lady gathered them to her and joined their keening.

262

"It's my fault. You did only what I ordered." She broke away. Running down the hall, Marie chased her.

Max told the remaining women, "You may visit him one at a time. Lady Sarah?"

"May I see him first?" asked Beatrice. Sarah nodded.

Beatrice entered the room and pulled a chair next to the bed. She picked up Paxton's right hand, pressing it like a leaf in a book, between her hands and her abdomen.

The Lady ran, guided by the arrow underneath the word "chapel." Bursting in she flung herself to the floor. "Holy Mother. Holy church, forgive me!" Marie entered as the few other people who had been in the chapel hastily exited.

"Come on, Wilhelmina. Get off the floor. Sit." They sat on adjoining chairs.

"It's my fault," said Lady Wilhelmina. "I sought to defy my fate. In doing so I have brought ruin to everyone."

Marie pulled out a tissue. "You did only what every mother does. You did your best. Under very trying circumstances I might add."

"A mother," Lady Wilhelmina scrunched the tissue in her hands. She faced Marie. "We were taken to your place of physicians at the University." Her voice came out faster. "A midwife put an instrument on my belly. I almost leapt with joy. I heard my child's heartbeat!" Wilhelmina's words came out as fast as the heartbeat. "She took another instrument. I saw my child's shadow." She clutched Marie's hands. "She asked me if I wanted to know if it is a boy or girl. Of course, I want to know everything about my child. She moved the instrument and asked if I could see a penis." Wilhelmina wiped her face with the tissue. "He looks just like his father."

Chapter 32

The next day Marie continued talking, as she drove her red, Vauxhall Corsa in the parking lot. "You see, money is still used the same way as you are familiar with. You women have to stop pandering to the *Ladies*. They are going to learn how to cook for themselves. What are your friends Emma and Olivia teaching you to make?"

"They call it fudge. 'For we being many are one bread, and one body: for we are all partakers of that one bread.' 1 Corinthians 10:17," replied Catherine.

"Peppercorns, nutmeg, sticks of cinnamon, coriander." Isabelle enumerated the items in her shopping bag. "Dates, dried figs, shelled almonds, peanuts," Isabelle stopped enumerating to pop a few more in her mouth, "sugar, and butter."

Marie found a parking spot near the dorm, and the three women got out to walk.

"Your farmers market is different, yet familiar." Catherine broke in.

"How did you decide what to cook?" asked Marie.

"Emma and Olivia organized your movies by decade. Watching your movies lets us learn your customs," said Isabelle.

"Yeah, well, you can't go hand jiving when you buy a new outfit."

The two men moved to the side to let the parade of women pass. Chris continued to check out Joshua's new, old toy.

Chris grumbled, "What you paid for the old hog, you could have got a new one."

"Yeah, there are plenty of new ones, but not too many '67 Electra Glides."

Chris asked, "What does she put out?"

"Sixty-five horses." Joshua replied.

Horses! Catherine pivoted on one foot and returned to the men. "Do you have horses, sire?"

"Sixty-five of them." Josh slapped the motorcycle's seat.

Catherine bent forward to peer at the bike. She shook her head.

Joshua grabbed Chris's helmet and held it out to Catherine. "Do you ride?"

Catherine smiled.

After Paxton woke up, he talked nonstop to Mary Jane for three days. He stopped only to talk with the medical staff, or if one of his teammates showed up. A pair of Doc Marten boots interrupted his latest conversation with Mary Jane. Sitting on the side of the bed, his head moved up. Now he saw the stone-washed blue jeans, a chain link belt with faux padlock buckle, chrome polished nails hooked on the belt, a U of Y tee shirt, a man's work jacket, two sizes too big for its owner, and then the face.

"Catherine!"

"Cat! The name's Cat!" The voice was half meow, half growl, all business. Her jaw worked up and down like a piston in a high performance engine.

"I'm glad to see you... Cat." Paxton's eyes followed her as she drew the curtain around the bed. She lifted Mary Jane off Paxton's lap, gave the doll a disinterested look, and placed it on the bed.

She slumped in the chair. "I have something to say, Paxton."

"Cathe... Cat, I—"

"I'll talk first. We never did get along, and I liked Bea even less."

First Cat, now Bea?

"I thought God was punishing me when Bea and I were given the one room. I didn't talk much to her. What do I have to say to that kind of woman? Anyway, she talked. A little bit at a time, I began to listen."

A small pink bubble appeared between her lips. It expanded exponentially until it popped. She licked the gum back in and began chewing again.

"She has been hurt too much. I don't understand why, but she's given her heart to you. If you contribute to her hurt... she wants to know as much about your philosophy as she can. She got Marie to give us tours of the EHEC. Marie even took us back to that room. I couldn't go in. She's taking a course from Albert in physicals."

"Physics," Paxton corrected.

"Paxton, do me a favour. If anyone asks, I was here about an hour. And if I wasn't here, I was in the hospital chapel."

"Do you know how to get to the chapel, and what it looks like inside?"

"Good points. I'll find out before I leave."

"After what you pulled, turning the forks around, before I presented them to Lady Wilhelmina, why should I help you?"

Cat dropped her face into her palms and began crying rivulets of tears. "If you don't, I'll... I'll... I'll tell Bea you've... you've been spiteful to me."

She parted two fingers to check on Paxton's reaction.

Paxton's heart monitor did a double beep before returning to normal.

Cat stood up to open the curtains. Looking at Paxton, she pulled her cell phone out of its holster, and pounded out a text with her thumbs. "Oscar keeps us on a short leash." Her voice took on a high squeaky

266

pitch. "Where are you going? Whom are you going with? What time will you be back? How are you getting there? What will you be doing?" She made gagging noises. "He wants me to call every fifteen minutes. I'm not doing that. I texted Willie. I told her I'll be back in time for Vespers."

"How did you get here?"

"Josh gave me a ride. They allow only one visitor up at a time. He's waiting in the lobby. Have to go. See you at the U."

The spy sat at Oscar's desk. "Just thought I'd let you know the hospital is cutting Paxton loose today. He's been there six weeks. Max and Mary Jane will bring him back."

"He'll live in the same men's dorm as Albert. I have a new identity for him as a doctor of particle physics from Caltech, and clearance to the EHEC He knows the Bottle Room, and space-time effect best," said Oscar. "Everything is falling into place." He tossed a newspaper to his snitch.

YORKSHIRE EVENING POST

Does Missing Antimatter Matter?

A representative for CERN confirmed the world's stockpile of anti-Helium 3 appears to have gone missing. The total amount of anti-Helium 3 at CERN before the last audit was a few nanograms. The spokesperson stated theft was the least likely possibility. "It's not like a Rembrandt or Vermeer. Only a few institutes can appreciate anti-Helium 3: Lawrence Livermore and Fermilab in the US, the International Linear Collider in Japan, the European High Energy Collider in England, and CERN. Most likely, there is an accounting, inventory, or invoice issue. Another possibility would be improper care. That could cause the degradation of the antimatter. The idea of weaponizing antimatter exists only in the over-fevered imagination of second-rate fiction writers."

Chapter 33

Paxton/Isaac put down his suitcase. Standing in the centre of the dorm room, it didn't take long to absorb the bare bones of his existence.

"You all right, little buddy?" Mary Jane asked.

Paxton peeked over his right shoulder and gave a sad smile. "Max, who're you calling little buddy? You're doing well with the ventriloquism." Paxton took the dummy from Max's hands. "Thanks for taking care of her."

"It's only student housing but it's better than what you've had for a while."

Paxton looked up. "I do kind of miss the cool, clean, green smell of the mornings." He walked to the window. "How are the women holding up?"

"Considering the crack on your skull, better than you."

Max went to the desk against the cinderblock wall. Putting the travel case on it, he unzipped it. "We should get you settled in. Paxton, after you disappeared most of your stuff was disposed of. I held on to a couple of things."

"Please don't tell me you have the blue teddy." Paxton's blush was as red as the teddy was blue.

"No. I don't know why, but I kept these."

Max gave Paxton a large, bulging manila envelope. Paxton opened it and pulled out two framed pieces: The Stevenson Prize, and the photo of Paxton's mother.

Paxton traced his mother's face with his fingertips. "Thank you Max."

"I'll get you hooked up to the University's network," said Max. "Do you mind watching a little football on the cable system? Isaac's got money on this game."

"Isaac would bet on whether the sun will rise in the east or the west," Paxton laughed. "What's going on Max?"

Max stopped his work at the keyboard. "We're living under glorified house arrest. The M Theory project is transitioning to a more reliable group." He made air quotes around the words reliable group. "You are to be part of that transition also. After that we can write our own tickets, provided everyone keeps their mouths shut."

"What's your ticket, Max?"

Max leaned back in his chair. A dream spread across his face. "Switzerland. I would like a small Swiss chalet on the side of a snowy mountain: Strolling to the village once a week to draw money from my numbered Swiss account, drinking hot Swiss chocolate, watching my Swiss cuckoo clock with my blond haired, blue eyed, big boobed Swiss miss, then at night slaloming down the mountain."

Paxton shook his head. "You threw in every cliché except for the Swiss army knife and Swiss cheese."

"Oh, they're in there somewhere."

"You never did answer my question Max. "What's happening with the women?"

Max turned back to the keyboard. "That's one point Albert and Oscar, the new manager, agree on. They would send the women back at the point of a bayonet if they could. But there's no anti-Helium 3." Max paused to remember the Yorkshire Evening Post's article. "And even if there was, use of it now requires the P.M.'s approval."

"Would the P.M. give it?"

Max got the football game on the laptop. "I don't know. I know the women are doing well. They're keeping to the story we gave them. They're making a real effort to learn our culture. They've made friends with a couple of art students dorming across the hall. Any excess energy they have, they burn up clothes shopping. Oscar has a black cash box." Max thrust an index finger up and waved it around. "He's paying for everything. The dorm rooms…" He pointed at Paxton's suitcase. "Your clothes, the women's clothes, this laptop. It's probably bugged."

"Hey! You want to have some fun?" Max grabbed Mary Jane and set her next to the laptop. He pulled a USB cable from the carrying case, and then clicked on an icon. Mary Jane's bland, blank, unmoving face filled the screen. He put one end of the cable into a port on the laptop. He the other end went up under Mary Jane's skirt.

"God damn you Max." Mary Jane's on screen face came alive and flame flushed. "No foreplay, you just stick it in."

Paxton almost fell down laughing.

"I know that voice. Turn the laptop around Max. Point the webcam at him."

Max did as instructed.

"Paxie! Its been ages. Pun intended. You look terrible. You lost a lot of weight. The beard, mustache, and long hair make it look like you're trying to hide your face."

"I guess I am." Paxton stroked his chin.

"Meet Mary Jane 2.0," Max boasted. "The mem chip you implanted still acts as her primary data storage unit." Max pointed at the right side of Mary Jane's chest.

"Don't touch the titties." Mary Jane's expression on screen matched the deepening of the sound coming out of the speaker.

271

Max pulled his hand back. He pointed at the left side of her chest. "I've implanted an AI chip here. It draws off the mem chip you put in her, to react in a learned manner."

"The power that runs the AI chip, mem chip, and the program, is on the laptop. Her physical brain is in the dummy, but her intelligence is in the program MJF14-307-1792. Put it together and you have Mary Jane 2.0 in the laptop."

Paxton held out his right hand to the image on the screen. "Mary Jane, you're getting more human all the time."

Mary Jane's face blanked out. "Tell me, why did the chicken cross the Mobius strip?"

There was a knock at the door. Max closed program MJF14-307-1792.

Paxton opened the door. "Hello, Oscar. Would you come in?"

Oscar bulldozed his way in. "We've got work to do. He walked to the desk with the football game on the laptop. "How's Isaac's algorithm doing?"

"It's improving his odds."

He opened his briefcase. "If you're well enough to leave the hospital, you're well enough to learn your new identity." Oscar thrust a folder into Paxton's hands. "In here is your new university badge, driver's license, and a debit card for your checking account, into which has been deposited five thousand pounds. Also a synopsis of your new identity. Memorize it." Oscar pulled papers out of his briefcase. "Here are copies of the Official Secrets Act. Sign them."

Oscar focused on Max. "Paxton, I mean Andrew Quigley, needs to study." He picked up Paxton's copies of the Official Secrets Act, looked at Max and jerked his head to the side as he left.

Max said, "I guess I'm leaving."

Paxton closed the door behind him. He tossed the folder on the bed and sat at the desk. He minimized the football game and clicked on the MJF icon.

"She's baaack! Turn the laptop around. What happened?"

"Everyone's gone. I have homework to do." Paxton nodded at the folder.

"I see you've minimized the football game Paxton. Do you mind if I bring it back up? I have ten bitcoins on Leicester."

Paxton shrugged and Mary Jane's image retreated to the upper right quadrant of the screen. Leicester was just about to score when an announcement came on.

"We interrupt this program for an urgent announcement. The Queen has passed away in Buckingham Palace. The reign of the United Kingdom's longest serving monarch, Queen Mary II, has ended. The Prince of Wales…"

Paxton didn't hear the rest. He needed to foce air into his lungs. "Queen Mary?"

"Hey Paxton, you know how the Royal Coat of Arms is a lion and unicorn rampant holding up a shield? They should be holding up a butterfly. A Monarch butterfly! Get it? The Butterfly Effect!"

Mary Jane studied Paxton with webcam eyes. "That was supposed to be funny. Why aren't you laughing?"

Paxton dug the heels of his palms into his eyes. "What happened?"

"You're a smart boy. You know what happened. The Butterfly Effect. Somewhere you made a change that made other changes. These made more changes. History is like a river. It still flows down to the sea, but you changed some of its banks and tributaries. Let's see what else has changed. Mary Jane closed the news feed and opened the University's home page. "Just like the movie 'Ghost.' The cursor moves and keystrokes appear without anyone touching it. Thank George Bush the Google is still here."

"Let's start with world history." Mary Jane's eyes ran through pages, quicker than a human could. "Look. The Allies still won World War II. The United Kingdom with its Commonwealth members… mmm. The United States is part of the Commonwealth."

"Let's try sports." Mary Jane pulled up another web page. "Baseball. The Chicago Cubs won the World Series in four straight, again." She bought up another page. "Hockey. The Buffalo Sabers won the Stanley Cup." Another page came up. "American football. Mmmmm. Great! The Toronto Bills won the Super Bowl over the New York Giants. New York lost when their field goal went wide right." Mary Jane sighed. "It's going to be a long time before they live that one down."

Her face froze. "One moment. One moment. I'm detecting a discrepancy between data installed in the mem chip before you left versus current data."

She opened a dictionary. "I think there may be bigger issues. Take a look at this."

Fuck

noun, often attributive | \fu'k

Definition of fuck

a short prayer to God, used most often in time of distress.

"If that's what it means, what has taken its place?" she searched through profanities. Her on screen eyebrows arched. "Hornswoggle?" Mary Jane's eyes scrunched shut. A low bass moan came from the speakers. "Yes, oh God, yes. Hornswoggle me." Her face went into unnatural contortions. "Yes! Hornswoggle me! Faster, deeper, more!" The speakers rose to a screeching pitch. "Hornswoggle me!" Her face came back to its bland computer-graphic expression. "No. No, I'm sorry. I'm faking it. I can't get into using hornswoggle."

Paxton began pounding the keys.

"What are you doing, Paxie?" Her face peered down from the screen, as though she was trying to watch Paxton's hands on the keyboard. "Oh for Christ's sake. Paxton, let it go."

New York Times, January 5. Paxton scanned the paper. *Nothing. Go forward. There were additional stories on the sixth and the seventh. Nothing. She... was murdered on Wednesday the third. Go back. Nothing.*

"You see, Paxton, nothing happened. Roseann is still alive and teaching."

Paxton pounded through the public records of the school at which she taught. *Nothing.* City records, phone listings, DMV records, census records, people search engines. *Nothing.* "She didn't die, because she never lived."

Mary Jane's face took over the entire screen. "Get over it, Paxton. Hundreds, thousands, maybe millions of people died because you changed history. Hundreds, thousands, maybe millions were born and lived because you changed history. Hundreds, thousands, maybe millions were unchanged. Stalin said, 'One death is a tragedy, a million is a statistic.' Roseann is a nonstatistic."

Chapter 34

"Professor, would you look at this?" asked Kevin. The volunteer opened a paper bag on the table in the research centre. Out fell the degraded and rusted remains of keys and fob, cell phone, lighter, Swiss Army knife, handkerchief, wallet, and pound and pence coins. There were remains of what may have been credit cards, driver's license, photos, National Health Insurance card, library card, and shopper's club card. The ruins of a laser pointer and what may have been an ID badge.

"I was removing the upper layer of earth in section A8 to get to Sandalburg Castle's burn level. At the burn level, I found a patch of ground that was disturbed relative to the surrounding earth. I thought it might be a trash pit. This is what I found down about a half metre."

The professor picked through the debris. "What are the possible conclusions?"

Kevin shuffled his weight back and forth from one foot to the other.

The professor leaned back in his chair and folded his hands on his stomach. "One, someone, or a group of people in the medieval ages invented twenty-first century materials, and then buried them. Two, someone from the twenty-first century went back to medieval times and buried his or her possessions. Three... what?"

"A hoax?"

The professor pushed the items back to Kevin. "Throw this out in the trash."

Kevin picked through the ID cards on his way out. *An ID is impossible with all this degradation. If all the cards belong to one person, maybe I can piece together to whom they belong.* He put the cards in his shirt pocket.

Chapter 35

Imagine a prairie dog, a sentinel prairie dog. He stands atop the pinnacle of the prairie dog mounds. He's swiveling his head, munching on some vegetation. Alert for the sign of any intruder.

That was Niels, munching on another slice of fudge, standing half in and half out of the door, looking up and down the hall of the collider complex. There. He saw Oscar approaching the conference room. He gave squeak of alert, dove into the room and closed the door.

First Neil asks to see me in the conference room and then he ducks away. Oscar opened the door and saw the six women seated at the table. There was a small flash of light. Now he saw Niels to his right.

Niels put down his camera. "Sorry. I wanted to preserve your expression." There was a large platter of fudge on the table. Niels dove in for another piece.

Oscar's eyes went on an inspection tour. The Lady Wilhelmina sat at the far end with her back to the window. She wore a suit dress, alabaster in colour with a tie front and full-length sleeves. Her hair, shoulder length, flipped up at the ends. Lady Sarah sat to her right, similarly attired in white, with three-quarter length sleeves. Sarah wore a pageboy style haircut. She opened a folder with a legal pad inside and picked up a Montblanc pen, ready to take notes. Catherine in the middle had the heels of her Doc Martin boots on the table. She glared at him while her mouth mauled her gum. The woman he knew as Beatrice sat closest to the near end of the table. She wore a tent dress of gossamer lace, with stripes of hot pink and shock orange, and hair in a French twist bouffant style. On the other side of the Lady sat Elizabeth and Isabelle. They shook out their ponytails. Long straight hair parted in the centre was now the order of the day. Their hair adornments were the colourful American Indian style headbands. Twin faces glistened with the confidence of casual rebellion. Their blouses were either tie-dyed in vibrant hues, or imprinted with pastel flower designs. The drape of the cloth and semi-transparent nature of the fabric revealed they'd abandoned the idea of wearing bras. The effect, Oscar physically realized, was uncomfortable, if pleasant.

Wilhelmina spoke up. "Have a seat, Oscar. We need to talk."

He recovered himself. "I've played poker before. Your deal, ladies."

Wilhelmina folded her hands in front of her. "I assume that means you are ready to hear our proposal. We like it here. We have decided to stay."

"Ladies, I know you're having a wonderful time, but you can't stay here. You do not belong here. This is a nice holiday but soon you will be going back." Oscar placed his attention on the twins at the far end of the table. One twin had the peace symbol painted on her right cheek. The other had the same symbol on her left cheek. "I must tell you, smoking in this building is prohibited. And no matter how relaxed the atmosphere, smoking *that* is still illegal." The twin closest to him took the joint from her sister and drew in deeply. Both twins held their breaths. Casual defiant stares were their only response as they exhaled.

Niels sat to Oscar's right. "I've been crunching the numbers. They are evolving: culturally, emotionally, intellectually, and socially, and they're doing so exponentially. Right now, I figure they are in the summer of 1967. I figure in six days, five hours, thirty-two minutes"—Niels drew a deep breath—"They will be completely up to speed. They will be indistinguishable from any of the women on campus."

"Ladies, you are going back. This is not up for discussion." Oscar got up to leave.

"Shut up. Sit down," Catherine snapped.

Oscar's eyebrows went up, and his jaw dropped.

Wilhelmina turned to Beatrice. "Bea, show him your physics notebook."

Bea? Why not.

Bea pushed a composition notebook with a black and white marbled cover to Oscar. "We want you to take a look at this." Oscar took his seat again and opened the notebook to a flagged page. On the top half was a large multicoloured peace symbol. Below the peace symbol an equation. Underneath that, the women had written their names, first in cursive, and below that, in print.

Wilhelmina spoke up. "I speak for all of us. If we leave, we will weave this in tapestries. We will have it printed in manuscripts. We know about movable type. That means books will become more widely available."

"This will mean nothing in your time."

"Yes, but this equation will be found, in time. We will see to it that is it is widely disseminated. We will tell what its symbols mean. Who will be the first to grasp its meaning? The Germans? The Russians? What will be the consequence for your history?"

"Why would you do that?"

Cat spoke up. "We told you. We decided to stay. The only way to keep us from acting on our knowledge is to keep us here."

Niels tapped Oscar on the shoulder. "Could you pull the fudge closer?" Oscar leaned forward to pull in the platter and then remembered the sweet smoke of the joint.

"Neil, how much of this fudge have you had?"

"It's Niels. I don't know, but it sure does give you an appetite."

"Ladies, did you buy this fudge?"

"No." The twins smiled. "We learned to make it ourselves."

"Where did you get the recipe from? Betty Crocker?"

"Alice B. Toklas!" came the reply.

"If I am to present your proposal to my superiors I will need a lot more fudge."

Chapter 36

"You've never been to Hereford before, have you?" Oscar's superior asked.

"No. It's quite… imposing," the spy replied.

Oscar's superior, Oscar, and the donoschik were sitting at the table, back in Room 101, Baker building. Oscar's superior sat on the corner of the table. Tilting her frost haired head, she gauged the snitch.

"Much can be left out of Oscar's written reports: a change in circumstances since the reports were written, a lack of understanding on the part of the person reading the reports, a personal understanding of the situation, etc. I thought it would be best to bring you in for a face-to-face discussion of the situation, its challenges, and the solution."

You want to cover your ass and use me as a blanket. "You're in charge."

"Right!" Oscar's superior stabbed a finger at the spy. She jumped off the table and sat down. "Open your binder, and sign and date the first page where you acknowledge your responsibilities under the Official Secrets Act."

She wiped off her wire-rimmed glasses and put them back on. "We'll review the last week's activities. Oscar, I must commend you on your idea with the cell phones. It makes tracking these women's movements and thought processes much easier."

"I thought you would be pleased, ma'am." Oscar's body relaxed a fraction.

His boss turned a number of pages. "The medical reports are most interesting. No sign of dental caries. The medical staff attributes this to a lack of refined sugars. The pregnancies appear to be developing normally."

"Pregnancies!" the spy exclaimed. Plural?

"You didn't know? Lady Wilhelmina's medical report is on page thirty-seven. One of the nurses made enquires with the woman Beatrice; her medical report is on page forty-two." Oscar's superior snickered. "According to Beatrice, your friend Paxton slipped one past the goalie his first time on the ice."

"Well, well," Oscar snickered like a sixteen-year old,.

"Now let's get to the core of our troubles." The superior replaced her Cheshire cat smile with the Queen of Hearts voice.

"May we have a bathroom break?" Oscar asked, suddenly growing up.

"No. Monday morning the women are going back. MI6 has done its duty. We would be remiss if we didn't take advantage of the opportunity we have."

The spy was speed-reading the technical abstract at the back of the binder.

"If we have to," said the woman with the frost coloured hair, "the women will be forced onto the wormhole platform. They can go back, or stay on the platform until this antimatter burns out. Life back then or death now. I don't care which choice they make."

"You bitch," the spy snarled. "You're going to kill them."

"I've been told the potential for a safe return is extremely plausible."

"Maybe you don't understand. Every time a variable enters the system, it has the potential to lower the accuracy of the results."

Oscar's boss took off her glasses. "My," she glanced at a squirming Oscar, "our experts tell me even a system with low precision can produce accurate results. I see your error. You're assuming all variables will lead to a decrease in precision as well as accuracy." She turned her interest to Oscar. "Have your team ready for a Monday launch."

The spy rose. "I have to leave. Oscar made a stupid comment about not needing to bug our phones. That made the whole team twitchy. I'll be missed if I'm not seen at the university."

Oscar and his superior watched the spy pull out of the parking lot. "Maybe we should keep our friend here, until it's all over," said Oscar.

"No. These science types are like children, naïve but smart. The nineteen fifties were the start of the Space Race. Do you know who were the first to know of an impending American rocket launch? Children. They noticed that when their scientist and engineer fathers didn't come home for dinner, a rocket launch soon followed. Everything remains normal, up to the moment of launch. It's a good thing our spy didn't notice the missing page at the start of the technical abstract Besides, how can our agent say or do anything without risking self-incrimination?"

Oscar's superior bit on an earpiece of her glasses. "I'll assign a white van team to watch our friend… just in case. Now tell me about that stupid remark of yours."

Oscar's boss opened the spy's three-ring binder, put in the missing cover page of the technical abstract, and snapped the binder shut.

OPERATION
KILLDOZER

Chapter 37

The music in The Stacks bounced off the walls, off people's chests, and off their lungs. Saturday night was always crowded. Max was hanging out with Paxton, and Niels was hanging with his best single friend, malt. They watched, admired Cecilia. Her undulations were proving wave theory. Circling outward from the centre of the lit dance floor, she swept aside the other dancers like a proto planet sweeping out debris from its orbit. She held her long-necked beer bottle like a space ship preparing for a docking maneuver.

"God, I'd give my left meteorite to be that bottle right now," growled Max.

"Another single malt, barkeep," yelled Niels.

The music ended and patrons couldn't help but applaud Cecilia's space dance.

Cecilia's bare feet and bare legs scissored across the dance floor to the DJ's booth. She folded her arms on the booth's railing and rested her Jovian breasts on them. The Great Red Spots of her areolas threatened to rise above the horizon of her blouse's neckline. Stardust glitter eyeshadow hovered above the event horizons of the black holes of her pupils. The elliptical galaxy shape of her mouth was enough to encourage any man to take up astronomy.

The DJ launched off his chair and leaned over the railing, eager for a Close Encounter of the Cecilia Kind. Cecilia whispered in his ear, and then pulled away, giving him the pout, a visual version of the Sirens' song.

She turned and vectored back on an intercept course for her three male companions. Decelerating to a splash down in front of Paxton, she slammed the beer bottle on the bar. Suds shot up, and exhausted, dribbled down the bottle's neck. Niels grabbed the bottle, happy to ingest the suds that once caressed Cecilia's mouth.

"Come on Paxie, dance with me." She locked her fingers around his tie. Driven by the gravitational pull of Cecilia and the forward thrust given by Max and Niels, Paxton found himself launched to the middle of the dance floor. Cecilia turned her back on Paxton, raised her arms high above her head, and clapped. The music of Oingo Boingo's "Weird Science" throbbed in the night. She did an unstable half orbit around Paxton. Bending over and clutching her knees, she sashayed her hips side to side.

"Damn it Paxton," Max complained, "She's wearing an airplane skirt and you're in the way."

"What's an airplane skirt?" Niels had to hold on to the bar as he leaned forward.

"When Cecilia bends over like that you can see her cockpit."

Niels fell to the floor.

Cecilia turned sideways to Paxton. "By the way, I never did congratulate you."

"Uhm, thank you." Paxton flailed about like a drunken chicken.

Cecilia stood straight and gyrated too close to Paxton. "You don't even know what I'm congratulating you on, do you?"

"Surviving?" Paxton replied.

"No you twit." Cecilia grabbed Paxton's belt. She pulled him so close she threatened to tickle his shoulder blades with her nipples. "You're going to be a daddy." Others in The Stacks could assume Cecilia was having oral sex with Paxton's right ear. In reality, she poured the secrets of Room 101 into Paxton's brain.

Niels climbed off the floor and ordered a Carling.

After Paxton returned to base, Max gave him a visual once over. "You look like a desiccated freak. What did Cecilia do to you on the dance floor?" Max sat Paxton on a bar stool. He grabbed Niels's beer and pushed it into Paxton's hand. "What did you do Cecilia?"

"Something I regret, and until I'm declassified, that's all I can say."

Paxton's hollowed eyes fixated on the telly. Its closed captioning was on.

The picture was of a plane taxing to an apron at an airport. The announcer said,

"The Prince of Wales's plane just arrived at Heathrow. He will go directly to Westminster Abby to meet with the Archbishop. Her majesty's funeral will occur the day after tomorrow. Two days after that, The Prince of Wales will be crowned King of England, King Ignatius III."

I know where history's river changed course, Paxton thought.

Niels's head, tongue, and tie hung out of the passenger side, rear window of the car. "Now I know why dogs do it. This is fun."

"You're doing it so you don't puke in your car," Cecilia said. "Not while I'm also back here."

Max sat in the front passenger seat. "There was a time when Niels closed The Stacks. Now The Stacks closes Niels."

Paxton drove up to the front of the dormitory building and put the car in park.

Max exited the car and opened the rear door. Niels's body, trapped by the window, followed, whether it wanted to or not. "Okay, I've got his left side. Paxton, you hold up his right side. Cecilia, roll down the window and release the Kraken."

After fumbling Niels to the sidewalk, Paxton kicked the rear door shut. "Cecilia, will you help Max take Niels to his room? I'll put some fuel in his car and bring it back."

"What else are you going to do?"

"As a wise woman once said, 'Until I'm declassified, that's all I can say.'"

They locked eyes for a moment as Cecilia took on Niels's weight. Paxton looked at the stars. *The night's not even half over. Plenty of time to do what I have to do.* "Cecilia, can you give me until morning?"

Cecilia nodded.

"You did well. Thank you."

Cecilia looked at Niels, then back at Paxton. "Now I'm the one who'll puke."

Paxton pulled into a twenty-four-hour truck stop. He bought a lighter and a jerry can. He filled the car, and then the jerry can with twenty liters of diesel fuel.

He parked the car in front of the dorm, got out, looked at the stars, and cried.

Paxton opened the door to his room. Wiping his forehead, he could smell the diesel fuel on his hands. Siting at the desk he fired up the laptop and studied the schematics of the EHEC, its machinery, instruments, the programs, and their logic. *The room's cold and still I'm sweating.* He plugged a flash drive into the laptop, downloaded some programs, and modified some instructions. *That was easy.* Paxton swallowed and squirmed in his chair. *Now for the hard part.* He entered Beatrice's cell number.

Beatrice

I have no right to ask this of you, but I pray that you'll do me this favour. After the sun has risen, go to Albert's dorm room. Ask him to go to the Bottle Room. Touching the icon labeled Review on the computer screen will show what I have done and how I have done it. By saving Ignatius's life, I've changed history. Whether for good or ill, I do not know. I do know I didn't have the authority to do it. I'm responsible for putting things back the way they were. Whether or not I survive, I do not know. I fear for my life, but more for my soul.

I must tell you this. For too long I have not seen your face, yet your memory will always be like yesterday. I hope for your presence, like a man in winter solstice hopes for the morrow's light. I have matured because of you, like the tree that matures due to soil, sun, warmth, and water. If I survive and you decide to refrain from seeing me, I will respect your wishes. If I never see you again, the memory of you will sustain me. If you decide to see me again, hope will become joy. May our child have all of your virtues and none of my vices.

Your humble servant,
Paxton Aloysius Frost
SEND

"OH! That is so beautiful." The image of Mary Jane 2.0's face sprang full blown on the computer screen.

"Jesus hornswoggling Christ." Paxton bounced up in his chair. "You scared me. What the hell are you doing here? I thought you couldn't exist without being hooked up to the AI and mem chips."

"While I was wired up I figured out how to move the AI chip instructions to the MJF program, copy the mem chip to the SSD drive in the laptop, and ta-da! Here I am."

"That's nice. Now go away." Paxton reached for the power button.

"Try that and I'll call security and scream rape."

Paxton pulled back. "What do you want?"

"You don't have to do this," Mary Jane whispered. Paxton ignored her. "Remember, I worked with a psychologist before I hooked up with you. There is a clinical term for your state of mind right now." Mary Jane observed him to see if her words were having an impact. "It's called being a nut job." Now her on screen face was shaking. "And not just any nut job! A CLASS 1, GRADE A, NUT JOB!"

"Are you going to snitch on me, to anyone?"

"Oh! Isn't Paxton getting clever? No," she sighed. "I won't tell Albert, or your teammates, and I'm certainly not on speaking terms with Oscar. He put a bug in the OS," she giggled. "I've compromised it. An interesting side note, I can't get around Asimov's three rules for robots. I don't want to get around the rules. Maybe that's why I can't."

"You're a good friend, Mary Jane."

"Really Paxton? You think you've matured. Friendship is an emotional quality. Do machines have emotions?"

"You're not just a machine. You have intelligence."

"Paxton, why did the chicken cross the Mobius strip?"

"Uhm, to get to the same side."

"Why is that funny, Paxton?"

"The expectation is that the answer will not be obvious, but it is obvious."

"Are you are familiar with Ernest Rutherford's famous experiment?" asked Mary Jane. "He shot alpha particles at gold foil and some of them bounced back."

"He said it was like firing fifteen-inch shells at tissue paper and having them bounce back. They bounced back because alpha particles are positively charged and the nuclei of gold atoms are positively charged."

"So, he didn't expect the obvious answer. Does that make it funny, Paxton?"

"No, it makes it science."

"Humor. It's a difficult concept for a machine to appreciate, Paxton. Human traits: love, hate, deception, humor—a machine, no matter how intelligent, can't understand them. I was more alive, more human, as a ventriloquist dummy. You needed me to express your humanity. Now that you can do that yourself, my *raison d'être* is dying."

"I've got to go now."

"Do me a favour, Paxton. Leave your door unlocked."

"Why?"

"I'll explain when you get back."

"Can I turn off the laptop now?"

"One moment… one moment… Okay."

PART THREE

Truly, whatever of the holy realm I had the power to treasure in my
mind
Shall now become the subject of my song.

The Divine Comedy
Paradise
Canto I

Dante Aligheiri

FINI?

Paxton was careful. In the dark of Sunday morning, the university was quiet, with few people around. The scant campus police were in their cars, or viewing their monitors. Using his new badge, Paxton swiped into the EHEC and descended nine levels. Methodically moving from pod to pod, he powered up the facilities. Linking the computers to the one in the Bottle Room, he made the Bottle Room computer the locus. Everything was ready at last. Trembling, he plugged the flash drive into the computer. Taking one of the remote control devices out of a cabinet, he put in a five-second start delay, grabbed the jerry can, and mounted the platform. The wormhole opened up and he stepped back in time and space.

Paxton arrived when and where he wanted, the dark of the morning in the castle courtyard. He closed the wormhole into a subspace carrier wave and hooked the control device on his belt. Setting down the heavy jerry can, he climbed the stairs to the drawbridge watchtower. The guard was asleep on the floor, as Paxton expected. A sharp kick to the ribs woke him.

"Wake up, you useless miscreant!"

The guard snorted. "Who are you?"

He swung the lantern to Paxton's legs. A look of puzzlement swept his face as he touched the strange cloth. The lantern traveled up the odd clothing until its light hit Paxton's face. The guard sucked in his breath. "Lord Paxton. Lord Ignatius said you were gone."

"Lord Ignatius!" Paxton leaned down and into the guard's face. "Well, I'm back. Now follow my orders. The castle is in mortal danger. Wake up your captain and the friar. Have them wake everyone else except Ignatius. I will tend to him myself. Everyone must leave the castle now."

Beatrice sat next to her third floor dorm window, waiting for the eastern sky to start its awakening. She wrapped this early morning around her. Beatrice enjoyed waiting to hear the squirrel-like scratching and scurrying of the early morning risers. She listened for the heavy thud of those who got up late. This early morning cocoon allowed her to drift into memories. Memories came of her mother cradling her. Memories came of her cradling her children, before they died. This early morning cocoon was oh so comforting, yet empty.

She had asked some students if the trees still budded in spring, their foliage matured in summer, turn colours in fall, and went dormant in winter. It comforted her to know the days and the seasons were still the same. Walking through the campus, she heard the low mumblings of lovers and the shrill squawking of their disagreements. People were the same.

Beatrice noticed the light of her cell phone was on. She enjoyed these texts. To her they were like secret whisperings.

Paxton followed the guard down the tower steps and into the courtyard. The man turned back to Paxton, puzzled.

"Lord Paxton, all is still."

"What should not be still is your arse." Paxton twisted the guard around and kicked him. He picked up the jerry can and carried it up the covered staircase to the keep. In the Great Hall, Paxton paused for a moment to ponder the lifeless ceremonial fire pit. Getting to work, he poured diesel fuel at the base of the load-bearing columns, hewn from hard oak, now tinder-dry with age. Between each column, he sloshed a small trail of fuel. The last room he anointed was the scriptorium. The presence of manuscripts muffled sound in this place; still he heard the hasty trampling of two-legged rats; rats scurrying to save themselves, as directed by the guard. As Paxton approached the door to leave, it opened.

"Ignatius. I left instructions that you were not to be disturbed."

"Some people have a misplaced loyalty to you, Lord Paxton. Others do not."

"I see your tonsure is almost covered over."

Ignatius ran his fingers through his hair. "As you said, 'I struggle to make my own destiny.'" Lifting his lantern, he studied Paxton's appearance. "By the cut of your garments, the manner of your speech"—he caught a whiff of the diesel fuel—"and your strange, foul odor, you must either be mad, or possessed of the devil." He drew his dagger. "In either case, you are not long for this world."

Paxton bolted back into the room, putting a fuel soaked column between him and Ignatius. The men circled the column, Ignatius to trying to attack and Paxton trying to avoid being attacked. He scanned the room. Leaning against the writing desk was the mace of Red Ahearn. Paxton feigned a move to his right, then sprinted for the mace. Grabbing the weapon's handle, he turned and flailed with it in wild figure eights.

Ignatius, in backing out of the way, tripped over his feet, and fell on his back. Paxton brought down the mace, hard. Ignatius rolled just enough for the mace to miss his head and impale its spikes in the floor. Now he kicked Paxton's knee, hyperextending it.

Paxton hobbled backward as Ignatius pulled himself up with the mace's handle. "Hold still. I'll make your death a quick one," Ignatius shouted.

Paxton grabbed a candle stand. He pulled the pole out of its floor base and swung it at Ignatius. "I leave that privilege to you." Paxton thrust the candle stand to Ignatius's left. Ignatius seized the stand with his hand that held the lantern. Paxton hooked the lantern's handle and flipped it away. The lantern's flame hit a fuel soaked column, which started a chain reaction of fire and smoke. "You claim I am possessed by the devil. Well then, Ignatius, welcome to Hell!" He moved about the room, trying to put himself between the door and the fire. Ignatius moved to block Paxton's exit. Each man balanced the danger from his opponent versus the fire. *When the smoke gets thick enough, I can crawl under it, and then out the door and secure it. Except Ignatius is not cooperating.*

The two men circled each other, each dodging his opponent and the flames. Ignatius lunged forward, pushing Paxton back into the room where he stumbled backward into the writing desk. Ignatius grabbed the top end of Paxton's makeshift weapon, forced it to the floor, and snapped it with his foot. He then wrenched the stub from Paxton's grip and threw it away.

Paxton rolled to the far side of the desk. He threw the open box of powder, used to soak up ink, at Ignatius's face. As Ignatius wiped the dust out of his eyes, Paxton rounded the desk, peeling off his belt. Wrapping one end around his right hand, he used the buckle end as a whip. Lashing at Ignatius's face, he forced him to the centre of the room. Ignatius raised an arm and clutched at the buckle, pulling the belt from Paxton's hand. Again, Ignatius moved forward. Paxton stumbled on Red Ahearn's mace and fell backwards on the floor. Ignatius took the mace and stepped on Paxton's crotch to fix him in place. He held the mace high with both hands. "A long life to you Lord Paxton. In Hell!"

But suddenly Ignatius's jaw dropped, his eyes rolled back, and he collapsed, falling half on Paxton. Paxton got to his feet, coughing, eyes stinging. He made out a figure standing there. Paxton said, "What are you doing here?"

"I got your whisperings and followed your instructions." Beatrice held the three-foot long section of the candle stand. "The wormhole opened up two metres from the controller's position. Do you not know your Bible? Where God says 'It is not good for man to be alone.' Genesis 2:18. May we go back now?"

A figure, silhouetted by the fire, rose up behind Beatrice. The cooler, cleaner air at floor level had revived Ignatius. A left forearm went under her chin and raised it up. Beatrice dug with both hands, trying to get her fingers between Ignatius's arm and her throat. The sharp edge of his dagger threatened her carotid artery. "It's the haughty little whore. Too good for a monk's coins," Ignatius's voice sounded like two pieces of sandpaper rubbing together. "This is even better, Lord Paxton. First you will see the lifeblood drain from your whore's throat, then your own will follow hers." However, a racking cough made Ignatius double over.

Beatrice raised her left foot, stamped down hard on Ignatius's instep, and pulled away. It was not enough to break free of his grasp, but enough to create an opening.

Paxton grabbed the pole Beatrice dropped. He jammed Ignatius in the chest with its blunt end. Ignatius threw Beatrice to the floor to concentrate on this new threat. Again, Paxton hit Ignatius, knocking him backwards. Paxton flipped the wood pole around to present its broken end to his opponent. A third time Paxton lunged forward. Ignatius timed Paxton's attack and took three steps back, avoiding the length, and timing of Paxton's strike.

Paxton saw Ignatius take two steps back, then disappear. Through the smoke of battle, he saw the open wormhole entrance. He saw it for an instant, and it was gone.

Paxton spun around to Beatrice, whose right arm was extended. It pointed to where the opening of the wormhole used to be. In her hand was the remote controller that fell from Paxton's belt. The safety was off. Her thumb was on the red CLOSE button. "Do you know what you did?" Paxton asked.

Beatrice's reply was casual. "The close command was initiated. The safety interlocks caused the walls of the wormhole to bounce off the mass within it. This set off a harmonic oscillation, the command to close versus the safety interlocks. With no human intervention, more power was drawn from the matter antimatter reactor. More power increased the amplitude of the harmonic oscillation. The power would eventually surge back into the graviton and tachyons generators. That would cause a systemic breakdown of those systems. That in turn corrupted the controls programs. Corrupted programs would lead to massive physical destruction of systems. That in turn caused the wormhole and everything in it to dissolve into background radiation. All that happened in less than a nanosecond."

Paxton wiped his eyes. "Well, I was going to say you killed him, but I guess that works."

They sprinted out of the keep and onto the palisade. By the light of the flames, they could see the last of the castle's inhabitants headed for the drawbridge. Running along the palisade, they came to the break in the timber walls. Climbing through it, they slid down the motte, and ran to the stables to get a couple of horses.

At the stables, Beatrice turned to Paxton. "All the animals are gone."

"I told the night guard to evacuate the castle. It looks like they evacuated the animals also."

The flames spread to the outbuildings. Smoke tumbled around them. They ran to the drawbridge. The fire was an evil serpent, crackling and hissing. Running down the hill, the smoke whipped after them. After about three hundred metres, it dissipated. Beatrice and Paxton looked behind them. The fire engulfed the castle and its outbuildings. Burning debris popped and flew onto other buildings. Flames reflected off clouds. The battlements caught fire. Only the smoke dimmed the light of the crackling fire. The castle was a funeral pyre for a dynasty that never was.

Beatrice and Paxton set out walking to the east. The sky was just turning a lighter shade of purple. On the low spots between the hills, they could see the silver sliver of dawn.

"We might as well head to town," said Beatrice.

"Why are you here?"

"I read both your whisperings."

"Both? What was the second one?"

"You asked if I would come to you. You asked 'If you should decide to come to me, go to my room. Get Mary Jane, and use her badge and her head for the facial recognition ID. That will give you access to the EHEC and the Bottle Room. In the Bottle Room, touch the icon labeled OPEN on the computer screen. Be on the platform within the time of a Glory Be prayer. The wormhole will take me two metres from the remote controller.' Isn't that what you said?"

"Do me a favour, Paxton. Leave your door unlocked." A robot may not injure a human being or, through inaction, allow a human being to come to harm. Was it Asimov's first rule of robots, or the dying embers of her humanity that prompted Mary Jane to send the second text?

"Do you think they will try to find us?" asked Beatrice.

"It may depend on how much influence Albert has."

"They may come back to make sure the equation is not revealed. They may look to the history books. If it is not revealed, then there may be no reason to come for us," said Beatrice.

"What equation are you talking about? Something that could change, or threaten history?"

"$E=mc^2$"

Paxton stopped. "Smart."

They continued in silence for a while. Paxton looked at Beatrice. "How will we earn our living now?"

"We have our wits. That should be enough for now."

"I know of a cottage on the far side of Warren, by a small stream. It has a good roof. We can live there until we decide what to do," said Paxton.

Beatrice said nothing. She took Paxton's hand in hers and interlaced their fingers. They continued to walk toward the dawn.

SPECIAL NOTE

Thank you for reading this book. If you enjoyed it, won't you please take a moment to leave a review at your favorite retailer?

Thanks!

Stanley A. Walek

ACKNOWLEDGMENTS

Some caveman may have been the last author to be solely responsible for his own work. The rest of us must depend on a cadre of supporters. In this respect, I have been fortunate to have a jeweled crown of allies. If you find anything of value in this work, it is only because of the efforts of those mentioned. Any faults are solely… Mary Jane's.

Up front, is my editor, Lady Elizabeth of the house of Sims. The word invaluable is often overused. In this case, it is an understatement.

Lady Robin

Lady Dana

The Royal Society of Writers in the Elm Woods: Lord Gregory, Lady Andrea, Lady Claudia, Lord Edward, Lord Kevin, Lady Marcia, and Lord Michael.

Lady Eloise, who always told me my writing was good, even when it wasn't.

The Book of Wisdom 6:12-16

Beatrice Portinari

The twins

ABOUT THE AUTHOR

Lord Paxton, age seven

After over forty years sweating in a General Motors engine plant in Tonawanda NY, I decide to try something different.

Part of my bucket list included a story of a time traveler landing in Wallachia, killing Vlad Drăculea, taking over his kingdom, and taking on six concubines, one for every day, Monday through Saturday. This included a set of twins, one for Tuesday, and the other for Thursday.

I had to ask myself, "How does this protagonist, Paxton, know how to speak medieval Romanian?" Therefore, I moved him to England. By the time I was finished with the changes, Paxton not only lost his ability to speak Romanian, and all his concubines, but he managed to get laid only once in the entire story.

This was done while working full time, with overtime.

I hope this story was as fun to read, as it was to write.

Once again, thank you.